T0129408

SPITE THE DEVIL

To Lee.
More than yesterday,
less than tomorrow.

SPITE THE DEVIL

Maude Aurand McDaniel

iUniverse, Inc.
New York   Bloomington

Anyway, the organ swelled slightly (Doug is very good with musical nuance), and the trumpet, played smartly by a small young man in a black mustache, tootled respectfully as the bride's mother, Beth, came in on the arm of an usher. Her gardenia corsage, trimmed in blue to match her lace suit, cut a swath through the other fragrances as she walked past me. It was a big corsage.

She entered the first pew on the left, with the large, fresh-flower-studded white satin bow on the end, opposite the one Mrs. Livingston had just settled into, a trifle frumpy in a light pink crepe dress that looked expensive but too tight. I had to admire Beth's poise as she glanced around, smiling serenely, before she sat down.

I wondered how she stood it. This was one family in the congregation I had never gotten to know very well, but I'd heard that Beth's husband had been steadfastly unfaithful to her for years. Now she was about to watch her only daughter come in on his arm and then take the same vows of love and fidelity Barney had flouted every day of his marriage.

Beth looked happy as a lark.

Well, you could say there's a lot of precedent for romanticizing love. Songs like "Can't Help Lovin' That Man of Mine," and a whole canon of country and rock about how he's bad but I love him, I can't help myself, I'll always take him back.

That's how lots of people think it's done, true love.

But I don't think true love is romantic at all. I think it's when you find a man you decide you can work with to create it.

At least, that's how it was for me with Dan, who was coming out from the sacristy, tall and dark and uneasy-looking right now, in his brand-new linen-texture alba, and his old green stole with the simple Maltese crosses on it from the days before stoles were considered *objets d'art*. His right temple throbbed visibly, as it always did when he was tense. After all these years, he still got stage fright at weddings and funerals.

A small voice shouted out from the pews three rows from the front, "He's wearing green suspenders over his nightgown!" The titter died down as the groom and his best man shuffled in from the side door, heads down, hunched with embarrassment in their slate blue morning coats and raspberry cummerbunds.

The congregation looked them over with interest.

Suddenly, the trumpet and organ sounded the traditional warning for "Here Comes the Bride," and all the guests got up immediately to check out the rest of the wedding party.

Beth still sat in her pew, and so did Steve's family, but it was a losing battle. Dan always instructs the relatives to rise only when the bride herself appears, a nice touch if only it ever worked. Congregations create their own momentum, and now, as always, the family chucked the agenda and got up too, so as not to miss the show.

Three bridesmaids, two ringbearers, one flower girl, and a maid of honor later, Marty floated down the aisle on her father's arm, looking as gorgeous as she ever would, drowned like Ophelia in fresh flowers, white lace, satin ribbon. Barney Graham, flushed and sweating in a new hairpiece, looked for all the world as if he really believed in the institution of marriage.

Good grief, he was crying.

From what I knew of Barney, though, he wouldn't remember this moment past his next drink. Still, should we give him credit for the thought, fleeting as it is? John Updike always does in his books, implicitly awarding salvation for impulse, regardless of intention, or commitment, or performance.

Well, today, maybe, I decided, because I saw him look at Beth and smile as he passed her, and one can always hope. (So much for hope. The next week I saw him at the movies with a new woman, old-young and battered-by-life-looking with bottle-red curls, so that took care of that.)

Doug one-upped the trumpeter with a flourish of organ chimes after the couple arrived at the altar. Although he was now the regular organist downtown at Our Saviour, Steve had gotten friendly with him while he was still playing here at Trinity, and had asked him to play for the wedding. Doug is always good at weddings, good at funerals, good at everything really, and I say it even if he is our son-in-law. And where was Grace, I wondered, as we sat down after the invocation.

Just then she slipped past the tall young couple next to me, and I smiled at her. How could you help it? She is so nice! Nice is a dirty word nowadays, but let me tell you, it beats nasty for living with, day in and day out. She's getting a little plump, like me, poor thing – our other daughter Joy is thin as a whistle – but she wore a navy-blue chiffon with a little capelet that hid the traces. She'd just had her blonde hair permed lately, and it gave her animation.

She was frowning. "Some more of Doug's fans," she whispered. "I had to talk to them."

It had to be hard, being the white wife of a black man who was increasingly catching the public eye, at least in Evittsburg, but she never said much about it. I had mostly given up pondering it by this time. We'd warned her fifteen years ago about the problems of an interracial marriage, and she had accused us of racism.

Maybe she was right. Dan and I considered ourselves enlightened, and I had brooded over her accusation at the time. Still did, maybe, a little. But things had gone better than we'd dared hope, especially since Gil had arrived, fourteen now, and beautiful.

Up front, a bridesmaid reached out and caught a ring-bearer as he ran past from a standing start.

"Where's Gil?" I whispered.

"Home practicing the piano. He didn't want to come, so he had to think up a good excuse, and I took him up on that one."

Everyone sat down. The family with the outspoken child was now busily taking snapshots, despite the bulletin, which pleaded for no flashes during the service. Their camera was a Polaroid, and they would shoot a picture, and then pass it up and down the pew, pointing at it and whispering, quite missing the wedding itself, rather like a modern version of the Platonic cave.

Marty's cousin read the scripture, obviously doing her very best. She was a good reader, and so she read fast to prove it. The tall young couple beside me giggled a bit, and you could hardly blame them.

Marty and Steve had chosen the Genesis passage about the man leaving his father and mother and cleaving to his wife. When Marty's cousin got to the part about cleaving, the young man next to me muttered something to his girlfriend, and they snickered. Well, you have to expect that with these archaic words, if you're going to use old translations. I never quite understood myself how "cleave" could mean to adhere to and to separate, both at the same time. Cleave and cleavage. I sighed.

Steve's brother got up then and read his assignment. It was the 13th chapter of I Corinthians, and he had learned his lesson listening to Marty's cousin. He read deliberately and well. With all the weddings we have, I get a little tired of I Corinthians 13, but if ever there was any cliché to insist on retaining, this is it.

"If I speak with the tongues of men and of angels, but have not love, I am a noisy gong or a clanging cymbal. And if I have prophetic powers and understand all mysteries and all knowledge, and if I have all faith, so as to remove mountains, but have not love, I am nothing."

Come to think of it, the problem is that such clichés *aren't* clichés anymore. I once knew a journalism professor, a young man who had been brought up in the most progressive schools and carefully guarded by his family against any of these old religious superstitions of his European heritage. Consequently he was into astrology. He was writing a book on the human need for love, as if this were a contemporary insight dating roughly from *The Greening of America,* with some ancient groundwork by Freud. He asked me if I had any good references on love, so I read him I Corinthians 13.

"Not bad," he said. "Kahlil Gibran?"

Steve's brother had almost finished. He looked up earnestly as he arrived at the climax. "Love never ends; as for prophecies, they will pass away; as for tongues, they will cease; as for knowledge, it will pass away. For our knowledge is imperfect and our prophecy is imperfect; but when the perfect comes, the imperfect will pass away."

The tall young man next to me snorted. He reminded me of Joy, who would never take anybody else's word for anything, even if they had actually experienced what she scoffed at as imagination.

"Now I know in part; then I shall understand fully, even as I have been fully understood. So faith, hope, love abide, these three; but the greatest of these is love."

"Bullshit," said the tall young man loudly.

Well, only loud enough for a couple of pews to hear, but it made a little stir locally. His girl turned red and looked furiously at him, and he set his chin stubbornly. I have to admit, it really got to me. Presently, however, everyone decided it was pretty small potatoes anyway in this filthy-mouthed time, and maybe they had misunderstood anyway, so they turned back to the wedding again.

Dan spoke to the bride and groom in that very serious tone he always bemoaned about himself, but never seemed able to overcome, and as usual, he was a little above everyone's heads. This time it was about the covenant of marriage being a part of the covenant of God with Israel, and how Jesus (neatly, I think) took the next necessary step in religious evolution to refocus a nationalistic, earth-based revelation on to a universal, spiritual one.

Everybody listened patiently. All congregations have personalities, and Trinity had always been unusual, tolerant and undemanding, grateful for Dan's emphasis on pastoral ministry rather than power plays. Long ago, he realized his strength lay in trying to embody God's love, not His authority.

The youth were a puzzle, but he tried. He had a tendency to trust their own self-confidence and expect more from them than they were really capable of doing. He labored to transplant the full-grown fruits of his own experience into green young minds, but they didn't seem to root. Hearts and kidneys can be transplanted, but everyone wants to grow his own insights.

Dan counseled all young couples before he married them, but year after year brought news of conflicts and infidelities and divorces, even from the most promising start. Now he didn't permit himself to hope.

"I give them about three years," he'd said, home from counseling Marty and Steve the first time. But this was a wedding, and I permitted myself to hope and so did everyone else – you could tell. Everyone maybe except this tall young man here, who was probably too sophisticated even to imagine the possibility.

I managed to calm myself down, and we sang a hymn, a good glorious one, "Praise to the Lord the Almighty," and everyone bellowed, in good spirits with the occasion and God, giving in momentarily after all to that elusive hope against so much evidence.

Steve and Marty had written their own vows, charming, endearingly naive ("I promise to meet all your needs forever") and whispered them at great length and inaudibly to each other.

I remembered I'd wanted to ask Grace about the rumor I'd heard that Doug had started a Sunday School class of his own at Our Saviour. She hadn't wanted to leave our church, but small-city organists are few, and full-time positions fewer. When the Our

Saviour job occurred in this southern Pennsylvania town, and Doug was called, it was not a time to divide the family. Dan had urged her to transfer membership from Trinity too. "Doug needs you with him," he said.

Now, I'd missed the legal moment, the proclamation of marriage, and we were well into the prayers. I noticed that, as everyone else knelt, the tall young man sat looking around with raised eyebrows and a small superior smile. Looking a lot like Joy, when she deigns to go to church.

He made me mad all over again.

Then Doug and the trumpeter swung into the recessional, Beethoven's *Ode to Joy*, and the bridal couple came down the aisle laughing (really, they were lovely, and God must bless them), and the music swelled – Doug's father Robey always said his son put the soul of the black man behind the console of the white man – and the cloudstruck sun pulsed through the highest stained-glass windows, strobing shards of blue and yellow and ruby-red upon the heads of the congregation, the wedding attendants, the vanilla-white bride. It stirred the essence of gardenia, stephanotis, and pink roses into breathlessness, the music drowned out thinking, and everything seemed possible.

Grinning now, the tall young man opened his mouth, and I could just imagine what he was going to say. Suddenly it seemed important to forestall him, no matter what, so I turned to him and said pleasantly, "Well, bullshit to you too, my friend."

Grace shook her head, and I was rather scandalized myself. Profanity has never been my first line of defense against the popular stereotype of ministers' wives as prim, self-righteous biddies. I never could see the point of using up one's last earthly resort on piddling provocations. If you shit and damn when the potatoes boil over, what do you do when the house burns down? So, to preserve my options, I say "darn" a lot. I've never had a whole lot of houses burn down, so this was a surprise to us all.

I didn't trust myself with the young man yet, so I made myself smile at the tall young woman and backpedaled. "What I meant was, some of us have been lucky enough to find out that love really can work the way that reading says, you know."

The girl actually paled. "My God, Jim, it's the pastor's wife!"

That ruined my chances of saying anything anyone would listen to, since the perceived value of any given comment nowadays is automatically canceled when the source is known to be the clergy. I hate the glaze that comes over people – I saw it happening now – who meet their first minister (or his wife) late in life. No doubt, the sanctimonious image is inevitable in an age when even just believing in God is considered by definition a sanctimonious act.

I sneezed.

"God bless you," said the young man automatically, then blushed.

The sun seemed to have gone back under its cloud for good now, and people were looking curiously at us, standing there silently, almost embattled. I smiled again, feeling the skin of my upper lip grit against my teeth, and turned toward the aisle.

Nobody stopped me.

CHAPTER 2

Doug played valiantly; as long as a warm body remained in the congregation was his policy. Grace and I looked at each other under cover of the music.

"I've known you for thirty-four years," she said, without a smile. "I still haven't figured out whether you're a conservative rebel, or a rebellious square."

Fair enough. I've never been sure myself, but it's not an uncommon malady, ambivalence. Most people who think at all, including Grace herself, suffer from it. Only Joy in our family ever seemed to hold unqualified opinions.

"Doug's having trouble," said Grace then, lightly.

"He seems to be having a good enough time right now," I said, listening to him wind up with the trumpet on a roll.

"Ah, well," she said fondly, "he deserves to have some fun. He's been run ragged this week."

"Three choirs getting him down?"

"If only that were all." She hesitated. "Dr. Brammer's a phony, you know."

I guess you only start pulling your punches when you get older. "No, I didn't. He's pretty highly thought of around town."

"He looks good, but he's all wind and no rain. You talk about bullshit" – she eyed me mischievously" – he's full of it. His preaching's straight out of the sixties encounter movement, but he never has much to say about God."

"Grace, everybody is embarrassed about God these days. Like they used to be about sex. This is the the 1980s, for goodness' sake.

We're modern and sophisticated, remember? No one takes religion seriously these days."

"People have started coming to Doug to get what Brammer doesn't give them."

"But Doug's a minister of music, not a minister of religion."

"Yeah. But even just talking to his choirs about how to sing the words of the music they're learning, they've picked up his strength, his faith, his enthusiasm, all the things Brammer projects only about his golf game. Anyway, Joan Chavez asked him to visit her mother in the hospital, and Andre and Jeneeva Jackson have been coming to him with their marital problems, and – well, it's not just minorities, either. It's getting like he's the pastor and Brammer is just running the place. Even Brammer seems to be sending people to him."

"Sounds like a can of worms to me. Can't he point to his job description – ?"

"Well, you know Doug. If someone asks him for help, he's not going to turn them down. Besides, he's only human, Mother. It makes him feel good to help people."

A most unLutheran shout came down from the choir loft. "Hey, clear out, you two. We can't keep on playing here forever." Doug beamed at us from the choir loft, with the slightly anxious face of the trumpeter beside him, seconding the motion.

We smiled and waved and looked around to see that we were the last ones left in the sanctuary. Time to tackle the post-ceremony ordeal.

From this point on, even good weddings are a bore. Mainly you wait for the photographer to take hundreds of unnecessary pictures to justify his bill, first of the wedding party, then of the guests doing a variety of things that will remain incomprehensible to all future generations. One creative studio I know of even used to take pictures of the church janitor sweeping up the rice or bird feed afterwards, but only the janitors ever ordered them, so the practice was finally discontinued, disrupting three janitors' photo album collections that I heard of afterward.

As we made our way down the receiving line, hugging and congratulating with all the indiscriminate fervor of practiced wedding guests, I thought about Grace's comment, that Doug felt good about helping people. I couldn't quarrel with that. I've never been one to tear a person down because doing good makes him happy. God knows, I'll take him any time over the kind of person who feels good about doing bad things.

I've heard Joy argue that there's no difference between the two, that they're both motivated by selfishness. But isn't there an important core of difference in the first place, between someone fulfilled by being "good," and someone fulfilled by being "bad?"

Not to Joy.

Come to think of it, she'd say, yes, there is a difference. She'd say the "good" person was more boring.

She's pretty innocent about it all, though. She thinks Christians believe "good" is going to church and saying "please." And they believe "bad" is pretty much limited to premarital sex. Even though she was born into a pastor's family, and went to church all her life until a few years ago, she ignores religious ideas of the power of evil, because she doesn't believe in that kind of thing. You bring up Hitler, and she says, "For God's sake, Mother." That's her argument, finding evil irrelevant.

As we stood outside the church door, I wished I had a cigarette. (Now, that's really bad, says Joy, although I never heard her say the same about her friends' cocaine habits.) I gave up smoking five years ago, mainly in response to her proddings, but I've never gotten past wanting a cigarette sometimes, like after meals and when I'm thinking hard. Or arguing hard.

"There you are," said Doug's deep voice, and he came down the steps to join us, strong, sturdy, four-square like his father Robey, in a gray suit.

Automatically, I checked out the other guests, a habit I haven't been able to break from the start of Doug and Grace's relationship. Happy in each other, they never seemed aware of other people's reactions to biracial couples, so far as I know. Still, always, I had felt it necessary to keep an eye on the people around us, watching out for trouble, as if I could see it coming and quell it with a glance.

But the wedding guests were in a good mood. They made way for Doug with smiles, and some, the younger ones, who had been in his choirs while he was still here at Trinity, stopped and spoke to him with a curious mix of geniality and awe.

Doug and I smiled at each other; we were close then.

"Hey," I said. "Grace tells me you're a great success down at Our Saviour."

He laughed and opened his big fist to show us three tiny nylon bags of rice.

"Beth sent these out to you," he said. "She noticed you missed the basket." The bags were prickly, tied in pink and deep blue ribbon, with the same tactile fascination of shifting mass as beanbags. "So Grace has been telling you about my people." Even then he called them his people, quiet and proud.

I bounced the rice bag up and down in my hand. "If they ask you to do too much of that sort of thing, I think you ought to go to Brammer. He needs pushing sometimes, Dan says, but after all, it's his work, what's he's getting paid for, not yours."

"It's okay. I don't mind. In fact, I kind of take to it."

The bride and groom appeared at the church door, framed by the roman arch and that shimmering glow of the newlywed young. Bombarded by rice, they fled laughing down the steps, into the waiting automobile, miming double-takes at its transformation by the other young into something out of Stephen Spielberg. They drove away, trailed by a flock of blatting cars.

We go to a lot of them, and nothing matches the horror of wedding receptions, unless it's graduation parties. One and all now, in our town, they are cacophonous with rock noise, so that the old folks flee as soon as they decently can, sometimes before the cake is cut, while those of us over forty but too proud to admit we can't take it, hold on with our teeth clenched and our smiles fixed, enduring.

Even if I didn't wear a hearing aid, it would be hell.

Still, this is the nineteen eighties, after all, and I've had to face the fact that many people love the music, even people I love, which is the hardest of all to imagine. They seem to have no thought for what the sheer noise of it stands for, a mindless, destructive anarchy that, deep down underneath, they really don't want in their lives.

But it's part of their youth, and no one is rational about that. One loves worthless, and worse than worthless, things if they are associated with the great expectations of one's youth.

Like a book review I read the other day, of a novel set back in the sixties, and heavy on the drugs, obsessive sex, the wasting of the young, and the trashing of the old, and then the reviewer concludes, I swear it: "This one will make you yearn for the good old days."

And she wasn't being funny.

So we sat in our best clothes in a fine hotel at lace-covered tables centered with orchids and roses, screaming at each other.

Perry Mandeville and his wife sat down at our table, faces as pained as ours must have been. Sixteen years ago, when Doug had auditioned as organist at Trinity, Perry had bristled at his color, as he was now all too ready to recall to anyone willing to listen. But from the moment he heard Doug play, he, in his own words, "bellied up like a bony old pickerel begging to be tickled."

He had a theory about it. It was, he thought, as if God made music a field of truce, like sports, where racism was suspended in favor of a higher goal, and then, useless, withered away as if it had never been. I always wondered, when Perry got carried away about the ministry of music, why he never mentioned the irony that the church itself, with higher ideas than sports or music, had not yet withered away its own racism.

It didn't hurt, of course, that Doug had studied with a student of Virgil Fox, and learned the old master's talents for showmanship. He was smooth, Doug was, but his every conscious intention was well-meant, and in this sinful world, you can't do more than that. God knows, he made Trinity come alive on top, as Dan's quieter ministry took hold below, and people turned out for him. Before he came, the choirs had dwindled under Mrs. Heislich's dapper direction. The organ sounded slick and sterile, too polished and genteel to stir emotion. Dan called regularly from the pulpit for a thinking, feeling church, but the thinking was little evident, and the feeling seemed almost gone too, until Mrs. H. resigned and Doug got the job.

"What would you be without God?" I heard him ask the choir at practice one night, and they thought of lives as joyless as their own often were, but without the extra dimension of trust and hope, and they answered, "Nothing!" Faster and louder, he said, "Who would you be without God?" and they answered "No one!" and sang their hearts out.

And these were white people, you understand, hardly a black face to be seen here on a Sunday morning in those days, which made it stranger than ever that Doug should have been so universally accepted, although he seemed to see nothing unusual about it. He was a member of a black generation a step beyond the one that had carried the heaviest burden of racism, and a step before the one that told itself that it did. He loved the idea of universality, and imagined that it had already happened. "Race is no problem," he insisted, "not any more." And, teasing, "Not when Bach can bring us together."

For its sheer romanticism, that bothered me, but it was his father, Robey Carlier, who put it into words, for once without the help of his beloved Bartlett's Quotations: "My aching Bach!" he roared characteristically. "That dude – he be white!" He snorted. "We get us a black Bach – then we talk!"

Well, anyway, I was fond of Perry, and of his wife, Mary Ann. Meredith Busche sat with us too, muscular and intense, with flecked brown eyes, like fur. She had lately gone charismatic, and it did wonders for her, but was rather miserable for the rest of us. She used to sell furniture at a local store and couldn't control herself. "We've got just what you want, praise the Lord," and "Here's your bill, hallelujah," or so I imagine, were reasons they fired her shortly afterward. "Blessed are those who are persecuted in the name of the Lord," she caroled and got a job in a Christian book store.

She was happy as can be, rather an argument for it all, because I had seen her otherwise. Two of her children had died in a motorcycle accident, another had chronic kidney problems. Her husband was no help; he worked in a supermarket, and spent all his time in the produce department. Maybe she had decided to give him a good reason to stay away.

Dan was sensitive about her. She went to him for counseling after her children's's deaths, and he thought he'd been helping when she turned charismatic. Strangely enough, she retained her membership at Trinity, and, to his bewilderment, thanked God copiously for Dan's part in her transformation. "At least she didn't lose her faith," he would say, a little dubiously.

Meredith's good friend, Jan Berry, so constant as to arouse foolish talk in this sex-obsessed age, was there too with her peasant face and belly laugh, refreshingly vulgar in small doses.

"Wasn't it a lovely wedding, praise the Lord?" shouted Meredith,
"The bride was so beautiful," I yelled back, and turned down my hearing aid. It worked better that way.

"This is the worst part of weddings! By the time the wedding party gets their pictures taken, I'm always worn out and hungry."

We discussed the problem at about ninety decibels and were still losing, so we lapsed into a little local pocket of inaudible silence, sipping at our drinks through those pin-holed stirrers, nodding madly at each other from time to time in the din. My hearing aid bounced to the beat behind my ear.

Just as everyone was on the verge of exhaustion, Dan arrived, and, shortly afterward, the wedding party was announced. They came in full of juice, obviously prepared to go on for hours. (Now that couples are sleeping together from their first date, wedding receptions last longer.)

Dan came over to take the chair I had saved him, and all of us watched hungrily as the bride and groom led the rush to the orchid-decked food table, picked up those little sandwiches I love when I don't have to make them, prime rib and ham, shrimp out of large iced bowls, tiny flaky cream puffs filled with chicken salad, dips and veggies and fruits and salads of all kinds, and homemade mints.

When our turn came, we checked out the architectural masterpiece of wedding cake on the way. It was arranged with fountains, pillars, and staircases with bride and groom on top, and tiny dolls parading up and down, dressed in the pink and dark blue of the wedding party. "There's no minister," I shouted to Dan. He raised an eyebrow. "He had the sense to go home," he yelled.

Eventually we got our share of the food, and I scuttled back to the table, although Dan, as usual, stopped to talk with Trinity members at another one.

"Why do I come to these things?" moaned Doug, downing three sandwiches in as many gulps, and two cream puffs in the next two. Grace pointed soundlessly at his plate with her fork, and he grinned and polished off two more sandwiches and six shrimp. The band had taken a break, and we could hear each other again, but the people-noise still rattled my hearing aid.

"He has to maintain his strength, praise God," said Meredith.

"Is Marty pregnant, Pastor?" asked Jan. There was a general choking noise around the table, but she didn't seem to notice.

"Even if I knew, Jan," he said, "would I tell?"

"Probably not," she answered cheerfully. "I heard she was, but you hear that about all the brides nowadays."

"Really?" said Perry, fascinated.

I was, rather, myself. I always believed ministers and their families should be above listening to gossip, and, God knows, they see enough real-life soap opera not to need the packaged stuff, but lately I had begun to believe that gossip isn't all bad. It goes naturally with friendliness and concern with each other, the news about lives. No gossip, no community.

So I was disappointed when Perry said to Doug, "I hear you're starting a Sunday School at Our Saviour."

Doug's mouth was full, and he waved his hands, mock-helplessly.

"Dr. Brammer asked him to," Grace said defensively. "He didn't volunteer to do it."

"So who volunteers?" said Dan, coming out of his particular daydream. "What age group, Doug?"

"Adult, singles and couples."

"The most rewarding of all."

"Right. For the first time, you know they're coming out on their own. Mama didn't push them."

"So what do you hear from Joy?" Meredith asked me.

"Not much," I said. "She's always busy at the *Item*." Joy is a reporter for the local newspaper.

A shout of laughter went up from the bridesmaids. Every one had missed the bouquet, so they decided to have another go at it. This time the tallest one scooped it out of the air and screamed in triumph.

"Actually, she drops in quite often," I added.

The band rematerialized suddenly, riveting my hearing aid.

"Joy's changed a lot," I said, and then wished I hadn't, because I didn't really need Meredith's metaphysical insights on the situation. "Well, not that much, I guess. She's a good kid." And so we sat nodding and smiling at each other, until we could decently get up and say goodby to our hostess.

As for Marty and Steve, I think it was about a year later, the week before Doug's FourFathers show, that Beth told me they had split up.

CHAPTER 3

The rest of that winter I remember digging in my heels against time. Looking back, it seems as if I had a premonition, but, if I had, I never noticed it.

What I do recall thinking was that I didn't really need time to pass so fast. Standing still in my life was fine with me. I never was the kind of person who sees progress only in doing bigger and better and more exciting things every year. Or month, or whatever. If you're happy and contented, progress lies in keeping it that way, not in trying to be more so.

Robey called that wisdom once, but, if it is, it's pretty low on the scale. More like common sense.

Robey also said, in that mocking black English he turns on at will when he wants to stir me up, "If you don be watchin out, Gramomma, you be gettin – whaddya call it? – alienated from society. Don nobody that's anybody nowadays calls settin still progress."

He was right about that, of course, but then Dan and I long ago realized that we are the ones who have become alienated from the mainstream. Still, it's my theory that, even if "wild and crazy" is the drumbeat of America, the world still needs some folks over here marching to a different one. If only to give the wild-and-crazies someone to contrast with. After all, how wild and crazy can you be if everyone is wild and crazy?

Say, it's good to be needed.

I reminded myself of that when I got home from the grocery store the next Saturday, and found Joy there waiting for me.

My heart skipped a beat when I saw her at the door: my baby, my darling ...

She ran down to help me bring in the groceries, her breasts batting away against her T-shirt. Mighty uncomfortable, I should think. "How can you stand not wearing a bra?" I said.

She sighed. "Oh, Mother, for heaven's sake." Then she noticed that I was huffing and puffing a bit (as unobtrusively as possible) and went on the attack herself. "Mother, you really have to get in shape."

Joy is very big on being healthy, or, at least, physically healthy. She goes religiously three times a week to a health spa called "Our Bodies, Some Bodies," a name of such stupendous inanity I grit my teeth when I hear it. "Religiously" is the right word here – all her spiritual resources go into her body.

"Oh, Mother," she would say, so I didn't mention that it looked as if her body grew sleeker every week with self-worship. The sacrifices she made and the homage she paid. The rituals of body-building, the liturgical dance of aerobics, the sacraments of yogurt and brown rice. All within the community of believers. Well, when you don't use your instincts toward what they're intended for, they're bound to home in on something else, and fitness beats crystals, I guess. (And I could be jealous!)

Anyway, her faith has been rewarded. She's a beautiful girl, drawn in a single taut line, always in motion or on the edge of it, as innocent as her name, dancing on the surface of everyone's life. Grace, whom Joy calls goody-goody, is the one who observes, who knows, if only from the books she reads, the grim truths Joy never imagines. And yet – Joy is so – lovable.

"Black jelly beans?" Eagerly she had started to unpack the bags, setting the contents out on the counter instead of putting them away, of course. "And more eggs? You've still got half a dozen in the refrigerator. All that cholesterol – "

I mustered my defenses. "The jelly beans were on sale, and you know we've already cut down on eggs." It was a sore subject with me, not just the eggs, but everything, all the old values suddenly turned into bugaboos by the new generation. "If you don't die of cholesterol this year, they'll probably find out next year that you die from lack of cholesterol."

I took off my coat, and she put her arm around my shoulders and hugged in that deliberate way some people have who've been told for years that touching and embracing are the panacea of the world.

"I got the morning off to go to the dentist," she said. "A filling fell out."

"So how's Jim?" He'd been our family dentist for years.

"Fine. He sent you his love, and Noreen said to tell you you're due for a checkup. I thought I'd spend the rest of my morning shopping at the Allegany Plaza. Want to go along?"

We spent some time in a discount store that had just opened there. Looking the way she does, Joy can put anything on and carry it off with class. She can turn cheap into the smart quirkiness required of women in her time and place. Looking the way I do, it's the one place in the area I can find decent half-sizes, for Evittsburg proper is not small-town enough to resign itself to the existence of fat people. Most of the stores still pretend nobody exists over a Size 14.

"How about this one?" She held up a monstrosity in blue and yellow, with no neckline and the seams on the outside.

"Don't ask."

"Guess what?" She hung it back on the rack. "I don't like it either."

We shopped in a growing atmosphere of requited approval. She found a belt for me I'd been looking for for years, which means big enough to go around, and I found a dress, black skirt and white lacy top she looked lovely in, agreed that she did, and bought.

"Hats are coming back in," she said, stopping at a display of them.

"Oh, dear, I hope not. I never felt so liberated as when we stopped having to wear them in the sixties."

She tried on what looked like a man's fedora in black felt. It was hideous, and she looked marvelous.

"You'd probably even look good in it backwards."

Mischievously, she turned her back. "Like this?"

"Darned if you don't look good any way you wear it."

She turned, smiling, and I smiled too. We were riding a gust of mutual benevolence, and I got little prickles in my stomach, the way I feel in an airplane taking off.

"Isn't there a Norman Rockwell painting with someone wearing a hat like that?" I asked incautiously.

"Oh, God," she said and threw the hat back on the counter.

"Now wait a minute, don't fly off the handle. It was men who wore them in those days, so that would preserve your modern credentials."

"Norman Rockwell was a jerk, and he painted a world that never was."

"His world did exist, right along with all the other ones. I know, because I lived in it."

"As a child, right? And it was a child's world he painted."

"But, by your standards, everybody was a child in those days. Even grownups. I lived by the kind of ideas children grow out of nowadays by the age of puberty. About six, that is. And I don't mean mother and apple pie either – "

"Mother!" Joy's voice was low but charged with fury. A woman, dragging a child like a Cabbage Patch doll by the arm, stopped and eyed us covertly from another counter. "Your generation never even noticed what was going on under your noses while all the nice stuff was going on. Blacks living like a sub-class, and capitalists gouging the poor – " Joy calls herself a modified socialist.

"That's true," I had to be honest, "but almost everybody was poor during the depression when I was little, so you didn't notice it that much. And then when the war came – you'll never know what the country was like during the war – "

The woman with the child drifted into Nightgowns, and Joy's voice rose. "Rockwell was hopelessly naive and painted a limited world – "

"But it was how he saw it, along with almost everybody else at the time. How can you downgrade art just because it doesn't agree with your trendy view of life? Nobody calls Velazquez a hack because he mainly painted royalty, or Walt Disney, because he concentrated on children – or – or whoever that is that puts out all those drippy paintings just because he specializes in drips – " in the heat of the moment I couldn't remember the artist's name, which rather detracted from the effect of my argument.

We glared at each other, embattled around the hats, but the spirit of our recent détente still lingered. It wasn't long before we had to smile at the ridiculousness of it all, and I don't remember which of us smiled first, maybe both.

"Well, so much for Norman Rockwell," she said lightly. "Remind me not to bring up abortion."

"Damn it, Joy." She could always find my buttons. "Quit labeling me. You know I'm not totally against abortion. Just that society has to be in favor of supporting life and reverence for life, with necessary exceptions, instead of implying that the choice is between two equal possibilities –"

"I know, I know," said Joy hastily. "Don't get started on it now." She shook her head and looked around pointedly. "I should have known you'd argue at the drop of a hat. Last time I went to church you got into a discussion with Meredith Busche, and that time you argued for abortion. My God, you'd battle to the death against self-assertiveness."

"Only if that side weren't being heard," I said, with dignity. She was right. I had been known to argue on opposite sides of the same question within the same hour, but what can you do when you're in the middle? And not wishy-washy?

"Where did you get so argumentive, Mother? It couldn't have been in church."

"That shows what you know about church." It was uncalled for, I knew, but I couldn't help saying it. The discussion with Meredith had been after church a year ago, and Joy hadn't been there since.

"Well, anyway. And it shakes me up, Mother, when you swear. Please try not to do that again." Apparently she and Grace had gotten together recently.

This didn't seem to be the time or the place to elaborate on my theory about the last-resort benefits of rare profanity. "Let's have lunch," I said. "My treat."

We went to the Chinese restaurant in the Plaza and settled into the ornate, red-gold ambience. I was boring and ordered sweet-and-sour pork; Joy chose I forget what, but it had to be prepared at the table and exploded and sizzled enough to make an occasion out of the meal.

"I saw Amazing Grace and Doug yesterday," she said, when the dining room had settled down.

"They seemed preoccupied at the wedding."

"Doug's awfully busy from what I hear. Devon Rickles, the religion page editor, asked me if Doug was ordained, and he's getting feedback that Doug's doing a lot of things Brammer ought to be doing – "

"I heard that, too – "

"It's none of my business, I guess. Amazing said he's never been so happy, even though he's rushed off his feet – well, how's your column going, Mother?"

I write a column in a little regional weekly called *The Evitts County Viewer.* I never could seem to place an article in any other publication, but somehow I landed this one, and through the years I had managed to pin down the territory. I'd collected a small but loyal group of readers, and I even come across one now and then.

"No change. I don't seem to be running out of topics yet."

"Not you, Mother." Joy's tone was abstracted. "I'm worried about Gil," she said, putting down her chopsticks. (Naturally she ate with chopsticks, which outside the East I consider an Occidental affectation.)

"What's wrong with Gil?"

She hesitated. "Mother, he's so beautiful. A golden boy, if you want to get sickly sentimental." But sentimental was my normal state about Gil, our only grandchild.

" 'Child of unmeasured grace,' " I murmured, an old phrase Gil always brought to mind.

"Oh, I don't know. Grace gets measured a lot since she joined Weight Watchers, and – sorry, that old sibling rivalry again." She grinned and picked up her chopsticks again. "Gil's lost some of that glow lately, I'm afraid. When did you see him last?"

"Same time I saw you last, at his birthday party a couple weeks ago. And we've talked on the phone since then. I thought he looked wonderful. Just fourteen and the whole world before him."

"Well, I don't know, maybe it's my imagination. But I saw him on the corner when I drove past Blaise Hill School on Friday, and he didn't look so good. And neither did the guys he was with."

Dear God, he couldn't be on drugs, could he? The first thing one's mind turns to nowadays, without missing a beat for denial or incredulity. "Have you talked to Grace about it?"

"No," she said, poking a chopstick at something congealing anonymously in the sauce on her plate. "No – "

"Do you remember, when Doug put that new swing in for him in the backyard? He was about three, wasn't he, and I guess it had never occurred to him that a person could have his own swing. Well, he got onto that swing and he swung for, oh, half an hour, remember? High and fast at first, like any little boy, but after awhile, just back and forth, floating back and forth, lost in his own little world of dream fulfilled. He looked like someone just admitted to heaven, and not an angel, either, but someone who knew bliss from the opposite."

"He cried a lot as a baby," said Joy, who never minded bringing down other people's flights of fancy. "But, even if he weren't my only nephew, I think he'd still be my favorite one. Friday I stopped and picked him up and took him home, so he didn't have to stand around for the bus."

I waited.

She shrugged. "He acted pretty much as usual. Talked a lot about photography – that's his latest love, you know – and I encouraged him, of course. But the glow – well, he didn't say much. And he sat the whole time looking forward. You know how he usually sits sideways, so full of enthusiasm, leaning over and looking at you when he's talking in the car?"

"Maybe he's just growing up – "

"Maybe – "

"I don't think he has many defenses. He's gentle, maybe too gentle for these days. Remember, Joy, when he caught that butterfly?"

She moved impatiently.

"I know, you have to go. But the butterfly – it was a Monarch – it came right after him. And, just sort of in a reflex, he put out his hand and caught it, and I knew it was a goner. What child of five wouldn't crush it? But with this great big glorious smile he opened his hand and the butterfly flew away, like the essence of Gil himself, all gold and free – "

"Mother --"

Obviously, I was getting carried away. And I pride myself on being pragmatic and unemotional!

"Mother, I want to talk about me for a minute. I can't put it off any longer."

She used to say the same thing when she brought home a note from the teacher. ("Joy has all the brains she needs to be a great success in whatever she chooses. Now, if she'd just use them!" Teachers weren't afraid to speak up in those days.)

"I meant to tell you at home, but nothing was right for it. It's not here, either, but I've got to get back to work. And I wanted you to know, so you wouldn't think I was springing anything on you. Je - God, how do I say it?"

"It's Scott."

We looked at each other across the table, while the waitress removed our plates. It seemed to take a long time.

"You and Scott – "

"We're moving into an apartment together tomorrow."

I readjusted my hearing aid. The news couldn't have been a shock. Dan and I had known it would happen in the end. "I don't understand," I had said once. "Sure, sex is fun, but even if that were an excuse, Joy's not just a teenager any more. She's bright, and she's so responsible in so many ways. And sure, sex is beautiful, but not in itself. Sex is grubby, sweaty stuff by itself, everybody out for what they can get. But when it means something, it's beautiful. And the meaning that makes it beautiful is commitment to each other."

Dan had to laugh. "One woman's 'sweaty, grubby' stuff is another man's 'time of the singing of birds,' as Robey would put it. And probably has." His voice softened. "Their experiences aren't ours, Ellie, and we can't expect everyone to think like we do." He mused a moment, and I knew that beneath the professional acceptance lurked the same hurt I felt, the feeling of personal betrayal of standards faithfully passed along, and then, so very pointedly, rejected.

Now I looked at Joy. "So what am I supposed to say? You know how we feel about it."

She shrugged, very distant now. "Yeah. I guess I'll have to resign myself to not being saved."

That did it. I took care to lower my voice this time, but the increased intensity probably only made me sound sinister. "All those years of Lutheran confirmation classes, and you still don't get it? Morality won't earn your salvation. Morality is the way you say thanks for it. By building the most lasting, respectful relationship with another human being that is possible in this world. Your generation's always talking about not exploiting people – but there's always this outstanding exception."

She stood up. "I didn't expect you to understand, Mother. Scott and I aren't in this just for what we can get out of each other. Did you ever hear of love? Excuse me. I have to get back to work." She was gone, the bill with her, leaving several titillated diners behind, watching me with interest.

The waitress, undeniably inscrutable, doggedly brought me a small dish with two fortune cookies curled up in the middle, like somnolent snails. The slip from the first one read, "This is the last day of the first part of your life." The other one read, "Present happiness gives way to future uncertainty."

It must have been a bad day in the fortune cookie factory too.

CHAPTER 4

Actually, things got better. Joy's news, after all, was no more than we had been expecting for weeks. And Scott, we hoped, might be considered a cut above the relationships we were pretty sure she had been engaging in for several years.

Though not much. His last name was Lease. He was a lawyer, much older than Joy, balding; he looked like George McGovern with a tighter, narrower face, but he seemed a conservative of the left, intolerant, self-righteous, puritanic about all the verities, as long as they were progressive.

The next Friday, Gil came out to stay over the weekend with us. Grace had to attend a weekend conference for real-estate salespeople in Atlantic City. She'd gotten her license a few months earlier, but the market had just taken one of its periodic downswings, and she hadn't had much action since. The conference was supposed to help, therapeutically, at least.

Doug's weekend was all taken up with rehearsals and organ practice. He was planning a spring choir festival at Our Saviour in a month or two. "He's got so much to do he doesn't know which end is up," said Grace, when she called to make arrangements for Gil.

Dan confirmed this. After the City Ministerial Meeting at Our Saviour on Tuesday, he had caught Doug on the run and made him go to lunch with him. "I think he appreciated a little relaxation for a change. Funny thing – he seemed wistful for the old times here at Trinity, where he first started out. Yet, from all I hear, he's taken Our Saviour by storm. Got a good start on the city too. Pretty unusual for a black who doesn't play on race any more than Doug does."

"I wonder if that was ever a deliberate decision – I mean Doug's sort of 'above-the-racial-brouhaha' stance – or if it just comes naturally to him."

Dan squinted into the distance. "He told me about it some years ago. He said, in college – that would be before he met Grace – he was taking black studies, but he wanted so desperately to play the organ and study the classics. He got patronized by the whites and mocked by the blacks. He was on the edge of a nervous breakdown, he said, when he picked up Galatians and was reading how, under Christ, 'there is neither Jew nor Greek, there is neither slave nor free, there is neither male nor female.' Strangely enough, it wasn't the racial reference, or the slavery reference, but the gender one that finally got to him."

"The gender one?"

"Well, remember, his mother was white. Pretty unusual in those days. I've always wanted to ask Robey about that, but I never had the nerve. Anyway, Doug says it came to him suddenly, 'Just because I have a black father, why does that automatically make me black? I've got a white mother, and I'm me! Why can't I love Duke Ellington, and Bach too?' " Dan sat back and put his fingertips together, remembering. "The more Doug talked the more upset he got. He said, 'I'm crazy about the organ! I'm crazy about the classics. Even if it were a matter of color, which it isn't, I have just as much right to them as any white man. My mother was white. They are my heritage too, and if I have two rich heritages, then that makes me luckier than your average bear, and I'm going to take advantage of it.' "

I cheered. "That sounds like Doug. But I don't know whether anyone can pull it off in this day and age."

"Mmm. Talk about being in the middle. Still, if he's inherited his father's self-confidence, he'll make it eventually. I don't know anyone more secure in his racial identity than Robey. A lot more than Doug, who works so hard to claim both identities."

I made apple fritters for Gil, his favorite meal, but he didn't show up for dinner. I got angry and then scared.

"I was sure Grace said he'd be here in the afternoon." I'd done the dishes, but you don't use up much energy these days rinsing them off, shoving them into the dishwasher, turning the dial. I was furious to find myself pacing the floor. (You do tend to pace when you're worried and sigh when you're unhappy, just like they say. It's humiliating.) Dan sat patiently trying to watch his namesake on CBS News. His right temple twitched. He'd always had that slight tic, but lately I wondered if it wasn't getting more pronounced.

He tried to soothe me. "Since no one answers the phone, and we can't get hold of Doug at church, there's not much we can do about it right now. It's too early to call the hospitals. We'll just have to wait. Gil's probably on his way, and he'll walk in the door very soon, protesting he never realized what time it was."

As an Olympic worrier, I didn't let that comfort me too much. It was based on no more information than I had, plus Dan's boundless confidence that all the world lies ultimately in the hand of God.

I'm not always so sure.

"He clenches it sometimes, you know," I muttered, poking a scrap of newspaper along the carpet with my toe.

Dan sighed and got up and turned off the television. He knew me too well to suspect I could keep quiet at such a time although, actually, I had just resolved to sit down and shut up until the newscast was over.

"I'll be quiet," I said, and turned the television back on. "I promise." A commercial flipped on, featuring one of those stunned and gaping faces caught in the zoom lens of some idiot warp of the human condition.

"I needed that." I snapped it off again.

Dan was amused. "The news is over," he said. "You didn't think I'd cut short my daily fix, did you?"

"You mean all that graphic evidence that God's gotta be up there in His heaven because He's sure as hell not down here in this world?"

"I know," he said, and put his hand on my shoulder. "It's not that I don't worry, you know. I'm not such a fool as to think that God protects us from suffering. The things I see every week, how could I believe such a thing? But I have to pace my worries. I work with them one by one, and leave the others up to Him. If I let them all surge in on me, Gil, yes, and Doug, and Leona Fuller (she's fine – did I tell you? The doctor said it's benign) and Conor Rademacher – by the way, he's committed himself to the psychiatric wing of the hospital for treatment."

That was news. Conor was a painter, fairly famous in the local artistic community for his representational portraits. They were universally considered deeply profound, because he never painted mouths.

"He called me today with a problem."

"Called you. I didn't even know he knew you."

"Karen Connally is his sister-in-law, and he'd heard from her about the time I counseled her, that awful year when her husband accidentally backed the car over their little boy? Anyway, Conor, poor guy, suddenly found himself last week painting mouths at last. Only they're all wide open screaming. And he cries every night, but he doesn't know why. It all started after he visited his father's grave in Pittsburgh for the first time since he died twenty years ago. Conor wanted to know if I thought it was a good idea to look for professional help, now that he's starting to paint mouths – "

"He could probably use a market consultant, too," I said meanly.

" – and I told him 'yes.' But I know my limits. Some of those doctors are pretty good up there on Seven South."

Then Gil walked in.

Joy was right.

The glow was gone, drained from his dear golden face, as if the sun had gone behind clouds. I thought suddenly that someday he would be as old as we were, and then how would he look? The strong chin, Doug's, and the crisp ringlets – although I hated it when they fell down his face a la Michael Jackson – the quirked eyebrow, which was Grace's, and Doug's broad cheekbones, which made him look kindly and generous. Which he was. Now the color of goldenrod, bleached by winter.

But he insisted there was nothing wrong.

"Oh, Nana," he said, in much the same tone as Joy, "you fuss too much. I was just out for awhile with some of my friends, and lost track of the time. I don't know what you're worried about." He warmed from grandfillial reassurance to youthful indignation.

"Mom and Dad think I'm old enough to be out by myself. How come you don't trust me?"

Trust, of course, is where the young have the old by the throat, gasping guiltily between faith and common sense. I used to think I had the perfect answer ("Don't you trust me to trust you? It's the others I don't trust.") but constant repetition had worn down its point.

Still, I fought back. "You know it isn't that I don't trust you, Gil. Sorry if this is an insult, but you really are pretty darned responsible – "

"Nana, you make me sound like a goody-goody – " Some of the glow burned back, kindling light and color.

"Now, Gil, would I accuse you of virtue? All I mean is that, for your age" – he groaned loudly.

I gave up, which had been his idea all the time, of course.

"Nana means that we trust you to keep on being responsible," said Dan, sounding about as helpless as I. He shrugged. "How about a game?"

They spent the rest of the evening locked in battle over the chessboard, while I turned off my hearing aid and worked on a column about trying to get along with the newest generation. It insisted on getting serious, so I finally gave up and went to bed.

CHAPTER 5

The post office was open Saturday mornings, and I had a manuscript to mail, as usual. Not that anything would come of it. I took Gil along; he was used to the ritual.

The only thing I had ever published was my weekly column, but not for lack of trying. I had been getting rejection slips for so long, I had even gotten beyond thinking it was original to joke about papering my walls with them, the sign of a really professional rejectee.

It wasn't that I didn't have a good idea why I kept getting rejected; it's just that it always came too late. Some sort of mail-change always took place between the time I sent something out, and the time it came back. My writing sounded so good, so creative and clever, for the outgoing mail, but when I reread it on its return, it wasn't the same article. Here was a pronoun with no referent, there an idea that lapsed into another one halfway through the page. A logical sequence of thought lurched unaccountably; a leading question went nowhere in the end.

It was obvious why I couldn't publish anything: my writing just wasn't very good. It felt fine going down on paper, but once separated from its premises by time, it died on me.

Also, I never went to Princeton.

Still, the truth is that I'm a literary version of that old esprit d'escalier, the poor soul who thinks up all her best points going upstairs when the argument is over. I'm at my most articulate when I'm vacuuming, or cooking dinner, or listening to Dan's sermon in church, except the time is never right to jot things down. Or, if I do, the vacuum howling, potatoes boiling dry, people staring, I can never recreate the spark at the typewriter later.

Sometimes I can't even read my notes.

My best writing is in response to others' ideas. What a reactor I am, a brilliant, incisive letter-to-the-editor writer! But I'm terrible at fiction. It's one thing to respond to pre-selected topics, with the parameters staked out and the battle lines drawn, and quite another to launch out into fictional anarchy. Fiction is frightening, the whole world to choose from, so many alternatives, and no assurance that you're picking the right, or even a better, one.

Being God was never one of my ambitions.

On the other hand, writing a novel was. More than anything, I wanted to write about the people in between, the ones reviled by writers since Mencken for being bourgeois, and then, lately, in one splendid sweep of Orwellian Newthink, totally ignored. They are, in fact, the ones who invented the novel and for whom the novel was invented, and who were once its most frequent subject.

But even more than writing about the despised middle class, I wanted to write about the middle people, the ones like me. People who feel torn between black and white, who live in the gray places between wealth and poverty, virtue and sin, belief and doubt, people who say things they wonder if they believe, not out of hypocrisy but out of need, people who sometimes find themselves secretly cheered by the advances of movements they basically disagree with. People for whom to be in the middle gives the appearance of being against both sides, when it really means that, to some measure, you're for both sides.

On occasion.

A line-balancing act, where you sometimes have to put your hands over your head, to escape the brickbats from both right and left. Very hard on the balance –

"Is that your book, Nana?" asked Gil

"No way, hon. If I ever get that book to the point where I won't feel like an idiot sending it out, I'll let you know."

This manuscript was to Newsweek's My Turn, and I had a little more hope for it than usual. For some reason, I thought it might be helpful to nonbelievers to discover that the Moral Majority is not representative of all Christianity, as they seem to believe. Perhaps they might be interested to hear that, in the creation-evolution argument, there is a widely-held Christian position which accepts the scientific theory of evolution in general, seeing it as perhaps the truest analysis so far of how God creates the world.

Silly of me to think anyone would be interested these days, but there you are.

The post-office clerk was used to me by now, though the business of weighing the envelope with, and then without, the stamped, self-addressed envelope, always seemed to tax his tolerance. Gil could hardly wait until we were out of the building.

"I've written a play, you know."

"I didn't know."

He had always laughed and cried to the occasion, but now he gave nothing away. His tight black curls glittered like polyester in the sun.

"It's about me."

I unlocked the car door for him, and he hurled himself inside to unlock my driver's door before I got there. As we backed out of the parking place, he turned to me, the old Gil. Last night's apathy was gone. This was the same open, spontaneous Gil, brought up by his parents to "universal" values, arrogantly white, no doubt, in one line, certainly defiantly black, in the other, but cheekily himself. Labeled black by people who live by labels on both sides of the controversy, but golden-faced, golden-hearted.

"Nugget," his grandfather Robey had called him when he was a happy little dirt-encrusted boy. "You are what you are," Robey would croon, as Gil crawled across the floor to him, and, lithely, or groaning with arthritis, depending on the day, Robey would lean over carefully, knees stiff, and pick up the child, rock him against his own brown cheek: "Don't ever let them melt you down, boy."

"Nugget," I said now, and Gil flushed a deeper gold. I expected, "Oh, Nana." Instead, he took a deep breath and burst out, "I've been protected, Nana. Not that I hold it against anyone, but I don't live in the real world, you know."

"There are four billion worlds in this one, as many as there are people," I said, braking abruptly as a pickup with a tickled dog loose in the back slowed down in front of us. "And all of them are real, in their way."

The dog braced itself and barked heartily. Gil grinned. "He reminds me of old Sin."

"You still remember him?" Sinnamon had died years ago, hoary with age and doggy virtue.

"Of course. I remember everything. Even the bad things."

"Why do you want to do that, Gil?"

His grunt was the wry, grown-up kind. "Don't you know? I have to use them. Like in my play, see? I used the time at Karen Barber's birthday party. And last year when I ran for eighth-grade president, and the white kids went around rolling their eyes and doing Michael Jackson steps, and the black kids called me names?"

That I remembered. It had caused some family trouble, of the kind that Dan and I, and Doug and Grace, for that matter, always tried to avoid. Gil had come home blazing, wanting answers, although he was already old enough not to wonder why the white kids did it. "But why do the black kids go after me, when I'm black too, Dad?"

Driven, Doug sounded more like his father than himself: "It's the whites that make us, Gil," he said finally. "We learned racism from the whites, and then we turn it on our own, well, like you, because you're not quite black and you're not quite white, and in this country you've got to be one or the other to have a place. That's the way the whites made it."

I was furious when Gil told me about it his next weekend with us. But I could see that what Doug had said helped him somehow. For the moment, it gave him answers. Still, stupidly, I had not been able to let it go. "Listen, Gil," I'd said. "Don't let anyone turn you against yourself. You're as white as you are black, you know, and you can choose to let the two mesh or else clash inside yourself."

Later, I took it up with Doug. "It didn't sound like you," I said. "You've always prided yourself on being objective about all this race stuff."

He blew up. "Even I, Mom," he said, sarcasm dripping, "even I can't always live up to my own ideals. Who do you think I am, Jesus Christ? Gillie was hurting. I was hurting because he was, and whatever I believe about original sin or the human condition – damn it, Mom, when you come right down to it, it's you whites in this country that started it all, and don't you forget it!"

"I don't," I flashed back, "and don't you forget that you blacks are pretty fast learners!"

I was disgusted with myself. I told Grace about it, in a welter of self-reproach, and she only smiled, but her lower lip drew up and tightened, as it had begun to in the past year.

When I told Dan, he said, "Doug's heard worse."

"But not from me."

Doug and I had made up, though, and things were maybe even a little better between us than when we had self consciously sidestepped the issue. Now Gil was hurting again, but I didn't quite know why. Perhaps it was a mistake to dwell on it.

I had to stop and pick up some pictures, so I pulled into the tiny parking lot of the fast photography outfit on Fair Street, and then sat there and listened while Gil poured out the plot of his play. It was called "Fencing," some not-quite-obvious connection with the Robert Frost poem, I gathered, and it was predictable but promising from where I sat, vignettes of a man such as Gil might be in another ten years, facing his past, reliving as an adult his childish rejections because of his mixed parentage, being unable to root himself in either culture, unable to face the future beause of the damage of the past, sensitive, unutterably vulnerable to all the hurts stored up in generations of braving prejudice, most of it, one had to concede, at least until recently, unabashedly white.

I wanted to be Gil's loyal, faithful grandmother, unquestioning and supportive on every count, but, listening to this brilliant, susceptible child, I could only be terrified for him. What's more, I had to face the fact that I was jealous for his white ancestry, and hurt, too, that it seemed to mean nothing to him. He might have been better off, I thought bitterly, if, like most white grandparents of mixed grandchildren until this generation, we had viciously ignored his existence. But I couldn't stand that, and put my hand out quickly to touch his arm, reassure myself that he was there with me.

He gave me a quick smile and kept on talking.

I listened, and watched a small tree by the front fender sifting swatches of sunlight over the hood of the car, and I yearned over him, and over his father's determined, dogged fight, against all the odds and the times. I prayed that these might turn right for him to succeed. But above all, I prayed that Gil might grow into his grandfather Robey's cheerful strength, however prejudiced and harsh it seemed to me sometimes.

I ached for Gil to get past vulnerability. If that was possible.

But he rattled on, and I made all the right sounds, and then we went in and got the prints, a few still from last Christmas, and Gil's birthday party, and a couple from Marty's wedding, and we sat in the car looking at them.When I sensed his attention shifting, I looked up smiling, to tease him about his male disinterest in weddings. Only then did I notice that another car had slipped in beside us, a Mercedes, no less.

The two men who got out of it didn't seem to notice us. One was lightly black, and the other was darkly white; both were young and slim, with eyes like olive pits. Unsmiling, they pushed open the door of the photography store and disappeared inside.

I turned to Gil. He was staring after them, more drained-looking than the night before.

"Okay, Gil, what's the problem? You look at those men like they're the devil incarnate."

But he only shook his head and turned his gaze out the front window. "It's okay, Nana. They're teachers at school."

I put my hand on his arm. "Gil, what's wrong?"

"Can we go, Nana?" he asked, tight-lipped.

"Gil, are you into drugs, somehow? Are those men drug-dealers?"

Staring at the dashboard, he shook his head.

"Gil, you know what drugs can do to a person. If you're doing drugs, or selling them, either one, you can destroy the rest of your life. And your family's too."

"I know, Nana." His voice was so low I could hardly make out the words. "I'm not doing anything with drugs."

I put my hand on his shoulder. "Can I trust you, Gil?"

The convulsive movement of his head could have been a nod.

I started the car and got out of there in a hurry.

The weekend passed rapidly after all. I didn't push him; maybe I was afraid to make any more of anything than I already had. Perhaps I should have, but I don't think it would have made any difference in the end. As it was, we had a good time, although we watched more television together than I approve of.

Gil talked incessantly about his play, which his ninth grade was putting on as their contribution to the Middle-School One Act Play Tournament. I hadn't realized it had gotten so far along. The performance was scheduled for the beginning of June, a part of the outbreak of spring festivities that always overwhelms everyone as winter schedules draw to a close. I hoped it would fit into mine, between the Mother-Daughter Banquet, and the Church Bowling Banquet, to which we were always invited.

Grace drove out to pick up Gil Sunday night, and I had a chance to ask her if she knew what Gil had been up to lately, besides the play. He had joined a new club at school, which he hadn't told me about: something, she thought, that had to do with drill teams and color bearers for school athletic activities.

"I'd check into it, if I were you," I said. "Gil seems guilty, or scared, about it, or something."

"I never got a hint of anything wrong," she said. "You can bet I'll look into it right away."

I sent Gil home with a big batch of his favorite soft sugar cookies done up in a shoe box. Doug liked them too.

CHAPTER 6

Spring exploded all over the place, like bombs planted by some benign terrorist, the sun blinding winter eyes, and fire in all the gray corners, forsythia, daffodils, tulips. After that came the hotter, whiter flame, dogwood, fruit blossoms crisping out little future cherries and apples, and lesser pink blasts among innocent bystanders, almond and peach and weeping cherry. Altogether, a superior spring, and the smell and taste and feel of it reached all the way inside the auditorium at Gil's school, the night his play went on.

Dan had rushed back from a viewing to make it, but we were still a little late. Luckily the side doors were open to let in the spring, and, not too publicly, we found seats in time for Gil's first entrance.

He came onstage as himself ten years from now, obviously delighting in the future. His conception of that far-off self was pretty conventional, I was relieved to see. (He had borrowed Dan's gray sport jacket, and it was only a touch too large). Anyway, no fright wig or hip threads, or whatever they call them these days. That was fine with me; nothing wrong with being conventional; as a human condition, it has a lot of precedent.

The interesting thing was that, even though Gil saw himself as a grown man in this play, he seemed to have trouble visualizing a life beyond the present. The play consisted mainly of flashbacks, in which he relived his childhood.

Or recycled it.

It started with his first day at school, when little Gil, played by a small, black first-grader with great dignity, entered his schoolroom filled with white children, and everyone stopped and stared at him in deadly silence. It was modeled after the "When you talk, they listen,"

E. F. Hutton commercials and got rather a laugh, which, I hoped, was what Gil had intended.

In the next scene, he was slightly older, home telling his parents about winning the school spelling bee. The children playing Grace and Doug were proud and congratulatory, seemingly unfazed by the fact that the word Gil had won on was "miscegenation." It was a point also missed by much of the audience, but they clapped and cheered when a large black boy playing Gil's grandfather burst onto the scene in a parody of Robey's bombastic character, and, barely waiting to hear Gil's story, announced in ringing tones, "You be what you is, boy, you be what you is." Everybody onstage hugged everybody else and segued into the next scene, which was a birthday party for the sixth graders at Karen Barber's house.

That hadn't been so long ago. I was there when he got the invitation in the mail – a card full of clowns and balloons.

"Do I have to go?" he'd asked Grace, but it seemed a *pro-forma* question.

When she answered, "I don't see why not," he only said, "Well, they better not do any of those post office games – I'm not kissing any girls," and ran off to play baseball.

Gil reproduced the party on stage as I have no doubt it occurred.

It was full of uneasy, half-eager little boys, and coy little girls who were completely in control of the situation. They played, so help me, Pin The Tail On the Donkey, and the Gil-actor, a white boy this time with a classic Italian complexion almost as golden as Gil's or even a little darker, enjoyed himself immensely in the ad-lib melee on-stage, managing to run into people with his blindfold on with all the enthusiasm boys usually show when mild mayhem is socially acceptable.

That game over, the girls said, "Let's play post-office." An older girl, playing Karen's mother, took an elaborate look around the party guests and said, "Not yet." So they played a prize-finding game, and then the girls called for post-office again, while the boys loftily ignored the fuss. Again, Karen's mother produced another game. Halfway through this one, the doorbell rang offstage, and in walked a black girl, playing Gil's only female black classmate, Pearletta Warren.

"Now you can play post office," said Karen's mother. "Now Gil has someone to send a letter to." And the curtain rang down.

"Subtle," commented Dan in my right ear, the one without the hearing aid.

The next scene was a considerable production, a kind of song-and-dance replay of the recent student body elections, at least as Gil saw them. Amidst a kind of micro-panoply of the national elections, the Gil-actor from the last scene campaigned vigorously for office, on the platform I remembered hating as soon as I'd heard it.

Grace hadn't much cared for it either. " 'Less noise and more toys'?" she'd repeated incredulously, when he told her, and he'd said, "Oh, Mom, it's just a snappy way of saying I'm for teachers shutting up a little, first, and then letting us have more computers in the school. Everybody says computers are the wave of the future, but we only have one in the whole school for the kids to learn on."

"Toys?"

"Mom, don't you see? It *sounds* good."

The Gil-actor worked up his support onstage, and the representative student body, six whites and three blacks, gave him their attention, while the grown-up Gil described the progress of the campaign, stage-left. When the Gil-actor walked off, the student body went into a choreographed response, with the blacks and three whites cheering for Carlier, and the other whites doing mocking little moonwalk steps and yelling, "Hey, Mr. Jackson! Dance, Mr. Carlier!" I wondered where Gil had picked up the minstrel reference – probably Robey.

Then they voted. The results were announced by a dancing principal, as bald and skinny as Mr. Forsyth himself, and the audience hooted and roared. Gil won the election and was installed as student-body president, but, as he stepped off the upstage platform, the whites and one black melted into the wings, and the other two blacks pelted him with paper wads and chanted, "Yellow Tom, yellow Tom."

And the curtain fell.

Gil must have felt uneasy with the musical format, because he dropped it for the last scene, which was short and curiously noncommittal, grown-up Gil in a photography shop talking to the clerk, who was wearing a hat with "God" on it. There was dialogue about negatives and inverted images and black-and-white and color. Gil handed over his film to be processed, and the clerk said, portentously, "We'll see what develops." Everyone in the auditorium groaned, of course, almost covering up the Gil-actor's concluding remarks. All I heard of them was, "Back then I wasn't sure. But now I know."

"What did he say there before the part about not being sure?" I whispered to Dan, but he hadn't heard it either.

It turned out that Gil wasn't the only one in the ninth grade who wrote, so we watched three other original, self-produced plays, one similar to *Lord of the Flies* in concept, another quite a pretty little romantic idyll of the Harlequin novel type, and the third an earnest plea on behalf of environmentalism, with riveting scientific and statistical information, delivered by children dressed as endangered species.

When it was all over, I had a healthier respect than ever for Ms Wood-Thomas, the ninth grade teacher. "All the work you put into it," I said to her afterward, and she smiled wearily, "Yes, but they did so much of it themselves, especially Gil. He's very special, your grandson."

I couldn't help but agree.

Intermittently through the evening I had heard Robey's unmistakable rumble underlining the audience laughter, and when the lights went on for good, Dan and I looked for him at once. He stood with Doug and Grace accepting compliments on his grandson's play, solid like Doug, but bigger, with broad black cheeks so shiny they seemed to reflect the changing light as people walked past.

His mustache parted in the center, and his forehead met his hair just in time to be called high. His head was big, topped by the tight curly hair he had worn the same way through all the electric-shock Afro fads of the '60s and '70s. "You can't see no head with all that hair," he told me once, unabashed, "only face. And I got me a good head. No call to hide it."

He wore cords and a good shirt, open at the neck. I had never seen him wear a tie in his retirement, nor had I ever seen him ill at ease. Perhaps his forty years of experience as a head waiter in a railroad dining car had relaxed him permanently in every situation. But what I admired most about him was that he never had any doubts.

"Ain he sumpin, that Gil?" I heard him say as we pushed through the crowd that had gathered around him. "Steady yo'sef there comin through, Gramomma," he called, and manipulating large hands, palms down, he seemed to clear a path for us miraculously. It was easy to see where Doug had gotten his magnetic authority.

Several people from Trinity were there, those with children at the school, the Swaneys and the Harts, and Donnie Hicks, Dan's secretary, whose oldest daughter, Jennifer, had played the romantic lead in the Harlequin romance. Robey, who sometimes dropped in to see Dan at church, and knew Donnie, said, "She set it singin, mam, that little play," sounding in his way courtly, with the outmoded title, rather than servile.

By the way, the black dialect was a put-on. Or maybe it was the impeccable "white" prose he could switch into at the drop of an eyelid that was the put-on. I never had the nerve to ask him which, although I let him know from time to time that I thought one of them was. It annoyed me for some reason; I think it was the suspicion of mockery. But Robey had only raised his hand loftily when I fussed and retrieved from his tremendous, Bartlett-based memory bank yet another running commentary: " 'White persons never understand.' "

Now he put his arms around my shoulders. "You a hard woman for reachin round," he said, an old joke between us, though funnier to him than to me. "You like our boy tonight, Gramomma?"

"Honestly, Robey," I said crossly, "all this Gramomma stuff. You make me sound like a white-haired old lady."

The chuckle from his barrel chest shook the two of us, and Dan grinned. He knew how I felt about Robey, love and irritation and respect all jammed together in a room with a very low threshold. Robey knew too, and released me, after a final hug, still teasing, " 'Old and godly and grave,' " he said, giving his Bartlett's Quotations another whirl. "But how about Gil?"

"It was a good play – "

"He workin on life," said Robey sagely.

"At least you got a mention," said Dan, more lightly than I was going to. "Sometimes El and I feel like the forgotten ancestors these days."

Robey's eyes glazed over slightly; this was another conversation we had had before. "He proceedin into the black age now; it don be easy."

"There was so much noise there at the end," I said. "Robey, did you catch everything he said – ?"

"Some," he said, as Gil walked up, with Dan's jacket neatly folded over his arm. His eyes were watchful, and they did not change in the round of hugs and congratulations that followed.

"Gil," I said, curiously, "you never said in your play what you grew up to be. You know – " as he didn't answer – "doctor, lawyer, Indian chief – ?"

"There are other things to think about first, Nan," he said, and I felt rebuked.

"Okay." I retreated defensively into my own childhood. "Do you know the first thing I ever wanted to be was a litter-picker-upper? Just so I could use one of those sticks with a nail in the tip."

He looked at me witheringly. "That must have been when you were about seven."

I'd done it again, treated him like a child. "Yes," I said, "yes, it was."

"What was it you said," Dan asked him, "there at the end, after the joke about seeing what developed?"

"Hey, Brian!" Gil disappeared frantically, like some kind of little brown bird I had seen out the window that morning – all his effort aimed at escaping the nest.

"Who was that masked man – ?" murmured Dan wryly.

"I really don't understand."

"He feelin black tonight, Gramomma," Robey said, out of the corner of his mouth, as he turned to shake hands with Brian's smiling parents.

CHAPTER 7

That was a big week.

The next Sunday night, Doug's Junior-Senior Choir Festival started off as a triumph and ended in Hallelujah. It was glorious, really, and all Doug's show from beginning to end.

The idea had been his to start with, getting together choirs from all over the city, both children and adult, for a grand performance, a festive celebration of God by all colors and kinds of people. Like a great stereo, the "wow" of his own real religious exhilaration blasted the heavens through these hundreds of extra speakers, brought to life by his baton.

Dan and I had worried about his adding so much more to his schedule, but Grace only shrugged when we mentioned it. I put that down to preoccupation with her real estate concerns. (Being firmly against massive real estate development, on the whole, I found it easy to imagine that she was fighting inner battles on that subject; probably I even hoped so.) Still, I yearned back sometimes to those early days of their courtship when Doug and Grace had seemed wound in a bullet-proof web of romance and security, no one more confident than they about the happyeverafterness of life.

As usual, we had trouble getting away. During dinner, Joe Caborolli came by. Joe's a member of St. Anne's, but all his life he's known Katie Markle, who's a member of Trinity, and eighty if she's a day. Katie's a born musician, always played by ear, though she never had a lesson, and made a living by it.

She started to play for the silent movies when she was fourteen, and then went on to play for Rita Durban's dancing school five nights a week, and then for churches, the Masonic choir, and the local choral group until they got too classical for her. She also does yoga and is probably the youngest eighty on record, lithe and clear-minded, what I wouldn't mind reaching eighty as, if I had to.

Joe refused coffee. "I just came by to tell you Katie's moved again, Pastor."

"So I heard." Katie moved every couple of years into a new apartment. She claimed it kept her young and only laughed when I accused her of hating housecleaning as much as I did, and moving instead.

"Well, she just went down another door, but they can't get the piano in. She's on the first floor now, but the hall's too narrow to turn the piano in."

"How about the window?"

"That's why I'm here, Pastor. Her son Tom says it's too much trouble for him and young Tommie; she should get rid of it. Katie's worse off than I've ever seen her. Could you come down and – ?"

"Okay, Joe, let me get my jacket."

By the time he got back, I was ready to go, and he still had to change. "We have fifteen minutes," I said, handing him a clean shirt. "What happened with the piano?"

"We got it in through the window."

The Festival was scheduled for 7:30, and we arrived at Our Savior only just in time. The place was packed. Anything with children in it gets the parents out, or at least church parents. We couldn't find seats in the back and had to walk all the way up the aisle to the front, which I hate. Okay, as a minister's wife, I'm not supposed to, but I do. Too public.

When we finally got settled, and Dan's twitch had subsided, I looked up at the chancel for the first time and caught my breath. Only the children's choirs were there at the moment, along with a bell choir down front, but there must have been close to 150 kids squeezed in: twelve local choirs, I read in the bulletin. Masking the altar, robed in twelve different color combinations, not all of them liturgical, they stood motionless, sweating, intent to the last child on Doug.

On the low green podium between audience and singers, Doug was compelling, even from the back. He gave off a sense of tightly controlled power, rippling muscle, not so much physical as emotional, vitality rolling in waves from the gathered body under his white robe, channeled along the large arms that moved broadly from the shoulders, flowing off the fingers, impacted in the eyes of the singers who seemed mesmerized, responding as one voice to his directions.

I'd never seen a church choir so attentive. In general, they have an attention deficit problem: members looking all over the place, checking out the pastor's reaction, bracing themselves against little Susie's wails during a pregnant pause, tracking old Mr. Lodge's progress out of the nave in the middle of the anthem. And children's choirs are the worst of all, trying to locate their parents, dropping their music, giggling through the second verse because it refers to bells tinkling – but not these children. Every child was fixed on Doug, finding validation for existence in that time and place in him, like cherubs in the presence of the Lord.

Musically, it was a stunning performance, but, I thought, it makes God superfluous. That's not what Doug wants. I soon forgot such trivialities, under the influence, for that is what great religious music done greatly is, an intoxication of the senses. Far from tranquilizing, it can turn you into a noisy celebrating drunk. I still don't understand that ravishing gift of Doug's, to be able to transform those poky choirs into reverberations of glory to God.

The evening was an uncommon blend of black gospel and white German Protestant tradition, but it worked. The piping of the children, like young birds open-mouthed for sustenance, the deep pedal-tones of adult males, the richness of even ill-trained women, all brought us into the company of saints, another world concurrent with ours, because those children up there were our children and those adults were our fellows, but all of us caught up in light and praise and unearthly grace.

As the last strains of *Ode to Joy* faded away, Doug turned around to the congregation, his face afire.

"Join us," he cried. "Praise God in the highest!" He strode to the organ, pushed the organist aside, and, left arm rampant, directed choirs and congregation in *A Mighty Fortress Is Our God*, that gigantic lyric to the the most mind-blowing idea of all, the victory of a personal God over all the mindless evil and tragedy of the world and our life in it. He drew a cry of faith and trust from all our throats, making way for God to enter – and Doug shone. I saw from where I sat, he shivered, he flamed, he burned.

"His kingdom is forever," we swelled, fixed on Doug.

He leaped off the organ bench and shouted, "We are what we are!"

He raised his arms, closed his eyes, and people cried, "Yes, Lord!" or "Hallelujah!" or groaned unintelligibly. I felt my own mouth open involuntarily and snapped it shut on a gasp. Embarrassed, I looked at Dan, and saw that his mouth too was open, and his twitch was carrying on like crazy. "But God loves us!" Doug cried, spreading out his hands, palms up, naked to the world, to his God.

"We are what we are!" he shouted, and this time the congregation cried out with him, "but God loves us!" and we gave ourselves, willed ourselves into the stream of emotion; where was the world, where was anything but this heartstopping, throat-choking chant that brought God into us, made God possible, maybe even probable?

"We are what we are – but God loves us! We are what we are – but God loves us!"

Right then I knew it for sure even myself.

CHAPTER 8

There was no hangover as such, not from the emotionalism or the fervor. A few times a month or a year or a lifetime such a moment will occur, at the sight of a sunset, or at a gift of art or love, and there are no hangovers. What lingers is awe that, in this prosaic life, such times happen, to make it easier – at least as I see it – to believe in God. A freebie, so to speak, to ease the harder giftless passages. And so I did not question anything that had happened that night.

Dan was not so complacent. He too had been carried away and respected the moment, but he knew then, more than I, the complexities of such times and emotions, the diffused presence of evil in good, and, on the other hand, the honeycombing of the good with the bad, the glorious with the squalid, the possibilities even within the slavery of mortality. We both felt new tensions in Doug, and Grace was more tight-lipped than ever, although that evening she had been caught up with us all, bright-faced the whole night.

Still, even mountaintop experiences stay us from our appointed rounds only temporarily. In this world, at least, we don't seem equipped to combine the two. St. Therese of Liseaux found it holy to say that she didn't see how it would be possible for a heart given to earthly affections to achieve union with God. On the other hand, I tend to think that you need to do your best with what you've got, which means not trashing earthly affections.

Grace called Wednesday before I got off to the Ruth-and-Naomi class meeting.

"Did you hear the latest?" she asked. "Kerry Hemling – you know her – "

"Vaguely." A young member of Our Savior, active in the youth work there –

"She's engaged to a computer operator in the Ag Department at the College." That was Evitt Community College, which ran an agricultural division of the State University. "She was at the choir festival on Sunday, and she got so worked up she put her diamond engagement ring in the offering. Pastor Bremer just about croaked when the ushers turned it in. Nobody knew whose it was until her fiance called yesterday and demanded it back."

"Did they give it to him?"

"Of course. We're not Elmer Gantry around here, you know."

"So how's Doug doing?"

"Not too bad. He seems easier since Sunday night, sort of more relaxed." She paused. "I guess you've noticed I worry about him."

"Yes, I've noticed."

"Well, I'm not really sure why. Maybe because he seems so wound up a lot of the time. But then, when you're so busy, that's bound to happen."

"Your father gets like that too – "

"Yeah, I see that old twitch going in his left temple sometimes. And, of course, there's Gil. The older he gets, the more I worry about him. But I'm hoping this new group he's joined at school will get some of that nervous energy out of the way. He stays in the house too much, he needs exercise. I mean, you can only write so many poems, and plays, and things – you've got to get out and do something, I keep telling him."

"Women worry too much. Maybe the feminists ought to look into that."

She laughed. "I consider myself one, and I haven't got a clue how to stop worrying. Leaving it in God's hands is all very well, and sometimes it even helps. But first thing you know, here it is back again in mine."

I roused myself. "I've got to get going. I'll let you know when I find out how to stop worrying."

"You do that."

The elderly ladies' class meeting was starting to look pretty good. Going to the Ruth-and-Naomi monthly get-together is like scream therapy. It gets everything else off your mind for the moment.

I'm a believer in integrated church activities myself, colors and sexes and ages working together in the Name that comprises them all and then some. On the other hand (Dan always said "On the Other Hand" was my middle name), if some ages or genders, especially the older ones who grew up in different times, feel more comfortable working together as a group, I see no problem, although for some reason I feel different about colors.

I go to the the Ruth-and-Naomis strictly in my capacity as pastor's wife. There aren't many church activities I feel this way about, and, in these liberated days, the pressure on parsonage wives to be unpaid assistants to their husbands has eased more than most people think. The things I do in the church I do because I want to, and actually, even the R/Ns fit into that category, once I get there. These people have become a precious part of my life, even if we don't always think the same about things.

Miracle of miracles, there was a place to park open on the curb, so I didn't have to run up through the pouring rain from the parking lot across the street. When I got inside, I found a good deal of milling about, because a leak had developed up in the roof, and the water was coming in two floors below through the parlor ceiling. It was dripping in a lively fashion all over the end of the sofa where May Benning was accustomed to sit to conduct the meetings. After the sofa was moved over, with the assistance of the sexton, and the church secretary notified, and a pot from the kitchen placed under the leak, and then another pot from the kitchen placed under a twin leak over the conference table on the other side, the room settled down, and the ladies composed themselves for devotions and the topic.

Irene Wilson, round-faced, with great round glasses on a small round nose, round rings on round fingers, rosy round cheeks and large round blue plastic earrings bobbing on round ears (were her toes round too, I wondered), looking something like a Picasso painting if he had only had a Spherist period, was somehow in charge of both devotions and refreshments. She was in quite a dither about it all, getting her recipes mixed up with her scripture lesson, but in perfect good humor throughout. Noted as a redoubtable cook, and a formidable topicalizer, she took pains to maintain her reputation, and today was no exception.

With spring in mind, she read from the Song of Solomon, "The winter is over; the rains have stopped; in the countryside the flowers are in bloom. This is the time for singing; the song of the doves is heard in the fields. Figs are beginning to ripen; the air is fragrant with blossoming vines. Come then, my love, my darling, come with me."

Then, recklessly, I thought, she swung into Psalm 138: "I thank you, Lord, with all my heart; I sing praise to you before the gods." Then she topped it off with Matthew: "Let the fig tree teach you a lesson. When its branches become green and tender, you know that summer is near. In the same way, when you see all these things, you will know that the time is near, ready to begin."

I hoped that the immediacy of Matthew might wipe out the provocation of Psalm 138, but Carrie Cathcart, Edvard Munch to Irene's Picasso, all dark colors and doomful, had bounded erect at the sound of the word "gods." (Which I'd swear Irene read extra loud and clear.) Carrie quivered, dyed curls a-tingle, until the Matthew was over, ignoring all that delicious millennialism for her one obsession.

"I beg your pardon," she said, in a steely voice, "but you must have read that wrong."

Irene had pushed her monotheism button. Sometime in Carrie's life she had learned the difference between many gods and One, and it seems to have changed her life. What she was before, I don't know, because we weren't at Trinity then, but I'd been told she rarely came to church, and was, in fact, piously involved in her bowling league at work. She was an excellent bowler. But, in perhaps the one light-bulb moment of her life, she somehow happened across the concept of monotheism and its reputed founder, and it turned her around, sent her to the Scriptures, transformed her life forever. It also did a lot for Trinity's bowling team.

Irene peered at her Bible. "No, that's what it says here, 'gods.' "

"Well, there's something wrong. Moses lived before the Psalms were written, and he was the great first Monotheist, you know."

"Yes, of course, Carrie," said Irene. "But maybe this Psalm writer hadn't gotten the word yet."

They both looked at me, but I wasn't about to enter the fray. Even less likely was I to mention that lately the usual doubts had come up among the usual revisionists about Moses' claim to the name of First Monotheist. I was on his side, myself, even with Akhnaten in on the action somewhere along the line, and I was tempted to share my own fascination with the speculative ties between the two, but somehow it didn't seem the place or the audience.

I may be too patronizing about the ladies or some of them, anyway, for Irene then launched into an astounding exegesis of the Song of Solomon, its traditional embarrassed (her word, not mine) glossing over as a symbol of the love of God for Israel or the church, and her own conversion to the idea that it was simply a beautiful and sexy love poem, so lovely the Biblical compilers couldn't bear to leave it out.

Furthermore, she read some of the sexy parts, as the women dithered a bit, and then delivered a lecture on the marriage customs of Syria, straight out of the dictionary at the back of her Bible. And all these old women, long ago more accustomed to sex than any young person dreams, even if they have always found other facts of life more appropriate to talk about out loud, sat still for it all and listened to her, as she finished up like a preacher, harmonizing the realistic and the figurative views under the heading, "God can be found anywhere if you have the eye for Him."

I was impressed, and so were the other women. "I didn't know that, Irene," said little, fragile Phoebe Rapp, after Irene wound down, flushed and exhilarated.

Meredith Busch, who had come in late, wasn't so sure. "You didn't use the King James version," she said darkly.

"The Good News is so much easier to understand," said Irene, without apology.

"We should use God's Own words at all times," said Meredith. She was unwavering and I had to admire her constancy, if not her accuracy. I noticed that she left early, before the refreshments.

"I think we ought to give Irene a round of applause for all her hard work," said May Benning, trying to get back control of the meeting. That turned out to be a mistake for after the clapping subsided, it wasn't the easiest thing to regain everybody's attention. Like iron filings suddenly released from a magnet, they fell into little soft piles of discussion all over the room, and May had to use considerable effort to centralize the action again.

She had an enormous amount of surprisingly dark hair, which she wore in a large bun down low on the nape of her neck, and it trembled and strained as she shushed and waved the hardest-case chatterers into silence once more and then went on undeterred by the occasional loud-voiced conversations that grew up like weeds along the way: "What'd she say?" "We have $500 in the bank." "That bank – they'll steal you blind before it's all over, those service charges and everything. Did you ever hear tell of having to pay five dollars if you get below a hundred? Why, I don't hardly never get above a hundred."

It was not too early, said May, for whom it was never too early, to think about Christmas gifts for the shut-ins, seeing as how the Ruth-Naomis shut down these days over the summer, and never really got going again until October. Here was a Santa's boot, made out of felt and old bleach bottles, which could be made by anyone, even those of us, she said, with a grim smile, who were not good at making things. May was a whiz at crafts, and some of us knew what she really thought of our clumsiness and squirmed until she took pity on us, which she proceeded to do once her point was made.

However, she said, she and some of the others would make the boots, if the rest of us would buy the candy to put into them, and by then we were so relieved that a couple of us (I and Vera Finch, locally famous for holding the last notes of hymns longer than anyone else) volunteered to do just that.

We voted to give various contributions from the treasury – "Seeing as we're loaded," said Irene, emboldened by her earlier success, all her circles spinning away – to the Lutheran Home in Washington, DC, and to the local food pantry, and to the Trinity youth group which was planning a trip to Purdue University for a summer youth conference, and to a family up the street which had just been burned out.

Then there was a lively discussion between the women who wanted to wipe out the rest of the treasury for good works ("God always takes cares of us") and the women who wanted to leave some in to start the fall nest-egg ("God helps those who help themselves"). This was followed by a reprise of the argument for those who had privately fallen into an information-sharing agenda about the burned-out family, its history and options, and weren't listening anyway. I was getting interested in that one myself, when May called for the vote.

The nest-egg faction won that one, and by this time the ladies were visibly falling apart, so Irene came out of the kitchen to which she had retired earlier (shouting out her vote for dispensing the remainder of the money to Lutheran World Action from the kitchen sink) and announced refreshments.

The offering, which had been forgotten earlier under the influence of the Song of Solomon, was hastily gathered as ladies fell off the edges toward the refreshment table, and then regrouped again for the Mighty Mite, which was everybody's loose pennies. We had all bowed our heads in prayer (checking out the refreshments on the way down, or at least I did) when May screamed, and we all jumped and opened our eyes again to find her dripping water off her back bun.

Another leak had opened right above her head, it seemed, and so we mopped her off and forgot to pray after all, and sent word to the office about the new leak, and gathered about the sandwiches (which they know I love) and Irene's special strawberry-cream cheese-topping dessert, laughing and all worked up. The Ruth-and-Naomi class had rarely been so exciting in the twenty years since all the Naomis had died off, and the Ruths, shocked and unwilling, had inherited their age and mantle.

I was eating my ham salad sandwich when Carrie appeared beside me. "I went to the choir festival," she announced without preamble. My mouth was full of rye bun so I smiled and nodded. "That son-in-law of yours," she said, nodding sagely. "I think maybe he believes in more than one God."

I tried not to choke. "Oh, I don't think so, Carrie," I said, coughing as quietly as I could.

She snorted, and then looked sideways at me. "I saw your other girl what's her name? – Joy, downtown the other day."

I nodded politely.

"She had that young man with her, Scott Leasure?"

"They've been – going together for awhile."

"So I've heard." She chewed at her false teeth, hassling them back into place. "Damn these things (excuse my French) – they never want to stay where they belong. Well, the young folks always have surprises for us, don't they?"

"Yes, "I said, "yes, they do."

I helped in the kitchen afterwards, more out of duty than pleasure. I try to do this a couple times a year, which is not enough to boost my reputation, but at least saves it from going down the drain. I hate that kind of work as much as I loathe housecleaning, but it's a chance to chat with a number of women on a more sustained level than the brief after-church exchanges.

As always, the talk centered about families. Unbelievably, May Benning, who's seventy if she's a day, still had a mother living, 92-year-old Effie Boyer, twisted with arthritis, but lively enough still, with a face hardly older than May's. They didn't always get along, hadn't for sixty years, but seemed to have arrived at some kind of a truce, or else an impasse. May's husband was long gone, about twenty years, and they had only each other. The two lived alone in their big house, rubbing up against each other with a kind of abrasive togetherness that stood in for affection, possibly even generated it.

"I took her out to visit this friend at the nursing home." May briskly snapped the top back on a half-empty whipped topping box and picked up the pile of dirty plastic forks. One of the R/Ns' continuing debates was whether you threw away the plastic cutlery or washed it for another day, and our hostess Irene was of the non-washing persuasion, but May blithely dumped them into the soapy dishwater anyway. "Sylvan Acres, the one that just opened after Christmas?"

I looked around for something to be busy about, but Irene had already assembled the dessert pans in the other sink and was running hot water over them. So I found a dishtowel and looked alert.

"We visited Marian Shoakey, she went in there last month, she worked at Merrill's Department Store in the children's department for twenty years, and then she opened up that little gift shop on Bow Street?"

"I know her," said Irene, scrubbing away. "Hair like a carrot, and always talked too loud."

"Well, she has a good heart," said May, "and a lonely life."

"It always galled her that she could never find a man who'd have her." Irene meditated over the dishwater. "Of course, look who's talking. I never did either."

Jane Post and Vera came in and found things to do at once. I never could figure out how people do that; how things I never notice need to be done turn up for others to find. Vera, whose unaccountable addiction to last notes masked an otherwise sensible personality, picked up a dishcloth, dipped it in Irene's dishwater and started to wipe off the counters. Jane, a silent wiry old lady with large pores, opened a cupboard and stood there shaking her head.

"You're right, Jane," said Irene definitively, many of her circles getting pinker as she worked. "Look at that mess. You just can't trust the Mixed Couples Class." That was the class I taught, next in line to be unnerved by mortality, when the last of the Ruth/Naomis got too feeble to do her duty. It was well-known however that the R/Ns had their doubts about their heirs, all those women who worked at jobs that left them little time for altar guild and church kitchen service, and the men, some of whom had been known to actually take their turn in the kitchen, but whom the R/Ns distrusted there on principle.

"They'd as soon lock the cupboards to hold the stuff in as keep it neat," said Irene, drying the pans she had washed before I even realized they were ready. Jane nodded seriously, and started to sort out the jumble of paper plates and cups and bottles of Cremora and bags and jars of coffee shoved onto the shelf at random.

"I was just telling about Mother visiting Marian Shoakey," said May imperturbably. "Anyway, they were talking and they got on the subject of men, and Marian said – I never thought I'd ever hear her say such a thing, and I just had to laugh and turn and look out the window so she wouldn't see me – she said, 'You know, Effie?' she said to Mother, 'you know, Effie, one thing I've always regretted?' And Mother says, 'What's that, Marian?' And Marian says, 'You know, Effie, I never married.' And Mother says, 'I know, Marian.' And Marian says, 'Well, Effie, you know that means I ain't never seen a man.' Mother didn't laugh, and she says, 'I guess not, Marian.' And Marian says, 'I wish just onct I could see what a man looks like before

I die.' And Mother looks at her, and says, 'Never mind, Marian. They ain't so pretty.' "

The kitchen exploded, and several of the women nodded vigorously at each other as they roared. The story was reported to the other ladies in the parlor, and even Carrie said goodby with a smile on her face, and not a parting word about Moses, or Doug, either one.

I do love these folks.

CHAPTER 9

I took two of the oldest Ruth-Naomis home afterward, and didn't have to help them much, because each one tried to help the other to show that she was the less feeble of the two. They managed quite well together. When I got home, Dan was there, a surprise in the middle of the afternoon. He was up in the bedroom, packing his small leather suitcase.

"Let me guess," I said. "You want a divorce."

When he turned around his pallor frightened me, but he smiled weakly. His lips looked bluish.

"Nothing to worry about, really," he said, the kind of mindless assurance that only compounds one's worry. "I just came from the doctor's, and he wants me in the hospital at once."

"In the hospital?" I stood there stupidly.

"Well," with an apologetic grimace, "I've had this pain down my arm lately. He thinks there may be some heart problem, or something – "

"You aren't telling me everything."

He shook his head. "That's all it is, really, oh, a little short of breath, when I helped move that piano. And I'm so tired." He put in pajamas, socks, slippers – I shook myself mentally.

"Shouldn't I be doing that for you?"

He lifted his head, the pallor relieved by a grin. "You never did before. Why start now?"

"This is hardly a time to joke." I pushed him aside and then winced to be manhandling him. It was strange to worry about such things with Dan; he'd always been heathy as an ox. He sat wanly on the bed, watching.

"A little shaky?"

"Only when you get bossy."

I packed the rest of his things. "Is it serious, Dan?"

"I hope not. God knows I have no intention of dying."

I sat down beside him and hugged him. Another time he might perhaps have persuaded me to think about other things for awhile on the bed together. Not now. What you do at times like this is pray. But if you pray for healing and it doesn't happen, then you have to deal with the idea of unanswered prayer. Far safer just to ask for strength. So I did, out loud, with Dan's hand in mine, willing health to flow through it into him, and God to pay attention.

Halfway through, I thought, how unfair, it's *we* who must make the adjustments, tailor our prayers, genericize our needs, so as not to set ourselves up for a let-down. Why don't You make an occasional gesture, like letting Dan off this time. I quashed it mid-prayer. You don't talk to God like that, and silently I apologized.

They put Dan through a whole battery of tests, including a stress test, which sounds like a ridiculous idea to me, deliberately pushing a sick man to his breaking point just for the purpose of locating it, although they told us it really doesn't work like that.

He couldn't have been too worn out though, because when I went in to see him after supper, I couldn't find him. "He's up in Seven South," said a nurse at the hall desk, checking a memo at her elbow.

"Seven South?"

She laughed. "Hey, not what you think. He talked us into letting him call on a church member up there."

Dan can be amazingly persuasive. I went back to his room and talked to his roommate, an elderly man also with a heart problem, on oxygen, and mad as a hornet that he couldn't smoke.

"The worst of it is," he grumbled, "when I get home, my kids won't let me smoke either. They've been bugging me for years about it, and this time they'll never give up." He scrunched down morosely under his sheet.

"Well," I ventured, "maybe it's just as well, with your heart and everything – "

"Listen, lady – ma'am." He got up on one elbow and fixed me with bright blue eyes above the tube trailing out of his nose. "I've been smoking since I was twelve years old, and it never did me nothin' but good. Why, if I was to stop now, that's what would kill me, not this stupid old ticker – " he punched himself in the chest so hard I recoiled. "Hi, Reverner – "

"Hi, Bill. Hi, honey." Dan still looked tired but his color was good. He stopped at the bathroom, which was cleverly concealed at the entrance of the room so that the room door and the bathroom door banged loudly against each other at the slightest provocation.

"They ought to make architects spend time in every building they design," he said wryly when he came out. "You hear doors banging all down the hall, especially, they tell me, in the wee hours of the night. You think you know all about a place – heaven knows I've visited here often enough – but there's nothing like being there." He crawled gratefully into his bed and touched a button along the side. The mechanism hummed, and the foot of the bed elevated itself alarmingly. "Oops." He fiddled with the buttons until he found the right one. "This part's fun though."

"Did Conor sign himself in on Seven South?"

He nodded. "He's still painting wide-open mouths, but he says they're not screaming any more." He laughed. "He didn't notice I was in pajamas, which is probably just as well, but can't help but make you wonder about him – " His smile enlarged to a chuckle. "Actually, I'm not so sure about myself. I forgot I was wearing them, and dropped in to see Clara Nash on my way back – they finally got her to the hospital, you know."

Crippled up and feeble as she is, Clara had resisted for three days the combined efforts of two large sons, one hysterical daughter, and Dan, who had been called to add his weight to the push to get her to go to the hospital. "You should have seen her face when she saw me walk in in my pajamas and robe."

He rubbed his temple thoughtfully. "It didn't help that I crashed the room door into her bathroom door just as she was coming out. Still, she seems a lot stronger. Her son, Jim, says she won't eat at home, and her sugar count is on a roller coaster. But she won't even listen to the doctor – "

I handed him *The New York Times*, which we buy every day at Fresh's Newsstand, and the day's mail. "Well, that's a bust," he said, glancing though the junk. "A new issue from the Philadelphia Mint – they must think up something new every hour on the hour – two sweepstakes, and three catalogs. What's this?" He turned over a severe business envelope with a hand-typed address and return address without a name.

"Oh, just tear it open, for goodness sake," but, as usual, he had to be neat about it. He opened the drawer of his bedtable and took out his little pocket penknife and carefully slit the envelope open.

"I got another rejection slip for my collection," I said lightly.

He paused and looked up. "The *Newsweek* My Turn one?"

I nodded. "I guess it still wasn't my turn. Well, it would have been a fluke, if they'd taken it, but even flukes happen sometimes, so they tell me."

"Ah, honey, I'm sorry. You can't help but have hopes." He held out his hand and we laced fingers and sat silent for a moment, rather like a miniature wake. He was telling me about his tests when the doors crashed, and Gil burst in, followed by Grace and Doug.

Hugs all around, and Grace glanced about conspiratorially, before she settled on Dan's bed, her legs tucked under her. "You're not supposed to sit on the patient's bed," she said. "Dad, how are you doing?"

"Fine," he said. "I amazed the doctors with my stress test."

"Which way?" asked Doug, dragging up one of the bright orange vinyl chairs from Mr. Teeter's side of the room. "I'll give it back when your company comes," he assured the old man, who looked dubious at all the energy let loose in the room.

Gil was investigating the room's amenities. "Hey, man," he said, discovering Dan's remote television control. Dan turned it on for them, and Gil and Mr. Teeter watched Wheel of Fortune together raptly.

Grace seemed unusually happy tonight, and I mentioned it to her after everybody had marveled sufficiently at both the miracles and the minuses of modern medicine. She beamed at Doug, and he reached up from his chair and laid his hand on her knee in a caress as sheerly affectionate as it was sexual.

"After two solid years since we've been at Our Savior," she said happily, "Doug's finally going to take a few weeks off this summer." She leaned over to kiss him gently, then looked up anxiously at Dan. "Do you think you'll be camping down at Cumberland in July? If the doctor won't let you, Doug and I could take the trailer out to Rocky Gap and set it up and you could come out any time you want."

Dan laughed easily. "Don't count me out, Grace. I think all I needed was a rest, and, God knows, I'm getting enough of that now. Mother and I'll be going down as usual, so you come whenever it suits you." Doug and Grace nodded at each other and smiled happily.

Those doors were as good as a family butler announcing guests. They banged reliably as Joy and Scott came in, abashed at the noise they made.

Joy had assured us early on that Scott hoped to be accepted as one of the family, loftily ignoring some muttered comment of mine about getting all the advantages of marriage without having to risk any commitment. "You keep hearing about how admirable it is to take risks nowadays," I'd gone on stubbornly, "but I guess that only applies to sex, or hang-gliding, that sort of thing. Not marriage, or stability, or anything like that."

Joy ignored that too, and later Dan and I had talked it over and decided that loving Joy was more important than giving in to our distress at her flouting of the guidelines we had handed down to her for living life most wisely. Above all, we didn't want to break the ties that bound us. We must be there if she needed us, and it turned out not to be awfully hard, after all, to greet Scott as part of the family, knowing that his misgivings were as great as ours. (When she'd first met him, Joy had reported gleefully how taken aback he had been to discover her father was a minister. She hadn't heard from him for days afterward. It was rather like being classified Untouchable, but we thought we were used to it.)

"I don't know how many visitors they allow here at a time," said Grace, when the greetings were over, but Gil and Mr. Teeter were glued to a car chase on TV, and it was obvious that nothing but the end of the program would unglue them. Keeping an eye out for the nurses, we all listened to Dan recap his day's experience for the third time.

The television noise seemed to be accelerating with the car chase, and Doug had to speak up to get over it. "You sure need a good vacation, Pop. Grace and I've decided to take you up on your invitation and camp with you folks this summer. Scott, think you can get some time off for a few days in July?" He looked affectionately at Dan. "It would be good for Pop not to have all that wood-chopping and water-hauling for a change."

"That's a great idea," said Scott, swallowing. "I've never been camping in my life, although I jog – don't I, Joy? – and I go to the BodyFit – that's a spa – religiously – um – regularly. I've always wanted to get out and experience nature in the raw, so to speak, get in harmony with it, as they say, get back to the elemental – "

He was trying so hard to please, making the effort, and I felt an unexpected kindliness well up toward him. "You and Joy will have to come visit us," I said magnanimously. "We go to this really beautiful park in Maryland only a couple hours south of here."

Dan seconded the invitation. "Come on down with the others. Gil loves it there, don't you, Nuggie?" But Gil and Mr. Teeter were too engrossed in the show to answer, and it was easy to see why. Somebody with guns was shooting somebody else with guns – just your average everyday incident – although without blood.

"That does it!" Grace scrambled to her feet. "Come on, men," she said. "It'll take us half an hour to get home, and I've got to work tomorrow."

Joy and Scott lingered for awhile afterward, and in my new-found tolerance for him, I was glad. Maybe there was more to him than the terminal trendiness I had seen originally. I have a bad tendency to kneejerk reaction against that sort of thing.

I had to get my column started, so I couldn't visit Dan the next afternoon, but I talked to him on the phone. He sounded encouraged, All the tests had come out okay, and Dr. Romajandi had told him that he might get out by tomorrow night, Friday.

I went in after dinner and found Robey there, engaged in a lively exchange with Dan about the postal system. The only person in the world who has more opinions than I do, I think, is Robey.

I noticed Mr. Teeter was pretending to be asleep, but regarding Robey from beneath his eyelids instead. I had no doubt but that

Robey knew it and enjoyed it, so I spoiled the fun for both of them and introduced them.

"How do you do?" said Mr. Teeter politely, and turned on his television. Robey just twinkled and expansively included him in his conversation until, in self defence, the old man turned off the set and pretended to go to sleep.

"Did you see this yesterday?" Dan asked. He held out the letter he had started to open the day before. Now it was scribbled over with notes in his handwriting.

I checked him out quickly as I took the envelope. He looked rested, his color was good, the tic was quiet. What you probably needed most, my dear one, was rest. Even doors banging regularly down the hall beats a telephone summons at four in the morning. Though that has to be, I reminded myself. It's part of the job as Dan conceives of his calling and – to be honest – as I conceive of it too. I may even have to come to terms someday with the idea that if his life is to be shortened by the press of his work, it will have been lived the way he wants to live and the way he believes God means him to live.

I opened the envelope. "It's from Lily Lyle Hadley."

"Our friendly neighborhood atheist, herself."

Robey perked up. "The White Fright," he said, with interest. "That's what they call her at AME Zion."

"I'm sorry to say that the Ministerial Association calls her Lily Nilly," said Dan, not looking all that sorry. "For her inclination toward nihilism, I believe."

I skimmed the letter. "And she wants you to debate with her! On television, yet! Dan, I'm impressed."

"Well, so was I. Until I realized that she probably picked someone she figured was an easy victory, instead of one of the great shining lights in town who has everything up his sleeve. Corliss was the one I expected her to go with; he's sharp as a tack."

"You mean you knew about this before?"

"The TV station's been kicking this around for several years. They brought it up with the Ministerial Association some time ago. Lily's been looking for a broader stage for some time now, I think, maybe even a national one, since she seems to have the state pretty well covered. I guess she thought a TV debate, even on a local station, would give her some publicity, some clips she can use in the future. Doug told me last week he heard she was planning to hold a whole series of debates over the country with local clergy. Falwell in Virginia, you know, that kind of thing – "

"Falwell? She puts you in the same category of Christianity as Falwell?"

"Most non-Christians do."

"Yes, but I've heard Lily is very knowledgeable about Christianity. More than most Christians. She must know the differences between you and Falwell."

"Well, she certainly knows I'm not famous, so I'm not really sure why she chose me. Maybe she wants to knock off some of the mainstream Christians before she tackles the Moral Majority. *Hors d'oeuvres.*"

"Well, you're not the most liberal minister in town either."

"No, Robinson at Prince of Peace probably takes the honors there. Did I tell you he preached his Easter sermon this year on the Resurrection as Metaphor."

" 'One more devil's triumph,' " said Robey sardonically. He looked bored.

It's always hard for me to remember that the everyday exchange of thoughts about theology and religion that interest Dan and me are so far from the minds of everybody else we come across that they think we're putting them on. I did an instant runthrough of my usual thought progression at such times, wishing I'd been born in the last century when such conversations were common. Then I took it all back, because I know I could never have stood 19th century restrictions and pretensions.

Only the fact that being religious was nothing to be ashamed of then. That I would have liked.

I handed the letter back to him. "So, will you accept?"

He looked astonished. "Did you think I wouldn't?"

"Well, you are in the hospital right now, in case you hadn't noticed – "

"Just for tests, and they haven't found a thing. Of course I'll accept. It's not until October anyway, and I'll have the whole summer to get ready physically and mentally. And spiritually."

"You really 'carryin the Word,' man," said Robey, " 'woofin round.' " He grinned.

" 'Dance! Whirl! Whirl!' and 'leap against the sun!' " Sedately mocking his words, he sat unmoving in his chair.

Mr. Teeter interrupted from deep sleep. "You was talkin' about religion. Somp'n' I've always wondered about – would ya mind if I asked?"

Dan leaned back on his pillow. "Go ahead."

"Well, see, Adam and Eve is the first people, right? So when they had kids and Cain got married, who did he marry?" The world's most-asked religious question.

"I'll leave you men to answer that," I said. Male chauvinism has its uses.

I kissed Dan good-night and left. I simply wasn't up to Mr.Teeter's outrage when he heard Dan's possible answers.

Hard to imagine, I know, but I was too tired to argue.

Dr. Romajandi's terra-cotta countenance seemed a shade brighter than usual when he delivered the doctors' final diagnosis. There did not appear to be any major heart involvement after all, he said stiffly, in his British-tipped accent; instead Dan simply had a bad case of nerve damage in his arm. A minor operation was available for this, when we wanted it, and meanwhile he could relieve the pain by wearing a pad on his elbow.

Not, continued Dr. Romajandi, that it would hurt Dan, from the look of his arteries, to slow down and go on the kind of diet that was good for anyone's heart. It made your life seem longer, Dr. Romajandi said heavily, even if it didn't extend it any. For a doctor who had come into this country just six years ago, he seemed to have the old American jokes at his fingertips.

Once we had slipped the octopus coils of the hospital, we went out and celebrated with an early dinner at the Old Evitt Circle Inn, by ourselves. Then we went home and called the girls and told them the good news.

"I feel like a refugee coming home," said Dan, climbing willingly into bed. "I wonder why it is that going out into the world, living there for a few days even, is like entering a danger zone."

"It might not be," I said curtly, "if you didn't always have to deal with problems when you went out. Even in the hospital, roaming around visiting people – "

He rolled over on his side, shoving the pillow in under his cheek to leave his nose free. "Whoever said it was right," he said. "It's a jungle out there." He was asleep before I got the phone turned down.

CHAPTER 10

For Sunday, Trinity insisted on going with the arranged pulpit supply, a large bearded man left over from the 70s, whom the synod was trying to push into gainful employment after a career of flashing encounter-group cliches as gospel truths. He seemed to have matured since the last time I had heard him, and, distasteful as those cliches have become to me, I have to admit that they could prepare a fertile soil for some in-depth growing. If a person were so inclined.

Monday Dan got out of bed and returned to work. Everything was back to normal. He had a Lutheran Home Board meeting, and then May Benning called to tell him that Effie had had a stroke. He postponed a marriage counseling and went up to the hospital to be with her and May until Effie died at 3:30.

He got home for dinner on time, subdued as always at death in life, but not so tired as I expected. I reminded myself once more that he had made this life for himself because it was how he needed it, rediscovering God all day long for himself and for anyone else who wanted him.

Just as we got up from the dinner table, Robey came in to find out how Dan was doing. Hitting the doorbell with his trademark Beethoven victory signal, he dispensed, as usual, with waiting for anyone to answer, but bounded in on his unusually small feet like a cat, or, rather, like an NFL lineman. Luckily, Dan was near a chair he could hold on to when Robey clapped him on the back.

" 'Sun-treader-life and light be thine forever!' " he said, perfectly seriously, and dropped onto the sofa.

"Glad you came, Robey," said Dan imperturbably. He got his jacket out of the closet.

"Don be dressin up for me, man."

"That'll be the day. No, I have to go out for awhile. I promised May Benning I'd meet her at the funeral home to help make the arrrangements."

Robey sat back. "Sure, Dan. I came to see how you were doing, and you seem to be just fine. Gramomma and I will shoot the breeeze while you're gone." Robey's eclectic mix and match of language was infectious, as usual, and I had to laugh as I waved Dan to the door.

"He probably would have had to fight harder to get out tonight if you hadn't been here," I said, when the door closed. "For that you have to help me do the dishes."

"For my usual fee," he stipulated.

"Right, one cup of coffee, and all the refills you want. But dishes first."

"Ah, anything for coffee, 'which makes the politician wise.' " he said, picking up the dish towel. "Is Dan really okay?"

I washed the coffee pot first so we could use it right away. "Yes, it was all exhaustion, the doctor said, and a super-sensitive nerve in the arm."

He filled the pot and poured the water into the machine.

"Christ, I'm glad," he said simply. I knew it was no prayer, but for once it didn't offend me. (Perhaps because he hadn't meant it to.) "There's a Chinese proverb in the Bart that always reminded me of Dan. 'Keep a green tree in your heart and perhaps the singing bird will come.' He's one of the few men I know who's kept that tree green."

He dried a dinner plate and actually twirled it on his right forefinger like a basketball. "Mah bones a'hummin tonight," he said with delight. "Gil needs him too," he went on just as matter-of-factly, catching the plate in his other hand. "There are things I do for him, and things Dan does for him, and they don't necessarily overlap."

The coffee maker sputtered and spit, and I barely waited for it to stop. After I pulled out the pot, a drop or two fell on the hot plate and danced around lazily. "Do you really think Gil needs help?" I asked, pouring two of the mugs I had just washed full to the top. The hot breath of the coffee-maker blew coffee fumes about, and I followed them with my nose.

"El, you is mah woman now," sang Robey, nursing his mug carefully to the kitchen table so it wouldn't spill. "You th only gal I know fills a man's cup to the top. Thout no nonsense about cream or nothin." He leered happily at me over the rim of his mug as I sat down.

"Well, we both take our coffee, if you'll excuse the expression, black." I sat down too, and blew at my own coffee, vainly, before I drank.

"You need a cast-iron mouth like mine, Gramomma," he boasted, and drank down his whole mugful, just to prove it. "This new organization he's joined," he went on, setting the mug down thoughtfully. "What do you know about it?"

"Not much," I said, trying to remember. "Just what Grace told me once, something about a drill team, or a color guard, or something –"

"It's called Wave Your Colors, and I like the sound of it. Rick Sites, the social studies teacher at school is one of the sponsors, and from what Gil says, they're emphasizing pride in your color – they're all different racial mixes – and they use the drill team concept as a symbol as well as the purpose of the group."

"Robey," I said uneasily. "You know I want to get beyond that now. Surely the time has come when there shouldn't be so much emphasis on color for its own sake."

I should have known better, because it was always a sore subject with Robey, and why shouldn't it be? "Well, ma'am," he said, getting up stiffly, straightening over the coffee maker as he poured out another mugful, "maybe the time is over for you, because the time ain never come for you. You ain never lived in 'suffer and dancin country.' " He sat down again. "Anyway, this Sites, he's black, Gil says, and the other one, who's a temporary caretaker or something at the school until he gets a job coaching, I think Gil said is white, or close to it, and they seem to be good for the kids." He gulped the coffee mightily and grinned. "Like Dan and me, Gramomma. We bring out the twoness, and that do Gil a lot of good."

I was dubious. "If you say so, Robey," I said meekly, and he grinned,

"Oh, Gramomma," he mocked gently, "you lie through your teeth."

"Well," I said defensively, "it sounds schizophrenic to me. I just don't understand why there has to be a black way and a white way – look at Doug – "

The explosion of air between Robey's teeth sounded like a hiss. "Yeah, look at Doug. He about as white a black man as ever I see. Take too much from his mamma, all that Bach, I keep tellin him – "

"But you use both cultures, God knows, you bounce back and forth between them like a gazelle. He's chosen what he likes, what's wrong with that?"

"Gramomma, I got proud shoes and they black ones. We only twelve per cent of the population. We cain afford to leave go any of it, or we gone our own selves." He stared into his cup. "Doug – he in his bare feet."

"I know, I know – " I sighed. "I guess it's a problem everybody has to solve for themselves, who to be."

He tossed off his third cup of coffee like liquor.

"Ah, Robey," I said, seized with sudden overwhelming fondness for this man, wounded as he was, as all of us are, who yet recklessly waved off aid from all sides.

"Don't 'Ah, Robey' me," he said, without a smile. "I've got my pride, and I mean to plant it in Gil."

Who could question that? "You plant your garden then, and we'll plant ours," I said lightly, and offered him a dish of ice cream.

About nine o'clock, Dan got back. "I see Robey found the ice cream," he said, throwing his coat on the back of a kitchen chair. "Did you leave any for me, old son, or did you gobble it all up by yourself?"

"She made me put half of it back for you," grumbled Robey, who shared with Dan a passion for the stuff. "Gramomma do look out for you, Dan. Mind me of Annaliese sometimes."

Doug's mother had died long before he and Grace ever met, and I had never been able to see her image clearly. She was a white German woman whom Robey had brought back as a war bride, after World War ll. Sometimes they spoke of her as if she had been an angel on earth; other times she sounded more appealing. It must have been hard for them in those days when mixed marriages were rarer than now; they must have lived a circumscribed life, which gave Robey the time when he was off from the railroad, to read so voraciously. He mentioned once how she bought "the Bart" for him, and would go out and buy the books his favorite quotes came from, so he could read the originals, black or white. I guess it doesn't matter if you're desperate to read, but it set up some interesting ambivalences in their lives.

And in Doug's.

Dan didn't bother to put his ice cream in a dish. "May Benning said something tonight." He pulled back his chair and sat down, looked around for a spoon, and appropriated the sugar spoon. He opened the lid of the ice cream carton and plunged in. "We were talking, you know, how I always do? About the one who died, what memories they have of them, how they feel, what they want to remember? Did you know Effie's been in that wheelchair for thirty years now, even before May's husband died? May said, 'You know, Pastor, if I didn't know better, I'd think God had it in for me.' " He ate out of the ice cream box with total concentration.

Robey was puzzled. "I wouldn't think you'd feel so good to hear that."

Dan looked up, a bead of cream on his lower lip. "May's lost three children," he said. "All she had: one as a child, and the other two more recently. I can't even imagine the agony of losing all your children – and her husband died twenty years ago. She's been caring for her mother for thirty."

Robey still looked puzzled.

Dan dropped his spoon in the ice cream box and leaned forward on his elbows. "Don't you see? I'd have been raving against God years ago. 'Why me, God? What have I done to deserve this?' Well, May entertains the thought, but she's worked it out through the years. Now she can fall back on what she knows is true, even if she doesn't feel that way right now yet. So she says, 'If I didn't know better – ' "

He stopped short at the expression on Robey's face. "You still don't understand?"

"Maybe I do," said Robey. "It's just that I was brought up to a more impulsive, well, say, spontaneous approach to religion."

"Really, Robey?" I said, getting in a dig. "I hadn't noticed."

Dan applied himself to the ice cream again. "Well, God has lots of room in his mansions." He scraped the box one last time.

"One thing I can say for my wife, Robey. She buys a mean box of ice cream."

"But not enough of it," said Roby regretfully.

Dan picked up the empty box and Robey's dish and carried them over to the sink and ran hot water on them, then turned around and leaned against the sink, balling up the wet carton. From my chair, I could smell the soaked cardboard.

"Robey, you'll like this. Ed Waring" – as funeral director for a good part of Evittsburg, Ed knew most of what was going on, and Dan depended heavily on him for the latest news. Don't tell me men never gossip! – "Ed Waring was telling me about a Baptist minister in Harrisburg – around Camp Hill where Ed's brother has another funeral home, I gather – well, this minister had recurring visions that Jesus appeared and told him to rebuild the Temple. In Harrisburg, we're talking about. He felt like a fool about the visions, according to Ed's brother, and he didn't say anything to anyone about them, at first, but they kept getting more and more compelling, until finally he's given in and he's starting a campaign for the funds."

" 'Cypress and gold leaf,' " said Robey dreamily.

"Well, that's a problem too. No one knows whether it's supposed to be Solomon's or Herod's Temple – it seems the dreams didn't specify. There's quite an argument shaping up – "

"Wouldn't that put you in a bind though?" I said, imagining it with some distress. "I mean, having visions like that. Just one could be anything, indigestion, maybe, but what do you do if they keep on coming? And how do you know that the visions are from God, and not just somebody, maybe even you, playing God in your head?"

" 'Vision beatific,' " murmured Robey, humoring our eternal religious talk. "The prophets had visions. Are they out of style among you righteous folks now?"

"No," said Dan, soberly. "But it's the same old problem, telling the false prophets from the true ones. Sometimes I don't even think they know themselves." He looked at me, the memory of an old shared struggle in mind. "When I went into Seminary the big push was on for 'prophetic ministry,' but I've opted out of the deliberately prophetic myself. There was a time when I worked hard at it."

He was talking about our first congregation, Cathedral Street, Baltimore, where racism had been next to godliness for some of the members. "But I think a real prophet doesn't have to work at the job. He simply is. Also, I found out you have to throw bombs, or at least dead skunks, to make people pay attention these days. So I took up listening instead. Healing, over surgery."

"A prophet must be awfully hard to live with," I said. "Some of the ones in the Old Testament sound like pain-in-the-necks."

"You could say that heavenly visions are a form of divine coercion," said Robey, mischievously.

"Well, you could say that," said Dan dryly; "I won't. But I pray every night not to be given one." He lofted the crumpled carton neatly into the trash can at the end of the counter. Surely he didn't mean it – sometimes a person can use a vision.

CHAPTER 11

Rocky Gap is a beautiful state park, not spectacular, but solidly lovely: heavily wooded camping sites, deer too friendly for their own good come fall, and decent public bathrooms. Except that the Ladies in Loop G is improperly leveled, and the water from the showers collects in the middle of the floor, looking sinister, and you skirt the edges distastefully, trying not to imagine what else it could come from.

In spite of that, we seem to end up in Loop G every summer, often at Site 200, because a small stream curves picturesquely around the picnic table, keeping you awake at night with those gurgling noises so widely reputed to be sleep-inducing.

We settled in late one warm Sunday in the middle of July for two weeks, as long as you were allowed to stay in one site. Everybody decided to come down and help us set up. I was glad because putting up the trailer by ourselves gets to be more and more of a burden every year.

Dan managed to back it into place without too much trouble, inspiring the girls into reminiscence as we wrestled with the rusty stabilizers and cranked out the sides.

"Remember that campsite in Canada when we got the idea we wanted the trailer at the very top of the hill, and we all had to push it up ourselves, because the car couldn't make the curve?" Joy shook out the canvas expertly, flicking off dead insects and leaves entombed in the window mesh over the winter. Everything smelled musty, as usual, but the little spots of black mildew didn't seem to have grown much since last year.

Rubbing absently at one, she went on. "I had to go to the bathroom so bad, but it was a matter of pride to get that trailer up there first. I remember, I almost wet my pants. Actually, I did wet my pants." She pulled the metal braces for the canvas out and up into place, as Grace disappeared into the trailer to accomplish her own traditional task, fitting the turned edge of canvas into the track above the windows.

"This isn't so easy any more, with long fingernails." Grace's voice was muffled, and the trailer shook as she slipped on the boxes of canned goods she was using as a stool. "How come none of this is as easy as it used to be?"

"Join the club," I said, parentally smug to observe my own offspring coping with the symptoms of impending middle age.

Joy was even less sympathetic. "That's what comes of having a cushy job where you can let your fingernails grow," she said, and neatly caught the wooden tent peg Grace lobbed at her. "Thank you, Amazing. Just what we need."

"Here. Mom, let me do it."

Grace handed the job over to Gil with relief and jumped to the ground. Gil loved camping and whatever was going on with him seemed to have disappeared for the moment.

"Listen to the stream," she said, standing for a moment, her head tilted. "I can smell new-cut grass too," she added, but no one else was in a mood to encourage her sensual celebrations when there was work to be done, so she went to help Doug and Scott set up the tarp over the picnic table.

Dan stood inside the trailer, eyeing the door distrustfully. Still quietly tucked up under the roof, a monster under wraps, it would presently be rubbing his patience raw; trying to slide it down into place was probably the most infuriating of all the odd jobs of camp setup.

"It's never gone in right on the first try yet," he said gloomily, "and it never will."

"You'll get it, Dan," I said and cravenly deserted him for my own job, the one I always snag because it's easy and fun, clamping together those snaps that hold the bottom of the canvas to the box of the trailer.

"If you can tear yourself away, Mom?" called Doug. "We could use you over here on the poles." So I helped Grace hold up the sidepoles on the tarp, while Doug showed Scott how to pound in pegs for the guy ropes. I watched critically, but Scott seemed to be getting the hang of it.

After we got the tarp up we all went over to enjoy ourselves watching Dan slide the door down, try after try, to get it into the right groove so the zippers on the canvas would meet. As usual, everybody offered advice, and Doug and Scott tried their hands at it, while Dan gracefully permitted them to make fools of themselves.

Fortunately, Gil had gone down to the beach by this time, or he would have had a go at it as well. Every year the men of the family have to find out all over again that, for purposes of proving one's macho handymanship, that door was a bust. Finally, Dan took the job back and chancing haplessly upon the appropriate pressure at the same time as the designated bird sang, slid the door into place.

Camping has to be relearned every year. By the end of vacation, you just about know what to do and how to do it, before you forget it all over again through the winter.

We had hamburgers for supper that night, and Joy made no protest at being expected to help Grace and me get them together and to set the picnic table while the men walked down to the beach to get Gil.

"If you want to stay over, Grace," I said, pumping away at the camp stove, "the trailer sleeps six, remember. And it's a two-hour drive back to Evittsburg."

"We'd love to," she said, setting out the paper plates and silverware, "but let's make it later in the week. Doug has a breakfast meeting tomorrow, and Gil's helping at vacation church school this week. He's doing the music with Heather Pepper – would you name your daughter Heather if your last name was Pepper? – anyway, she's a ball of fire with all kinds of ideas about camp songs she learned at church camp last year. He's the only boy they could get to help," she added proudly.

"Hey, Amazing, how about teaching the little kids 'Like a Virgin' or 'Material Girl'?" said Joy mischievously, one eye all too obviously on me. But, like all great generals, I choose my own battleground.

"How about you, Joy? You and Scott want to stay over? Separate beds, of course, and no night-crawling."

"Mother." I swear she looked shocked. "What an expression." It was always curiously rewarding to shock Joy, a kind of perverse version of child rebelling against parent.

"Thank you," I said modestly. "It seemed appropriate to the outdoor theme. Well, how about it?"

"You know Scott's not much of a camping type, but we did bring along a few things, just in case. He said he's really looking forward to spending his first night out of doors, sleeping on the bosom of Mother Earth."

I grunted and turned down the gas, which was frying away the hamburgers like magic. "I knew I should have paid for the leaner meat. Is everything ready?"

"Everything but the corn. I'll check it." Joy picked up an aluminum-clad ear off the grill over the fire ring and gingerly peeled some of the foil down like a banana skin. "Perfect. Singed to a turn, the way I love it."

"Lucky, JoyWorld, because here come the men," said Grace. Two minutes later we were all seated around the red-vinyl tablecloth under the tarp and I remember feeling so contented, as we held hands through the drifting aromas of corn and hamburgers, that I didn't even get annoyed at Scott's insistence on keeping his head up and his eyes open through Dan's prayer. I always check to see, just in case there's been a change of heart.

After the men washed up the pots and pans, another neat family tradition, we all took a walk around the loop and then down to the beach again, with Gil as our roving scout. As we emerged from the path onto the gravel roadway that led to the beach, he took off with some friends he had made that afternoon.

I squinted into the light still reflecting feebly off the lake. "Grace," I said, "Gil certainly seems to have dropped some of the burden he was carrying when school ended. Did you ever find out what it was all about?"

Doug answered for her. "No, but I don't mind admitting that I'm glad it seems to be done with." He hesitated. "I'm pretty sure it had something to do with race, and he's never had to cope with that very much before." Another pause. "You know, I was lucky, growing up. I never had any really cutting experience of prejudice, and I would get so impatient with Dad when he'd go on about it. So I forget sometimes, in spite of things that happen, how pervasive and subtle it can be. I guess I didn't think Gillie had much reason to think about it until I saw that play of his."

"I don't think any American, black or white, can escape being prejudiced one way or another these days," said Dan. "Nobody's perfectly neutral; it can't be done." He took my hand to help me up over the grassy hill that led to the beach. "I've always thought the trick is to make yourself rise above it, get beyond it in yourself, kind of finesse it. You accept the fact that it's there in you, but you pretend it isn't. You go with your head instead of your conditioning. If enough people did that, it would lose its power, eventually,"

Doug's face set. "I call that begging the question. Is that what you do with me?"

Dan was silent. Finally, he said doggedly, "Doug, you must know that there was some of that going on when we first knew you."

Doug too was silent. Grace took his hand and looked anxiously at me. Dan hurried on, stumbling a little. "It works the way I said, Doug; racism loses its power when you do an end run around it, even if it's there. It turns into one of those ripples that gets stopped before it produces another ripple – you know – his laugh sounded a little forced "-- what I call Spite the Devil? When one evil thing doesn't just automatically produce another evil thing, but comes to a dead end, just sort of shrivels away. And that's what appened about you, Doug. Whatever racism we came to you with, it's gone now --"

"Except the raised consciousness." I felt compelled to see the thing through, "Which, you could argue, is a form of racism in itself."

"Man being the self-conscious animal that he – or she – is," said Dan, heavily trying to lighten things up, "who can expect automatic attitudes in these times? Intention and behavior are enough to start with - the spontaneity comes after."

Doug looked up wryly. "My whole life, you know, is based on universals, that the only answer is total color-blindness."

Grace put his hand to her lips and looked at us defiantly. "What's wrong with that?"

"Nothing at all," I said, "only it's easier said than done. You mean to wipe out all affirmative action, Doug? All the busing ¬?"

Doug turned to me impatiently. "No, Mom, of course I don't mean that. I'll admit I've wondered from time to time whether they do the job they're supposed to do. I've even thought maybe there should be a time limit on them, say twenty years, or thirty, the span of one generation, or some provision to have to renew it every so often. That way, maybe blacks would be encouraged to make something out of the opportunities while they last. Then things might slip into a colorblind situation more normally, with both sides on an equal footing."

The conversation lapsed under the influence of lounging on the grass at the sandy edge above the beach, though Doug still looked troubled. Of us all, I think, he was the idealist, the gentle soul who cared until he hurt, bled concern for anyone in need, expected the most from himself and others.

Grace put her arm around him, and he leaned his head on her shoulder, as they watched Gil running in the shallows with his friends. Gil should have put his swimsuit on, I heard her murmur, but Doug only laughed and put his hand, palm up, upon her knee, the pale flesh of it turned up so vulnerably I held my breath until Grace laid her own on top of it.

The faintest of twilight breezes stirred our hair, and everyone seemed motionless as the shadows lengthened, almost statues in the dusk. Joy sat, with Scott at full length, head in her lap; Dan and I crosslegged in the grass, hynotized by the dying sun, gold upon the water.

From the fields across the lake, through the megaphone of evening, floated the mooing of cows left out for the warm night, poignant as doves, and then one of those inscrutable self-introductions of the quail, unusual at that hour, "Bob-white," but only once, as if he dreamed it was daytime, before silence filled in the spaces again. It seemed that time fed in one side and out the other while we rested there in perfect harmony.

Joy screamed and jumped up. "Gillie! I'll kill you!" He had tossed a plastic cup of water over her and Scott, and fled now, taunting, back to the water's edge. The four adults chased him down for a terminal water battle, and then they all turned, soaked and breathless, to dump courtesy cups on the rest of us before racing back to the lake. It felt cool on my throat, and Dan kissed me, laughing, wiping the drops off my breast with his finger.

CHAPTER 12

The Carliers took off in the Chevy van, shouting goodbyes, and Dan and Scott occupied themselves building a fire, while I got out the lantern.

"Want me to do that, Mom?" asked Joy.

"Would you?" I asked gratefully. "I don't mind putting in the gas and pumping it up, but lighting it scares the dickens out of me."

"Mom," said Joy, after I had handed the lanern over to her, "I heard you talking to Grace today about those things on your arm."

"Yes?" I was surprised. "The doctor says they're nothing to worry about. I was just telling her what a shock it is when you've been young all your life and healthy, within reason, and then these things start happening." I motioned to my hearing aid. "The ears and the eyes – and all those ridiculous things you don't hear about much that start popping up on your skin, the moles and strange-looking things like these, that they used to call devil's tits, and drown women for as witches back in the 1600s. But they're not malignant or anything –"

"God!" A huge rush of flame burst out the tip of the lantern and she backed away, reaching gingerly for the knob to turn it down. "This thing needs cleaning or something. No wonder it scares you."

"Just let it gush out," I said, from a safe distance. "That's what your father does and it works every time."

"Whew!" She got it under control and shook her head. "The joys of camping." She cleaned the mantles carefully, running the little metal finger over them again and again as the light flickered in response. "I'm glad those skin things aren't serious, but I was just wondering why you never tell me about things like that, things that bother you or that you think about. All we ever do, it seems, is argue."

I was astounded. "I never thought you'd be interested." I sat down beside her on the bench. "We're so opinionated, you and I, and the opinions we hold are so – strongly opposite."

She laughed and set the lantern in the middle of the table, then eyed it dubiously. "The bugs'll get all over everything."

"Hang it on that big nail on the tree. Since it's there we might as well use it."

Reaching up carefully, she said, "Really, I don't want to stop the arguments. They keep me on my toes. But it would be nice to talk about normal mother-daughter things, too, don't you think?"

I considered it. "If there are any we could agree about."

A husky voice came out of the dark driveway behind us. "Somebody here from Pennsylvania?"

A large thin man in shorts and a large fat woman, her upper body cantilevered away from huge hips, strode into the lantern light. Dan and Scott came up from the fire and we all introduced ourselves; they were the Greeleys, Dayton and Nora, from the campsite below.

"Just taking our evening walk around the loop," said the man. "We spotted the P-A license on your car, and we thought we'd find out your home town."

"Our old stompin ground!" cried Greeley, when Dan told him. They settled into our lawn chairs to celebrate, and Dan, always the sociable one, settled in with them. "We're from Gunther Park."

Mildly irritated to have to be outgoing, I handed around soft drinks.

"So what's your line of work?" asked Greeley, Dayton call him, he said, or even Dub, like his friends did, when they admitted they knew him. He stretched out and put his feet on top of the fire ring. He pointed to his wife's drink. "How about this new Coke? I won't drink it until they put the old stuff back in the stores."

We talked about that, and hijacking, and terrorism, mutually disapproving of them all, ending up in a quiet shared halo of companionship.

"Your fire don't seem to be drawin good," he said, kicking the concrete ring. "I'll maybe have to look at it." He leaned closer. "The air ain't comin through."

He got down on his knees and rearranged the wood according to some arcane pattern of his own that set the flames leaping wildly into the air. "That'll do it."

He dusted off his knees and took back his Tab from his wife. "My boy taught me that, after he went to Boy Scout camp. I never knowed how to make a good fire before, always wimpy like yours."

Dan and Scott looked rather shamefaced, and I hoped they'd watched him to see how he did it; we always seemed to have trouble getting good fires, and Dan was always fooling with them.

"It's them concrete things," Greeley went on cheerfully. "It goes easier in the metal ones, or jis pile up some rocks around, that works good. Always use standin deadwood; you don go roun pickin up logs off the ground." He looked critically at our supply. "They don let you cut here without permission, but you can buy some wood that looks better'n that. Whadja say you do?"

"I'm a minister," said Dan, "and Scott here's a lawyer. You're right about that wood. It's left over from some I went out and got in a friend's woodlot. He couldn't go along, and I just chopped up what I found on the ground. Standing deadwood, eh? I'll remember that."

Dub had lost his cool, sitting on the edge of his lawn chair, about as well as you can sit on the edge of a lawn chair, looking vastly alarmed. "A minister."

The chair gave warning, and he sat back unwillingly. "God, I haven't been to church lately, Reverend, but I'm going to start back pretty soon, with Nora here, I promise." The revelation took all the starch out of him, but Nora perked up at once.

"Which church do you pastor, Reverend?" she asked, her body thrusting up out of her chair at an acute angle to the arms. With horror I noticed that the aluminum tube leg showed a hair crack right beyond the bend, and started willing it to hold. Or praying, which can be the same sometimes, God knows.

"Trinity Lutheran, on Jefferson, in the North End."

"Oh, I've heard of it. I'm Congregation of Jesus Christ, out near us there in Gunther Park. Rev. Staley, do you know him?"

"No, not personally." I remembered Staley; he had founded the Congregation himself, an autonomous little group that he now ruled with an iron hand in an iron glove. He was one of the most fundamentalist of the Evittsburg ministers, and a voluminous producer of letters-to-the-editor of the local newspaper.

Joy's eyes glittered. "That last letter your minister sent to the paper," she said. "He certainly seems to think a lot of the guy who bombed the abortion clinic downtown."

"Oh, we all do. He's President of the Directors' Board, you know. We all stand behind him, because he's only saving life, all those poor little babies in the garbage cans and screaming in the womb and everything. We should do something to save God's little babies, vengeance is mine saith the Lord, he will make thine enemies his footstool, he has delivered thine enemies into his hand. Isn't that right, Mrs --?"

"Heyer," I said.

"Mrs. Heyer. That's right, isn't it?"

She was so confident of my support, I didn't want to see her face when I answered, so I picked up a stick and poked the fire with it. "Well, I'm not sure about doing exactly 'anything.' "

There was a pause. "You mean you thnk abortion is okay?" Her blasted expectation hit me like destroyed innocence.

"No, I think it's an abomination," I said, and she looked relieved. "But I don't believe in terrorism to protest it." I took a breath. "What's more, abortion should be kept legal as a last resort. On the other hand," I hoped it would help, "we should offer all the alternatives first, and put the weight of society behind them. Just like we do about smoking."

She looked slightly bewildered, working it out. Finally, "You mean birth control?" she whispered in a breath as bated as any I'd heard lately.

"Of course."

Unfortunately, that did it. Visibly widening the hair crack in the leg, she pried herself out of the chair and collected her husband, who seemed to have overcome his initial revulsion at learning Dan's work, and was delivering a lecture on the management of the state and federal park systems. They shook our dust from their feet in thirty seconds.

"Well, that was a quick visit," said Dan, regretfully, rejoining us around the fire. "I was hoping to break out the popcorn before they left."

Joy gave him the aluminum-foiled pan and a hotpad to hold it with. "Nice of you to volunteer, Dad." She raised an eyebrow. "Hey, Mom, welcome to feminism."

It was really annoying.

Once Dub had cured our fire, it stayed healthy the rest of the evening, in spite of everything Dan and Scott could think to do. It was perfect for singing around, I said, and Gil would have loved it, but, if he couldn't take advantage of it, the rest of us could use it as God had intended campfires to be used. So, a trifle self-consciously, against the grim silence from the next camp, we sang "Down By the Old Mill Stream," and "I've Been Workin On the Railroad," and "Let Me Call You Sweetheart," all of which dated from before the youth of everyone present.

When Dan pulled up the lawn chair Nora had so hastily vacated, I showed him the crack. "They all do that, sooner or later," he said. "I'll sit quiet." So I gave up warning him about it, and concentrated on singing, taking Scott by surprise, I think, for I have been told I sing just badly enough to make strong men weep. "It's not that you can't sing," said Grace kindly, when she was about twelve; "it's just that it might be better if you didn't."

However, Scott made a quick recovery, assisted by a punch in the ribs from Joy, and we sang a few more oldies before Joy started "We Are The World." "Sorry, folks," I said. "That's one I don't know."

"You're kidding," Scott said. "Everyone knows "We Are the World.""

Joy shrugged. "I believe her," she said. "Brace yourself for the rock-and-roll lecture."

Here I give myself points. There are so many obvious things one never ever dares to say about rock music, but this wasn't the time to get off on that, and "We Are The World" was certainly not the song. So I hummed along, and actually even learned the part about, "There's a choice we're making/We're saving our own lives." Anomalous words.

In the lively night beyond our discords, the three-beat katydids chimed in with an occasional four-beater, as argumentive as I am, against the drone of locusts and the crackle of fire. The trees sighed faintly above our heads, a bird shifting for the night, leaves touching briefly, sounding existence.

Scott shivered. "You know, I thought I'd love it, and I do. But it - it kind of scares me --" he said. His candor caught me off guard again. "I really am a city boy, you know, brought up in New York and Chicago – my folks moved a lot before they got divorced, and Evittsburg --" his thin features pinched, as if he wished he had never brought up the subject, or, better yet, never touched down anywhere between New York and Chicago -- "well, Evittsburg's almost like being out in the country itself. And this is even worse." He jumped as a particularly outspoken katydid opened up near his ear. "It's frightening."

"Whatever inspired you to come to Evittsburg?" asked Dan curiously.

"Well, I was working in New Jersey, and Mr. Sackett" -- of Sackett and Ginevan, the local law firm Scott worked for -- "knew my boss and they needed a young corporate lawyer, and right then I really wanted to leave New Jersey --"

Problems at work, I wondered, or an unhappy love affair? Joy was poking around in the fire with the stick I had used earlier, her face determinedly noncommittal, and I was suddenly shaken with sadness for her and an intense need to sterilize the world, as I had once sterilized diapers, formula, teethers, of all troubles for her and every other helpless young one facing age, and old one facing worse -- but I couldn't. The only options lie between helping each other through the bad times -- or compounding them.

"Is it the noises?" Dan asked. "There's really nothing around here that would attack --"

"Oh, no, it's not that. It's -- I don't know -- maybe -- hearing things, that, you know, were being heard a hundred years ago. And nobody knew me then. And they'll probably be heard a hundred years from now, and nobody will know me then either. It's not like that, in New York, where nobody knows you, of course, but you're still part of it, and it will all probably change before you do --"

Joy still poked away with the stick. "But that's how life is," she said. "We come and we go, and that's all there is to it. No real meaning, except what you put into it yourself. In the end, there's really nothing to do but brace yourself. And do what you can with your own little slice of time."

And, you know, I understood exactly what she was saying.

Scott nodded, staring into the leaping fire. "And when your tree falls, the other trees will remember it and carry on your memory." He shivered again and his chair creaked. Briefly I worried about its giving way; all these chairs were in terrible shape. "But then they die too, and you're gone forever."

"Not forever," said Dan. "God still holds you in His consciousness, where he always did, where it all exists to start with -"

Even in the shadowed firelight, I saw Scott's face redden, and he opened his mouth. "You know," I said, making a show of coming out of deep thought, "one thing I can say for rock music is, it's one kind of music I can hear even without my hearing aid."

With a loud crack that definitively silenced the katydids for yards around, two legs of my chair broke and pitched me backwards, where I sat, still in the green-and-yellow-webbed seat, laughing like a fool.

CHAPTER 13

Scott and Joy left the next morning after a decorous night, poor things, with Joy in the crank-out bed opposite ours and Scott on the mattress in the trailer box. Breakfast was pleasant, carrying on the spirit that had resulted from my making an idiot of myself the night before. They had picked me up, the two men hauling at my arms with Joy anxiously helping from behind, and we had gone about the bedtime chores in a mutual jollity of inquiries for misplaced toothpaste tubes and advice on avoiding the puddle in the Ladies' bathroom.

By 10 AM Dan and I were alone, and the dishes were almost done. It had already gotten hot; the sun filtered sulkily through a veil of haze that seemed to bind the heat around the earth like a bandage.

"Do you want to swim?" asked Dan restlessly.

"You've forgotten that I haven't felt like inflicting the sight of me in a swimsuit on the general population for years."

"You're too self-conscious." He puttered around, picking up a crumpled tissue, a scrap of paper from the ground. "It's so hot. Maybe I'll put on my suit and go down later."

I was closing the campstove when he reappeared in his yellow-and-black striped trunks. "I always said you were a fine figure of a man," I said, clothes-pinning the dishcloth to dry on the tarp rope. "And you look like a fine figure of a bumble bee in that suit."

"Really?" he said, brightening up. He walked over and put his arms around me from the back and nuzzled my neck. "Bzz, bzz," he said, his voice somewhat muffled by the fact that I was checking out the surrounding trees for nosy strangers.

I can't help it, that's just the way I am.

"Nobody around," he said. "I already checked for you." It helps when you share some of the same characteristics, or at least understand them.

Reassured, I said, "No honey there," and turned my mouth toward his, settling in for awhile.

"We'll get to it," he said. And we did, in a morning as silent as a pond, with only a faint ripple of water sounding from the stream, and the world somehow held at bay outside the canvas of the tent trailer.

"Come swimming with me," he urged then. "That's all nonsense about how you look in a swimsuit. Trust me," he winked outrageously, "after all, I know more about your body than anyone else."

I lay on my elbow, drawing lines from one hair to the other on his chest. "Like a dot-to-dot drawing," I said. "Look, it's a pine tree. You've got a pine tree on your chest."

"I wish I did," he grumbled. "It's humiliating to have all that bare space in between. I always wished I had lots of hair on my chest. I even used to rub hair tonic into it, when I was a kid. And I still had only those nine."

He zipped down a window and put his arm around me, then took it out again. "It's getting hotter. I never did understand how I could be hairy-armed and so smooth-chested."

"Actually, there's twelve here," I said. "You haven't counted lately."

He laughed and gave me a quick kiss. "That's true. I have had other things on my mind in recent years. Back when I was 17, I must have had more time."

I rolled over on my back. "Growing up is so -- well, everybody says it's agonizing, but I never thought that was exactly right. If I was agonized, I never knew it. I just thought whatever it was was normal. Nowadays, kids are made to be so self-conscious about themseves." I discovered a spider hanging by a thread above our heads.

"Not that I'm implying that she's an adolescent," he said, "but do you think that Joy will ever settle down with a solid guy?"

"Maybe not until after I die."

"Are you serious?"

I watched the spider ride his thread like a child in a swing. "Joy and I are alike in so many ways, I think she has a horror of being my clone. For instance, she'll fight letting God in her life, because that's our biggest difference."

Dan was pursuing his own line of thought. "It's not that an atheist can't be a solid guy, of course -- though I think Scott's more of an agnostic -- so many of these young ones are, from what I can see, seriously concerned with honesty and actually expecting they can get all the answers at some point."

"And Grace. Dan, have you noticed that she doesn't seem as -- well -- unscathed as she used to be?"

Dan smiled fondly, and the spider swung lower. "Ah, well, she's what, good Lord, 34 now, and life is going to show a little --"

"Yes, but there's something else. I'm not even sure she's all that aware of it herself. Sort of a puzzled look -- she's the one like you, Dan, and I hate something going on that I can't help her with. She's not like Joy, she'd accept whatever I could do for her, but --"

"This is ridiculous," said Dan firmly. "We spend far too much time worrying about the kids. Next we'll be getting on Gil, and we don't have time, because that spider is about to land in our eyes." He sat up. "Come on swimming with me. I'll guarantee your body to anyone who looks cross-eyed at you. I'll tell them I just did the 5000-mile checkup."

He leaned over and kissed me and then detached the spider at the roof and carried it, rapidly climbing toward his wrist, over to the door. On the way he picked up my jeans and shirt, opened the door, and threw them on the picnic table, glued the spider thread neatly to the outside canvas, and then gasped, a great, noisy, artificial make-believe gasp.

"Oh my goodness!" he said. "There are a thousand people out here looking at us. You'd better put on some clothes." He pulled my swim suit out of the bathing suit bag and threw it in the door. I put it on, and we went swimming and had a wonderful time, though I can't speak for the innocent bystanders.

That afternoon, Dan began making preparations for the debate with Lily Lyle Hadley, reading, making notes, thinking, while I sat near

him at the cold fireplace with my feet up on the rim, finishing off
-And Ladies of the Club.

Reading that book is like stepping bodily into an Ohio
community of the last century, one of the few literary reinforcements
to tranquillity to come out of the last twenty-five years. I said so to
Dan, and he looked at the size of the book and grimaced. "Looks
like you've got to begin with a pretty good stock of tranquillity just
to start it."

"Why, tranquillity? Persistence, maybe --"

"I mean, if you're worried about the end of the world coming any
time in the next century, you wouldn't dare start it."

I laughed. "So -- do you think you could?"

"Sure, why not? The world's always coming to an end for
somebody. I never did believe in suddenly changing your whole
lifestyle just because you suddenly knew for sure your life was ending
tomorrow."

"No deathbed conversions?"

"I'm more interested in lifetime ones."

"How about Lily Lyle Hadley's conversion?" I asked slyly.

"Not a chance of it. Even if she had the impulse, she'd stifle it,
maybe even herself, before she'd give in. Her whole identity is tied
up in being an atheist. Nothingness is her reality. If she ever allowed
herself any doubts about the possibility of God's existence, she'd
wipe herself out, by definition."

"Well, so would we, wouldn't we? If we decided God didn't
exist, I mean? Wouldn't that be wiping ourselves out too? Especially
if you believe, like you said last night, that we all exist in God's
consciousness?"

He thought how to put it. "It seems to me that faith can co-exist
with more doubt than doubt can with faith. Because if faith is ever
right that God exists, then it's always right. He can't exist some times
and not others. But, for an atheist, if that perception of God's non-
existence is ever right, it's only right for that moment." He brooded.
"There must be a better way to put it." He shook his head. "Anyway,
I always feel sorry for people like Lilly Nilly."

"Sorry for her? She's made a mint, and stands to make more." I
lowered *-And Ladies of the Club* carefully to the ground, avoiding my
toes. "How about some lemonade?"

"No, thanks. But I could use some ice water." He leaned back in his chair and closed his eyes. "Poor soul, here she is spending her whole life obsessed with -- guess what? God! Challenging not just the existence but the very nature of something she doesn't even believe in. She spends half her life with his name on her lips."

He held the glass of water, drops beading and dripping unnoticed as he stared into space. I thought of an exercise I had once read about how to enhance one's Zen capabilities: put your finger in the air and stare at it, and then take it away and see if you can still focus on the point where it used to be. Dan looked as if he was succeeding.

He put the glass down. "You know," he said, "to be an atheist, you've got to believe that every single person who ever had an experience of God was either a fraud or a fool. Every single one, El! If even one of those millions of experiences down through the ages was valid, it cancels out the whole premise of atheism. Just one experience, El, from the very first one in the world, say, whoever he was, Adam's, down to yours." He shook his head. "Maybe I'm a fool too, but I don't have the presumption to pronounce such a judgment on so many other people, even aside from my own beliefs."

I hardly heard his last words, thrown back by his reference to something that had happened years ago, when my father was so unhappily heeding Dylan Thomas's foolish young admonition not to go gentle into the night. When the Alzheimer's had him by the throat, and I couldn't bear it, something very quiet and important had happened, simply an assurance that someone loving was with me that we call God. I had been so sure at the time, but curiously, I rarely thought of it any more.

"It's very easy," I said, "to rationalize a religious feeling, put it down to nerves, or hysteria, or something."

"Like God's voice speaking, in John, and some people called it thunder." He rubbed the icy glass against his temple. "And some didn't, of course."

CHAPTER 14

Grace and Doug came down with Gil on Friday. The weather had turned cold and the sky gleamed a heavy dull white, like ironstone. Gil leaped out of the van, all ready to go swimming, and loped toward the beach at once, his body almost lemon in the clouded light.

Grace came along more leisurely, carrying a plastic bowl of potato salad in one hand and extra lawn chairs in the other, and then Doug, loaded down with firewood.

"Hey, hold on," yelled Dan and jumped up to help them.

"Don't let him take that heavy stuff, Doug." Grace shook her head. "Men! Gil gets away before we can put him to work, and Dad leaps to the harness like an old warhorse."

"Old?" said Dan indignantly.

Doug eased his load onto the ground. "There's more out in the trunk. I remembered Dub's lesson and specifically asked the guy who was selling it if this was standing wood."

"I thought he was going to hit you for implying he didn't know his job." Grace shook her head.

"I was all ready to duck," Doug assured her. He hefted the wood expectantly. "I can't wait to get at it," he said. "There's something about chopping wood that does a lot for me. Gets rid of my hostilities, I guess," he added apologetically, as if he really shouldn't have any. "But first we're going to go for a good row."

I sighed. Doug always worked so hard when he played.

When we walked down to the beach, Gil was hard to find, now that he was no more bronzed than all the other tanned bodies lying around in the non-existent sunshine.

"There he is, over by the boathouse, talking to the girl in the green bikini." Doug looked at Grace, and his creases quirked. "Am I mistaken, or is he getting more interested in girls than he used to be?"

Grace smiled her quick, no-holds-barred smile. "No, you're not mistaken. And the interest seems to be mutual."

She and I sat down on the grass, while the men set off for the boathouse. "Doug's really been looking forward to renting the rowboats," she said, taking a scarf out of her jeans pocket and tying her hair off her forehead with it.

"Sounds like fun," I said dubiously.

"I told him, as long as he's willing to do the rowing, I'm willing to do the sitting."

I approved of that. "How's the job going?"

"Not bad, considering the market. I almost sold a house yesterday, but the wife decided the lawn was too big for her to mow."

"A truly liberated woman. And how's Gil doing these days?"

"Oh, he's fine now. I think all that stuff in the spring was just a stage he was going through. You know, puberty and all that."

Well, that was a relief. Two rowboats out on the lake seemed to crash headon, but a minute later, one emerged from the other's bow: a trick of perspective then. "Miracles do happen."

"Do you really think so?"

"I often wonder how many happen without our knowing it. When something doesn't happen, you never know that it might have."

"Or vice versa," she said, with a throb of hilarity in her voice.

"We're living in a world of miracles," I went on, stubbornly. "When you come right down to thinking about them, air and water are sort of miracles, aren't they, and fire and earth? If you lived on Mars, say, could you have thought of any of them on your own? Water's always fascinated me. Who would ever have invented something that slips along like that, and still stays solid and deep, and yet penetrable in a pool or frozen hard as a rock, or even moving in the air – "

"I know how your mind works, Mother. Next, we're all going to be miracles – "

"No woman is a sage among her own offspring." I subsided as the men walked up, beaming.

"Okay, girls. The Heyer-Carlier Excursion is due to leave in two minutes sharp."

Gil consented to go along, leaving the girl, whose name, we learned presently, was Windy Kellogg, poor thing. However, flatulence appeared not to be a problem, and I managed not to speculate out loud on the new generation's tendency to name daughters after meteorological conditions, especially adverse ones, like Windy, Stormy, and Misty. Still, I couldn't help imagining to myself a profusion of Aunt Windies, Grandma Stormies, and Cousin Misties in another fifty years or so.

I also noticed that, after they parted, she looked back at him more than he looked back at her. "Gil looks like he's turning into a lady killer," I said. "I think he takes after you, Doug."

The large rimless glasses Doug had taken to wearing lately slid down his straight-bridged nose as he laughed. "Oh, no doubt about it. The only woman I never did captivate at first sight was you, Mom."

I thought about that. "You know, you're right. It took you a couple weeks to get around me. Funny. I thought I hid that all very well."

His hand squeezed mine quickly as we walked. "Well, I really did have some kind of an idea of the problems you were having." We stepped onto the dock. "A lot like my Dad was having about Grace."

Doug and Dan had rented out two rowboats, disappointingly aluminum, so that they thunked in the water, instead of slapping like proper wooden rowboats. The females in the group contented themselves with token stints as rowers before allowing the men to take over, and Gil enforced an equal time agreement with his father. So we all had a good morning out on the water, rowing around the lake more or less together, stopping when the rowers got tired, which I was glad to see, happened no more often with Dan than with Doug.

Pulling in close to the shore where trees shaded the water, Dan and I rested alone in the most limpid silence, magnified by the muffled clap of water against the boat, a bird of some sort chiming up in the woods. The sun, newly out, sprinkled showers of sequins on the water between shadows of leaves.

Smelling the hot green July, feeling the cool rip of water between my fingers, I saw Dan look over at me, and felt us joined as much as ever we were when straining to reach oneness in bed.

"Let's never go back," I said. "Let's stay here forever."

He stored an oar, and dipped his hand into the water. Then he looked up and smiled into my eyes. "Why not?" he said. "Yes, let's. Forever."

You say these things but you don't do them.

The park ranger drove up while we were eating supper and leaned out of his window. "Rev. Heyer?"

They sat in the driveway and talked a few minutes. Dan came back looking troubled, as the ranger's car backed out and went on down the camp road.

"Perry Mandible," he said. "He's had a heart attack and Mary Ann called and left a message that he's bad."

"Oh, Dan. Would you like me to go with you?"

"No, it's okay." He swung up the step into the camper and reappeared while I stood there. "I'll just take my dop kit here and use the clothes at the house. Take care and don't miss me. I'll try to be back tomorrow."

Doug started forward. "How about if I go along for company?"

Dan was astonished. "On your vacation? No use ruining things for all of us. This is something I have to do, Doug, but you don't. Anyway, it's only a couple hours' drive. I'll be there before dark."

With a wave he drove away, and Doug and I went to sit down again with Grace. "Next to my Dad," he said to her absently, "I do love yours."

Perry Mandible died that night, and Dan stayed over until morning. He got back in the afternoon, just in time for our planned trip to the Compass Inn at Ligonier Tuesday.

CHAPTER 15

Dan had insisted on his return from Evittsburg the night before that we should stick to the planned expedition. "It sounds good," he said. "I met Lee McDonald at the funeral home today, and he was telling me that it's an old drovers' inn from the early 19th century, not big but authentic, and not so crowded the guides won't take time for you."

"He's the one who plays the bagpipes, isn't he?" I seemed to remember a gentle, kilted, sandy-haired man, all wrapped up in his music, so to speak.

Dan chuckled. "Yes. I told him I'd trust his word about the Compass Inn, even if he did have terrible taste in music." Poor McDonald came in for a good deal of teasing about his musical preferences.

The van was full of noisy conversation and laughter. Even Scott was animated, maybe because we were away from intimidating nature. Just people sounds here, against the background noise of engine.

Gil was all over; you couldn't keep him down. He went up to sit beside his father for awhile but when he reached over to turn on the radio, Doug shook his head. "You know how it fills up Nana's hearing aid."

When we stopped for gas, Gil came back to where Scott sat by Joy.

"You can see better out the front window," he said innocently. Scott grinned and got up.

"I should be jealous," he said. "But seeing as you're a blood relative – " He went up to the seat next to Doug, and they carried on a conversation about cars and motors for longer than can be believed.

Still, sitting quietly wasn't Gil's thing. Before we got out of Evittsburg, he had coaxed Dan into doing bird trills, and suddenly the van was filled with cascades of flutey notes, like no known birdcall, but entrancing as a music box.

"Oh, Dad," sighed Joy. "If I only had a dollar for every time I used to try to do that. Remember that day I got you to teach me, but I couldn't learn? I was so mad. I thought it was just a genetic fact that I should be able to do it."

"You were mad. I was sad," said Grace.

Joy looked at her curiously. "You too?"

"Boys whistle better than girls," said Gil confidently. I thought Joy would nip that little sprout of male chauvinism in the bud, but she only regarded him with amusement. "Grandpa's teaching me how to do it." To our amazement he whistled quite a passable phrase. "I'll teach my own sons and hundreds of years from now our descendents will still be trilling away, carrying on the ancient tradition." The combination of child and adult in Gil was startling sometimes.

"Good, Nuggie," said Dan, and trilled a particularly beautiful cadenza, worthy of any number of generations of offspring. It shrilled in my hearing aid, and I turned it down.

"Actually, as a straight whistler, I'm pretty good," said Joy, from a distance. "Gil, guess where I whistled my very first whistle of all time? In church during Dad's sermon. What a shock. I'd been trying for weeks, but I had no idea I was going to learn at that moment – "

"I remember that." Grace's tone was wry. "I remember thinking if I'd done it I would have gotten heck."

Dan had stopped, and I turned my hearing aid back up. "Mmm. I wonder if that's true. We always tried to treat you both the same."

"Well, the older child always has more required of her, I think," said Grace. "Now, in Gillie's case – " she turned to him across the car, teasing – "Gil, you're both the oldest and the youngest. Do you think more is required of you as the oldest or more is allowed from you as the youngest?"

"More's required of me," he said, without hesitation.

"But no more than you're capable of," said Joy, putting her arm around him. "No drugs, no smoking, all we've talked about, Gil – "

He wriggled free with dignity. "You know what Grandpa says – 'You are what you are and don never forget it.' "

"In *Les Cage Aux Folles,* Zaza sings 'I am what I am,' " contributed Scott.

"I've been hearing that all my life," called Doug from the front. "Long before *Le Cage* or, for that matter, Lake Wobegon, ever came along."

"I've never been quite sure," said Dan. "Doug, does your dad mean we should live up to our highest protential, or not be dissatisfied with what we are?"

Doug squinted against the sun. "I always thought of it as living up to something, a challenge," he called back finally. "With all kinds of dimension to it, depending on where I was coming from. When I was little, I connected it with Popeye. You know, I yam what I yam, and spinach and strength, and not just some puny little guy who was black and second class, but full of muscle and punch."

"Then, later, when I read in the Bible where Moses asks God what His name is, and God says, 'I AM THAT I AM,' and the whole thing got deeper, you know? It's there in Job too, when the poor guy asks God what this awful life is all about anyway, and God sort of bullies him, says, where were you when I created the earth and all that. He's saying 'I Am' again, pure existence, declaring himself in the middle of the agony of life, and saying, 'I am, I exist, just know, feel my presence in your life, and you'll bear through.' And when it's all over – Scott, man, don't look at me like that. It's okay to talk about God as if there is one, you know. It's not being fanatic or crazy – "

Scott straightened up. "It's all so different. It takes a little getting used to. Like people seriously debating whether the earth is flat – "

Joy laughed, a high nervous sound, and the rest of us were silent. It isn't easy to see yourself through others' eyes, but I suppose it's therapeutic.

"So, anyway," I said, "that's the history of Robey's You Are What You Are. Popeye and God."

"Not a bad combination," said Dan pacifically.

Winding around on the country road, we took in the spectacle of hill-to-hill shag rugs of corn and clover and pasture, set among forested slopes, with here barns and houses and there, cows and a deer Gil glimpsed ecstatically down a gully.

"The heartland of America," Scott called back to Joy, and he didn't even sound sarcastic.

Maybe it was just as well that he and Doug had drifted back into a comfortable exchange on the subject of computers, for back in the van we were knee-deep in nostalgia.

"Do you remember?" said Joy, "when I used that flashlight Grandpa gave me on you during your sermon?"

Dan's whole face displaced itself in laughter. "And Stella Straw thought it was the Holy Spirit shining out of my eyes, and said I was a true prophet of God." He shook his head.

"She was the one who laundered her church money, wasn't she, Dad?" asked Grace.

"Laundered her church money?" echoed Gil, fascinated by this spate of events that had happened in his world before he was ever known to it.

Dan nodded. "That's how we found out she was sick, you know, the week she died. About a year after Joy's flashlight escapade, Stella broke her hip, and after she got out of the hospital she never left her house. I visited her, of course, and every week she sent in her offering by the folks next door. She'd put it in the mail box, and they'd pick it up and bring it in. Well, she had the idea that money was dirty, not worthy of God, or something like that. So every Saturday she'd wash her money, bills and all, in soap and water, and she'd hang the bills up to dry with clothespins on a little rubber rope in her bathroom over the tub. She showed it to me once. And then she'd iron it, and for years, every Sunday when the money was counted, here was this beautiful crisp money in Stella's church envelope.

"One Sunday when the Sadlers opened her envelope – remember the Sadlers, girls? They counted the money for years, right after church, and then went out to dinner afterwards at the State Hotel, and everyone always kidded them about using the money from the offerings – they opened Stella's envelope and the money was as dirty as everyone else's. They called me at the house, feeling silly, but – "

"I remember that," cried Joy. " You went over to the house, and she was lying on the floor."

Dan nodded. "She'd felt so weak Saturday, she just couldn't make herself launder the money as usual, and she put it out early without laundering it. The next morning she fell getting out of bed."

"What did you do?" asked Gil.

"Called the ambulance. She kept apologizing all the way over for not having her money clean, if you can imagine that. She died the next day."

"How about the Sadlers?" asked Joy.

"The Sadlers?" Dan looked puzzled. "I guess they went out to dinner as usual."

"No, I mean, did you ever find out if they had been embezzling all that time?"

Dan laughed and shook his head. "Sorry, Joy, I hate to ruin your day, but they were quite honest. Good people, both of them."

"Well, they could have been stealing away all those years and nobody knew it," said Gil, defending his aunt. His attention suddenly turned outside the window. " Hey, not bad," he said, sighting a slim young thing on the sidewalk, her hair all tied up and jutting out a la Madonna.

"Decadence on the very streets of Berlin, P-A," said Joy, amused.

"Have you ever noticed how pretty all the young girls are these days?" I said generously, rather spoiling the effect by adding, "No matter what they do to themselves."

"Yes," said Dan.

"Aren't they always?" said Grace.

"Not when I was young. Only the occasional lucky girl – all the rest of us were duds. Nobody wore makeup, except for lipstick, and nobody had many clothes, or knew how to wear our hair – "

"And you walked through the snow for five miles to school every winter," said Joy playfully.

"Well, no, I lived in the city about one block from school. But some things were different then, you know, really different – "

"On the other hand," said Dan gallantly, "even if you didn't look beautiful to yourselves, you still were, I bet, to the boys, and to the Stella Straws of the time, too."

We got there about 2:30, and it was pretty hot, even for early August. The Compass Inn is a perfectly ordinary little tourist preservation and reconstruction: the center building a small log house originally put up in 1799, with a limestone addition from about 1820. Like a thousand other historical attractions around the country, it's lovingly resurrected, restored, and cared for by local volunteer labor.

I love the memory of it, because it was the frame for one of the nicest, most uneventful, ordinary, happy family days we ever had together. Who wouldn't hang in her heart such a picture, wreathed forever with fresh flowers?

We parked behind the house, next to the reconstructed barn, and walked up the path to the back entrance, past little plots of zinnia and transplanted jewelweed. Big smiles from the guides as they met us, dressed in early 19th century garb, two women and a man, a two-dimensional postcard picture in real life, with the low range of the buildings in the background separated from the sky by nothing more than roofline.

Gil was entranced. History was not a new idea to him – he'd been to Washington with his class last year, and we had taken him to Gettysburg. Robey had made sure he was up on Martin Luther King, Jr., amd Malcolm X, and Roots, and black history. Occupying a prominent place on his dresser at home was an arrowhead, the discovery of which, along the C&O Canal near Cumberland, had formed the pinnacle of his eleventh year. But he fell for the everyday charm of the Inn.

You entered the barroom on the stone side, through the wooden door with a glass window which was shuttered against drunken importunity with a sliding panel fastened with a wooden pin. The wide planked floor, the dark polished tables set with the usual pewterware, horn spoons, ancient three-tined forks with bone handles.

Old decks of cards without numbers: "They couldn't read so they didn't have numbers on their cards," explained the small elderly guide in her kerchiefed dress. It didn't sound quite right (surely it would have been easier to learn twelve numbers than to compare dabs on a card every time, but who knows now?) but it was a revelation to Gil. It had never occurred to him that illiteracy had not always been a function of racism, and, more surprising, that the world had once adapted to it.

He examined carefully the bear furs hanging on the walls with the claws still attached, the teapot in the kitchen with its cantilevered extra handle for pouring without taking it off the fire, the meat grinder with its punishing wooden pegs. He didn't spend much time in the Ladies parlor downstairs, and upstairs he looked at the children's toys for only a minute. He seemd more interested in the guide's heavily ironic description of the beds, three and five to a room, each "limited to only five persons a night, even when business was brisk."

In the grassy back yard with its stepping-stones, he looked in silence at the bee skep centered in pale green lemon balm, which the guide picked for us to taste. Another guide, a large handsome woman with her kerchief slightly askew, explained the beehive oven, the cabbage shredder, the homemade yeast and fresh loaves of bread it produced, the box of soap she had made herself, her hickory broom with shavings from the handle left intact and bound at the other end to brush the brick floor.

He wasn't much interested in my own personal favorite in that kitchen, a deeply carved wooden "rolling pin" my fingers ached to stroke. It was used, she said, to press the whey out of cheese, and its smocked ridges and hollows seemed carved with infinite care, almost as good as love.

He gazed, fascinated, at this domestic chemistry lab, at the large stone crock on its troughed stone base, filled with wood ashes from the fire to be soaked with water for making lye. At the smithy he watched the man in cotton shirt and brown pantaloons display the large bellows, the fittings for the anvil, round hoops for barrels, the hubs of wagon wheels. They were art forms in themselves, with their shadowed recesses and shades of light, but with the added nuance of purpose.

Dan said absently, "We never give them credit for their ingenuity. After all, *we* have computers."

Gil only frowned in concentration, bending over to look at tiny wood wedges pounded under the metal rim of a huge wagon wheel to tighten it a hundred and fifty years ago. In the barn, finally, he sat with us on the little wooden benches placed for tourists and listened as the guide warmed to his job.

A neat small man with glasses and a quick smile, he told us he was a retired army man, and he was full to the brim with history. Like a lover he caressed an original Conestoga freight wagon, and told us old stories about them, and the harnesses, each with its own string of bells, ranked on the wall.

In the gift shop I bought a fly swatter with turtles petit-pointed on it for May Benning; she collects turtles and was caring for my plants while we were camping. Grace bought a brass candlestick with the little lever on the side you can raise the candle with as it burns down. The men poked around waiting for us, as men do, while Gil coaxed Joy to retrace the tour with him so he could take pictures with his Instamatic.

We waited for them on benches along the walk, watching a few other tourists who had come in after us. One of them, a jolly-looking little plump man with the face of a well-shaven Santa Claus, broke his stride as he came past, and I noticed he was looking at Doug and Grace, holding hands.

I cleared my throat loudly and stared directly into his eyes, as one doesn't in the normal course of the social amenities. He blushed rosy and turned abruptly, bumping into a woman in the party in his haste.

"At it again, Mom?" asked Doug, amused.

"I didn't mean to cause an injury," I said, "but I don't think it hurt him to have his prejudice called to his attention."

"You don't know that he's prejudiced," said Grace comfortably.

"Here comes the Nugget," said Dan, and Gil and Joy came up, giggling.

"Did you see that little man who looks like Santa Claus without a beard?" asked Joy. "It was the funniest thing. The minute Gil and I came out of the door his head turned the other way as if it had been on a string, and he tripped and fell into my arms. He was so apologetic, but he kept looking over my head the whole time, really weird."

"He's not weird," said Doug. "Your mother merely terrorized him."

CHAPTER 16

We ate at a fine restaurant across the street from the Compass, a modest country-inn-sort-of-place, with less modest prices for an assortment of semi-gourmet meals. It had a cool and pleasant atmosphere, with the touches of tablecloth and fine wood and bad lighting that are generally held to constitute ambience.

Gil was quiet, but there was a throbbing beneath the surface, a vibrancy that affected us all. Grace and Doug looked at each other with brows figuratively lifted, and Grace asked tentatively, as mothers do, if Gil felt all right.

As sons do, Gil answered impatiently, yes, of course, and ordered spaghetti.

Doug unfolded his napkin and spread it on his lap. "So, Gil," he asked with elaborate casualness, "what did you think of the place?"

"Well, I like history, you know," said Gil, impassively adolescent. "It interests me how – uh – everybody has their own history."

The arrival of the salads got our minds off any further educational values that might be wrung out of the day's events.

"My God," said Joy. "I don't know if I can eat all that, and linguine, too."

"Sure you can," said Gil. "I'll help you." Scott volunteered to manage her onions.

We all sat back, cushioned in content. Gil's enjoyment lent the day his glow, so that we basked in it. Strangely enough, I felt that, for Dan and me, and Grace and Doug too, it wasn't so much his personal pleasure, but the fact of his age, his generation. It was almost like being reassured that the past, all its efforts, all its hardships, of which we automatically became a part with his entrance on the scene, would not be lost and forgotten, continuity broken with the newest generation. The one with the Michael Jackson dance steps and the punkish hairdos.

Here, see, was one of them, and he cherished it.

Scott wanted to play Scrabble that night after we got back to camp, and he got the fire going, and the lantern lit. After some good-natured goading from Dan and Doug ("Can't we just sit around the fire and burn marshmallows?"), we finished out the best family day ever with no more than token differences.

As when I challenged Scott's *scint* ("It's a kind of South American lizard," he said) and Joy said, "Mother, you really must learn to trust Scott once in a while."

And Grace, saying absently, as she sorted out her letters, "I've got terrible consonants, but my vowels aren't bad," at which Doug observed, with a frightful leer, "So I've noticed." She clenched her fist and laid it fearsomely against the folds of his chin, and shoved, and he laid his hand over it and brought it to his mouth, kissed it absently, and laid out words worth 32 points. Family violence like that.

Scott won, after a hard fight, with *rehabilitate* double-ended with *rage* and *emission* for 53 points. A couple of *e*'s were still kicking around but it was the last *r* everybody was looking for, and he drew it with cries of joy amidst general expressions of disgust.

Ah, God, it was a good day.

The next morning Doug chopped off the big toe of his left foot.

Joy and Scott were still asleep, but Dan and Grace and I were groggily consulting around cereal and coffee as to whether we should try to make the camp worship service at 9:30 when a shout, then Gil's cry, sounded from the old stump over near the fire which the men had been using to chop wood on.

Gray-faced, Gil burst over to us. "Dad!" he gasped. "He chopped his foot off!"

We rushed over to where Doug still stood, looking in horror at his left foot, gushing blood. Then he sat down slowly on the ground.

Dan grabbed off his belt and knelt beside Doug, feeling inexpertly for pressure points in the thigh. "Oh, God," he said, "it's been years since I took first aid. I'm going to have to try a tourniquet. El, quick, drive over to the office and get help."

Once I located the keys, it was all very simple, really. One of the rangers on duty jumped into her car and drove back to the site to help while the other dialed 911. Doug was on his way to the hospital in 20 minutes, with Grace at his side. Dan followed in the car, right after Joy and Scott came out of the trailer yawning, to find out what the siren was all about.

By then Gil and I could manage a strained smile at their bewilderment, and assure them that they had not been lacking in all human concern to have slept through most of the emergency. Then Dub showed up, lingering in the driveway until we noticed him and invited him to come up. He seemed to know what had happened (I'm sure everyone around the campsite did) and immediately offered to clean up the mess over by the stump, a job I hadn't even wanted to think about. After that, he asked to pray with us, and, as we all held hands he prayed simply, "Dear God, please let your presence hover over that good man who was hurt here today." He waved a shy, sideways wave, and disappeared back into his campsite.

After he left, the rest of us sat around the picnic table in similar states of aftershock, thinking much the same thing. Only Gil had the nerve to put words to it: "Do you think Dad'll still be able to play the organ?"

None of us knew for sure, but the silence was too painful to sustain. "Sure he will, I bet," I said sturdily. "He didn't lose the whole foot, you know, it just looked like it with all that blood. Just the big toe, I think. And he always wears special shoes anyway, doesn't he? Sure, he'll be back playing before you know it. I'll bet you – a dollar."

And I don't even approve of betting.

Gil considered the offer. "No," he said, finally. "Because if I bet against it, I'd be betting against what I want to happen."

But he looked cheered.

After everybody got dressed we went to the hospital, taking along the van and a change of clothing for Grace, who had only had time to change her pajama top for a shirt. They were still in the emergency room, but Grace looked fairly calm when she came out to the waiting room.

She held onto Gil very tight. "They decided not to try to sew it back on," she said. "But he'll be okay, Gillie, I'm sure of it."

Out at the camp again, Joy and Scott dispiritedly packed their things and left for Evittsburg. The others had stayed in town, and Dan got back to camp around 9 PM with the good news that Doug was doing very well and had already laughed off any uncertainties about his organ-playing.

"He's very up," said Dan. "Doesn't seem to be too bothered about it."

We got back to Evittsburg in plenty of time for Perry's funeral at eleven. Mary Ann waited for us in the church parlor with a good number of friends (from both within the church and out of it) and the open coffin against the wall. "We had so many plans," she said, clasping and unclasping her hands.

I remembered suddenly. "You had reservations to go to New England this fall, didn't you?" For some reason that made it even worse.

I've always teased Dan that he threw the best funerals in town, but it's true. Somehow, after one of Dan's funerals, low-key as they were in his almost hesitant conversational style, you felt more lifted than depressed at the end, willing to wait, that's for sure, but almost at the same time, expectant.

Actually it felt a lot like being pregnant.

After the interment, we returned to the fellowship hall, where the women of the church had set out food for everybody. This custom, which had fallen into disuse for some years, had turned out to be the best way to deal with the casseroles and cakes and breads and salads people made to show their sympathy, ministering physically to the sorrowing, as, in fashionable books, the characters administer sex for consolation.

So, when death happens, you either get fat or you get emotionally messed up.

CHAPTER 17

The television debate was scheduled for Saturday, September 14, at 7:30 P.M.

Dan met with Lily Lyle Hadley later in August to finalize the details. It was the first time he'd ever seen her face to face, and he was impressed. "She's much smaller than she seems on TV," he reported, "but she's just as formidable, knows what she wants, and means to get it. Kind of scary, really, like one of the early martyrs, or something, only in this case she'd die for her non-faith. It seems to be her mission to remove God from the world." He shook his head. "After this debate, she's got a whole schedule of them waiting for the go ahead across country."

"That puts a lot of pressure on you, doesn't it?"

"I doubt if it really makes any difference one way or another. She's bound to go on with her plans, no matter who comes out on top. Assuming anyone does."

"What format did you come up with?"

"No formal structure. Just to carry on a discussion as if we were in somebody's living room. Jason Held will sit in as a kind of moderator to make sure one of us doesn't run away with the thing."

"Jason Held? I thought he was the sports announcer."

"Yes, well, it seems he's interested in religion too, and he was the only one at the station that would touch it with a ten-foot pole. He has ambitions to get a talk-show going on issues of interest to the community – you know, sit local opponents across from each other and discuss school consolidation, historical preservation, that sort of thing."

EVTV was to carry it live, and there was quite a bit of fuss in town about it, mostly owing, Dan thought, to Lily Lyle's publicity agent. Dan felt there was a certain amount of upsurge in interest among the clergy themselves: "Now that it's gotten more publicity than we expected, some of them kind of wish they had gone for it themselves."

Early in September, a large ad appeared in the Evittsburg *Item*.

LILY LYLE HADLEY
in discussion
with
Reverend Daniel Heyer
Does God Exist?
And Other Questions
Saturday, September 14
at 7:30 P.M.
EVTV

After Dan protested, the ad reappeared with a proper Lutheran "Pastor" replacing "Reverend," and the additional line "Representing the Evittsburg Ministerium" below his name.

"That'll be a blow to some of the guys," said Dan, when it ran.

"They know about it, don't they?"

"It was announced at the August meeting, but a number of them were on vacation. They may be upset at being 'represented' by such a flaming liberal."

"You radical, you."

"Yeah, well, I'm a fanatic to Lily Lyle just for believing in God, so I guess it all balances out."

The congregation was excited about it, and everyone was eager to do everything possible to help, although nobody could think of anything.

On Friday, Dan came in from his hospital calls, laughing. "I went to see Bill Cable, after his appendectomy," he said. "When I asked him if he wanted to pray with me, he said, 'Sure, Pastor, if you think it'll help you.' "

I laughed. "Did it?"

"Did it what?"

"Help you. I noticed you were up last night several times. You couldn't even sleep when you were in bed. I missed your snoring."

He shook his head. "Something like this: you can't help but stay awake and worry about it, planning and thinking and praying." His left temple beat steadily, and he saw me looking at it. "That's another thing," he said bitterly. "Sometimes I wonder if that's why Lily Lyle picked me to debate with. This damn tic will go over on TV like a lead balloon."

"Just make sure your other side is to the camera." I took out my hearing aid and massaged my ear where it rubbed. "Have you got your argument planned?"

He shrugged. "I've made one big decision. I'm not going into anything deeply theological, unless she brings it up first."

"No St. Augustine? No Thomas Aquinas, no Luther – ?"

"Namedropper," he said. "And what did you get with that degree anyway, except me and the kids and our eternal love and gratitude? When this debate is over, we're going to sit down and do something about your future. I've been feeling guilty long enough."

"I have my column. And I write all those other things that yield a steady income of rejection slips." It seemed important right now not to take him too seriously. I looked across the table at him. "I don't want to change the rules on you in the middle of everything. I've seen too many people unhappy, too many marriages break up, because women thought they had changed when what had really changed was the culture." I slipped the hearing aid back into my ear. "On the other hand," I allowed, "people do change too. I never dreamed at 35 how much changing I still had ahead of me."

He chuckled. "I see you can still keep two opposing thoughts in your head at the same time." He sobered. "You know, you're probably the one who should be debating Lily Lyle. With your combativeness – "

"Combativeness!" I folded my hands angelically and cast my eyes to heaven. "Me? Your passive, submissive helpmate? You jest, sir. No, really, it just boils down to trying to define myself, and redefine myself, as I grow in a world that never stops changing. *Cogito ergo sum*, and all that. It just comes out as pure argument."

"Ah," he said, and the pause grew. Then he sighed. "We're all tempted to be God," he said tiredly. "One way or another, every one of us, the original sin." He leaned his elbow on the stack of morning papers on the table, and rested his chin in his hand, index finger across his mouth, and looked at me quizzically. "I look forward to seeing you argue with God someday."

"Well," I said lightly, "I doubt if He needs much work done on His Own Self-definition, so He won't argue back. That's no fun."

"Meanwhile, it's too bad you can't practice on Lily Lyle. You'd knock her dead." I remember we both laughed.

The day of the debate we had a quiet, early dinner together about 5 o'clock. Neither of us ate much. "I've got a nervous stomach," said Dan afterward, patting it beneath the dark suit and clerical shirt he'd put on to face Lily Lyle.

He took a deep breath.

"Just like me," I said, "when I have to teach Sunday School. I still get a terribly tired feeling when I have to speak in public, this enormous lassitude, as if I can hardly lift a finger. Then after I get out the first sentence, it's gone."

"Exactly," he said. "I read somewhere that the opera star, Lily Pons, used to throw up before every performance."

"Really?" I considered that. "You'd think it would have wrecked her throat for singing. Maybe the acid cleared it all out for her – "

"Well, I'm not going to find out." He got up and stretched. "I think your carbo-loading scheme yesterday is beginning to work."

The morning newspaper had run an article about sports heroes preparing for their events, so I had given him spaghetti for dinner the night before. "Steak tonight and a baked potato – guess I'm ready for the marathon."

" 'Let us run with perseverance the race that is set before us.' " I felt smug for having remembered a Biblical quotation, word for word. "I wonder if Saint Paul knew about carbo-loading."

"More to the point, Ms. Heyer – did they eat spaghetti two thousand years ago?"

"Tomatoes – I don't think anyone ate tomatoes then."

"Probably used clam sauce."

The foolishness was relaxing, and after we cleared the table, Dan kissed me. "For two cents, I'd invite you to bed, and say the hell with Lily Lyle."

I fished in my pocket and pulled out a nickel. "I must have known I'd get an offer."

"Wow," he said. "Double my price. It's a deal." He grabbed the nickel and mock-dragged me to the steps. "So long, Lily."

"Pity I'm not built like Scarlett O'Hara," I said. "You could carry me up with devil-may-care arrogance – "

"Ouch." He dropped me unromantically to the floor. "I always wondered how Clark Gable's back held out up all those steps. Obviously, he was younger than me – blast and damnation." He put his hand to his back. "Ellie, I've got to go."

I waved him off and resolutely turned away before the car got out of sight, just for good luck. In fact, I'm not superstitious. It's just that I have this very modern conviction of the pervasive ironies of life.

Even enlightened types seem to hesitate to tempt coincidence.

CHAPTER 18

As Dan drove away, Robey's old black Ford grunted into the driveway. Robey and Gil tumbled out uproariously. " 'Good Morning, Revolution!' " shouted Robey, and I turned back to greet them.

They had obviously been having a serious conversation.

"Ask your Gramomma, Nugget," rumbled Robey ominously, setting his feet firmly in the center of the walkway, so that Gil, younger and faster, did a quick end run into the grass to get around him without colliding. "I'm no expert in that department. My day's been and gone, and, unlike some old folks I know, I'm not afraid to admit it." He grinned, not believing a word of it.

"Robey, your day's not past in any department," I said, holding the door open. "Except in the departments you want it to be."

"Go ahead, ask your Gramomma," ordered Robey again, turning Gil around to face me like a guilty child. But Gil only hung his head and grinned, luminously.

"Then I'll ask her for you," said Robey. "Gramomma, Nugget here wants to know how to kiss."

"Grandma, I do not!" cried Gil, beaming, and twisting out of reach. "I only said I'd have to learn someday if I wanted to go out with Tammy."

"Who's Tammy?" I asked,

"Oh, this new girl in school." He looked up and down and around. "She's well, you know, beautiful."

He considered the matter, his head to one side, grave and thoughtful. "I never saw anyone so pretty." He sounded very young for this day and age, and I thought again how everyone starts at Square One. Lucky for humanity, but what do you do to prepare kids for the world? Morality as old-fashioned rules is unfashionable, and as advice it's ridiculed. Only experience works. So do you go upstairs and kick them in the teeth when they're asleep to help them grow up?

Robey looked at me, his brow lifted. " 'Never give all the heart,' " he quoted solemnly, " 'for love will hardly seem worth thinking of, to passionate women, if it seem certain – ' but we don't know if she's passionate, do we, Nugget? 'They never dream that it fades out from kiss to kiss.' Had to be a man wrote that – "

"Oh, I don't know. Women know men better than you think they do," I said. "Gil, do you really want to know how to kiss a girl?"

He took a deep breath. "Yes, Nana." He raised his head like Robey about to quote *"Morituri te salutamis."*

Once a decision's made, I don't lose time. "There are three ways of kissing. Of course, I'm not sure about young boys." I looked doubtfully at Robey.

"Oh, carry on, Gramomma," he said, in his low boom. "You just claimed to know all about us." He settled quite comfortably into the loveseat, which I had to admire, because it was hard and small and knobby, and nobody had ever done such a thing until Robey came along. But then, Robey was always comfortable. "Carry on. Maybe I'll learn things I never knew before."

"It's just that I know things have changed these days," I said helplessly. "All I know is what I learned back during the war. And since, of course," I added hastily.

"But, Nana," said Gil, too innocently, "I didn't know you were allowed to kiss boys during the Civil War."

"Smart alec." I made a face at him. "Now listen closely. You asked a question, you're going to get an answer. HOW TO KISS A GIRL. Number One: the first-date kiss – that is, of course, if you are planning to work up gradually for the fullest enjoyment."

Gil squirmed. "Yes, Nana."

As the only advocate left in the country of virginity until marriage, I was pleased to hear it. I even stretched matters a bit. "No kissing on the first date, then," I improvised recklessly. "That way you can both go home and take stock of the evening and decide whether you like each other well enough to go out again without sex getting in the way."

"Pardon me, Gramomma," interrupted Robey humbly. "Isn't sex more likely to get in the way if they don't kiss? They'll be wishing they had and want to try it out, even if they had a lousy time."

I weighed the matter judiciously. "At your age, Gil, sex is going to influence your decision, no matter what you do, right? But, if you ask me, it's unfair and humiliating and downright condescending to assume that just because someone is a teenager, and the glands are working, he turns into a critical mass of palpitating body parts. Or she," I added, responding belatedly to Joy's gender sensitivity training. "So it's a good idea to remind yourself beforehand that you *are* a teenager, subject to overload, and you need to work out an agenda."

I nodded decisively. "The second night's good enough for the first kiss. It's not like you don't have the rest of your life to get on with it. Come on out to the kitchen, so I can work while I talk."

We departed for the kitchen, where I had dessert under way for the evening. Robey got up with an exaggerated groan and followed us, straightening out the rug Gil had kicked up along the way.

"Oh, good," said Gil, eyeing the pound cake in the package on the counter. "I asked Mom what you were having and she didn't know. Peach Sweet Cake. What else?" Apparently sex hadn't pre-empted all his attention.

I was prepared for a big evening. Potato chips, pretzels, all the crunchy junk foods, dips for big if not gourmet appetites, even some fairly substantial appetizers, because Dan would be ravenous when he got back, win or lose. "Better start the party before the show goes on," he'd said. "These things are totally unpredictable and even though it's not formally juried, so to speak, there's bound to be a perceived winner. And Lily Lyle's – well, let's face it. Lily Lyle is brighter than I am."

I'd scoffed at that and thought of his whole self, and I said, "God wouldn't let you down, I'm sure of it."

"Oh, Elinor," he said wearily, "you know that's not how it always works."

How did it work?

"Okay, Gil," I said, "you can open that can of condensed milk and then we'll do something interesting."

He picked up the can opener. "But you were going to tell me how to kiss," he said, fitting it awkwardly around the lip of the can." We have an electric can opener at home," he muttered defensively as it slipped.

"Don't believe in 'em." I opened the freezer and took out the plastic box of peaches I had frozen in August after camp. "These are the last peaches left," I told Robey, who had flopped into one of the kitchen chairs with his feet up on another. "It was a terrible year for peaches. How about some coffee?" I poured him a mugful.

"Nana." Gill finally got a good grip on the can opener and cut away like a trooper.

"Okay, okay," I said, leaning back against the edge of the refrigerator in lecturing posture. "Avoid looselip."

Robey choked on his coffee.

"For your first kiss," I went on briskly, "you make sure there's life in the lips, but you keep them closed. Don't leave anything hanging out, like you see on TV. And avoid the frontloader effect until you know what to do with it." I stuck out my lower lip and illustrated messily on the back of my hand. "Some of the ones you see on TV you could pick up cartons with."

Gil watched, quite struck. After all his years of watching television, he had apparently never thought of opening his own lips while kissing. Or had he? Surely he wasn't all tht innocent; nobody could be nowadays.

Could they?

I felt a sudden pang of doubt. Sometimes innocence is its own safeguard, and more fun, too. It wasn't the first time I'd thought how God's giving us the potential for His Own self-awareness had permitted us to choose to abandon the comforting excuse, and enjoyable exercise, of animal impulse. (If the Adam-and-Eve story with its Tree of Knowledge really applies in some way to an evolutionary fork-in-the-road of human futures, as I believe it does, had the Neanderthals, or someone like them, perhaps opted to stay with animal instinct, dooming themselves to a dead end, compared to others who chose to forge blithely ahead into the unknown world of good and evil perceived as objective concepts?)

"That'll do for a date or two," I went on, "and then when you decide you really like her, you start – well, what can I call it? – well you start – I guess nuzzling's the word." Since I'd gotten myself into this I had to stay with it, so I nuzzled the back of my hand. "I guess you'd have to relax your lips just a little for that," I said doubtfully.

I heard a snort from the table. 'Sounds like a horse, Gramomma."

"That hardly applies, Robey," I said coldly. "All right, Gil, pour out the milk into this bowl and add that lemon juice there. The point is that, while your mouth is relaxed, it's not loose, right?"

He worked mechanically, lost in some dream I thought could better be postponed. "No hanky panky with the tongue, you understand?" I said sternly. "Leave that until you're engaged."

Robey's laughter boomed again. "The old-fashioned girl, for sure. Me, I say, 'Kiss till the cows come home,' " quoting God-knows-who out of Bartlett's. He certainly wasn't making this any easier.

"Okay," I said. "Gil, you should know that there's some difference of opinion about sex these days, and I'm giving you the one I believe in. It's old-fashioned and out of date. But I believe virginity before marriage has practical advantages, which is why society came up with it long ago. One is that it helps to bond a good marriage, if that's what you want, and makes the marriage relationship special, different from any other connection."

"This is cool," said Gil. "Look at how thick the milk gets. It turns into that thick sauce, just from the lemon juice."

"Some kind of chemical reaction," I said. "Well, anyway." I collected my thoughts and decided I had said more than enough along that line. Except, maybe, "The people who disagree with that haven't improved a thing, including human happiness and satisfaction, and they're starting to complain now about the conditions their own ideas have brought about, even if they don't see the connection."

Oh well, the advantage of being a grandmother is that you're expected to lecture. "So, Gil, don't be in too much of a hurry to move along. Give the first stages their full quota of enjoyment, and then you won't be so bored that, by the prime of life, you're frantic to try even the unhealthy stuff."

"It's kind of a hopeless cause, don't you think, Gramomma?" drawled Robey lighting up a large cigar without permission.

I shrugged and got him an ashtray out of the cupboard. "Not necessarily. The pendulum will swing, though I doubt if I'll live that long. Then I'd be worried about the other side of it, puritanism, repression. I don't want those either, you know. Of course, repression is going on right now all over the place. Repression of innocence against the victim's will."

Robey shook his head. "The ones I've seen weren't too unwilling."

"Nana," said Gil thoughtfully. "What do you do with your hands?"

The silence from the table was challenging.

"Okay," I said. "At the first level, you could hold the girl's hand, or even put your hands on her shoulders. Alternately, you might need to turn her face toward you gently so, if the kiss happens, it won't land awkwardly on her ear. At the second level, put your arms around her and gently pull her toward you for the kiss. As time goes on, you can passionately pull her forward. On the third and succeeding levels, you won't have to worry about your hands. They'll know what to do all by themselves."

Relieved and slightly bored, Gil went in and turned on the television.

"Professor Elinor," said Robey, leisurely removing his feet from the chair and rising into a deep bow, complete with a rococo flourish of the cigar. "There's nothing like the analytical nature." He sat down again. "Although I have always tended to believe that 'a culture is in its finest flower *before* it begins to analyze itself.' Italics mine." Thoughtfully, he put the cigar back in his mouth. "If I had had the benefit of your advice forty-five years ago, I might never have married Anna."

"Really?" I had to admit to being curious. In the years of our friendship, he had never talked much about his wife, and we had never felt easy inquiring into it..

Robey's eyes followed the trail of the smoke, as little puffing sounds from the cigar hardly registered against the distant television racket. "That would have been a mistake. She was the best thing that ever happened to me, and she gave me Doug, the second best thing. The moment I saw her, in that church in Antwerp, I loved her. The first night I went out with her, I slept with her, and she got pregnant. She went through hell, both over there and after I brought her back here. Europeans are not so racially tolerant as they think they are, especially when sex is involved. And living over here as a mixed couple was no way as easy in those days as Doug and Grace have it. But she never looked back. And she always loved me as I loved her. Ridiculously romantic, but true. It's why I can't hate whites or their works, either one, as much as I would like to sometimes. I knew one who showed what they could be – "

"What happened to her, Robey?"

"Cancer."

The front door opened, and the family erupted into the silence, bringing all the world along with them. I checked Doug out of the corner of my eye; he looked good and was walking naturally. He'd started back at the organ and was hoping to get into his organ shoes by Christmas.

"Hey, Mom," called Gil, suddenly the expert. 'Look how this works. All you do is pour lemon juice into that can of milk and it turns into that sweet sauce Nana uses on peach cake."

Joy came out to the kitchen with her jacket still on and peered into the bowl. "I'd forgotten about that, Mom. Still fascinating, isn't it?" She pounded Gil on the shoulder. "Good job, old bean." She made mock obeisance to Grace and Doug, and went on to hang up her jacket.

"Gramomma has just been giving us the benefit of her wisdom," said Robey, removing his feet from the chair. I fixed him with a stare, and he put his cigar back in his mouth.

"Gil and Robey and I were just discussing life," I said, handing Grace the bowl of sauce to put in the refrigerator. "What time is it?"

"Almost 7:30," said Doug. "time for the ritual slaughter of Lily Lyle Hadley."

CHAPTER 19

Robey took over the recliner with no apologies, and Gil flung himself prone in his usual position, hugging the big blue velour pillow Grace had made for him. He had a similar one at home, purply-red to match their mauve and gray color scheme. The blue pillow matched ours, which is pragmatic – whatever doesn't fit the other rooms works just fine in here.

Scott stretched out on one elbow on the piano bench, looking supremely uncomfortable with his legs dangling off the end, and soon enough he joined Gil on the floor. Grace and Joy squeezed, poking each other, onto the dismembered parts of a sectional sofa that had proved too long for the living room. Doug sat on the floor at Grace's feet, and I settled into Dan's worn red easy chair.

On the television, a picture of a woman bicycling through an endless expanse of sand cut to an Olympic sprinter running up the steps with the famous flame, cut to joggers churning along in singular mindless purpose, and, over the shots the smooth tones of the voiceover poured some commercial message so totally unrelated to those images that I've forgotten what it concerned.

A couple more commercials, and then the first shot of the studio, with *"Does God Exist? And Other Questions"* superimposed in Gothic script, over the scene. Very pretty, but surely a subliminal invitation to consider the whole issue an outmoded one, and I suspected, with no evidence whatsoever, the fine hand of Lily Lyle behind it.

Whatever I am, you can't call me non-partisan in such matters.

"There's Grandpa!" Gil was thrilled. He'd get some mileage out of this at school on Monday, regardless of whether Dan and his side came off well or not.

Dan looked good, I thought, if a trifle tense. He had forgotten to sit so that his left temple was away from the camera – Lily Lyle again? I was getting paranoid. But the tic didn't seem to show much in the front shots.

I looked critically at the clerical shirt and collar. We had debated whether he should wear them; he had decided to, as a matter of integrity. I was against it as a matter of provocation. "Maybe I want to provoke her," he said, and I answered, "You will, you will, why add insult to injury?"

The set consisted of blue padded pedestal chairs grouped around a coffee table finished in golden oak, with an effect that reminded me briefly of the old blue-and-gold high school colors of my youth. On the table sat a large glass pitcher of, presumably, ice water, and three glasses at the ready. Strictly conventional, but the background showed a certain amount of originality. Lily Lyle sat to the viewer's left, and behind her the wood-paneled wall registered a simple tongue-and-groove, lined pattern, But as it stretched around behind Jason Held's chair in the middle, the vertical lines made cumulative, Max-Escher-type changes so that by the time they reached Dan's chair, they had turned into organ pipes, a nice touch.

Then the camera moved in on Lily, and I got my first good look at her. The final credits ("A Jason Held Production") flicked off her face with a computerized swirl, and the viewer looked into two very blue and beautiful eyes, brilliant as sapphire, that picked up all the blue in the stage set, including Dan's dark blue suit, and threw it out like a laser.

I was glad there was no studio audience to be hypnotized by them, and somewhat reassured as the camera moved back and showed Lily Lyle as a whole. She was less than small, she was tiny, sitting like a child, with enviable spaces between her hips and the side of the chair. I thought for a moment that Dan might have to contend with the image of bully, but as she came into focus, her feral wariness dispelled any lingering impression of fragility. This was one tough lady, a wizened whirlwind of a woman, every inch of her focussed on destroying the terrible perversion of human potential she saw before her, in Dan, for heaven's sake.

Ethereal as a cloud in a white linen suit with a tatted lace collar, she looked as if she had never drunk a cup of coffee in her life. She had a decided chin, and her hair was cut in that no-nonsense man's cut that women choose when they have more important things to think about. Runnels of wrinkles cut through her face as if it had lately eroded, but above them all presided those mesmerizing eyes, and the impression of girded fury. It was almost a relief when the camera moved on to Jason Held, whose sporty young face looked appropriately noncommittal as he ceased chattering with his guests and waited for the camera to start getting serious.

The music – a Vivaldi also used locally for a real estate commercial – swelled up and out, and Jason smiled affably.

"Welcome," he said, "to the first of a series of debates about matters of interest to thoughtful people throughout the world -- and also here in Evittsburg. I'm Jason Held and my job in these programs will be mainly to stand by and allow the principals to interview each other. We are fortunate to have the prominent atheist Lily Lyle Hadley as our challenger today. In our informal format, she will be debating Dr. Daniel Heyer, who is appearing on behalf of the Evittsburg Ministerial Association."

The camera moved, seeming reluctant, from Lily Lyle's unsmiling gemlike stare to Dan just in time to catch him awkwardly waving off Held's doctorate. "No, no, just Pastor," he said, half audibly, knocking his mike off his tie with a series of thuds and crackles, while the camera switched back abruptly to Jason. The MC bent a not entirely benevolent gaze on Dan, waiting until someone had fixed the mike again. "My mistake," he said, "I imagine. Sorry. Then you have not studied beyond the usual requirements to be a – um – pastor in your church?"

Dan had recovered himself in time for the camera. "The Lutheran church requires four years after college for ordination," he said, managing to sound retroactively amused at his bad start. "Too bad none of it included TV technique. Beyond that, as it happens, I have an STM – that's a Master of Sacred Theology – for two additional years of study."

Lily Lyle was not the woman to let the train leave the station without her. Leaning forward from the waist, she rode over Jason's response like a hawk stooping over prey. "How nice for you. To have mastered the sacred." She appeared to hover for a moment over the subject, then abandoned it for her earlier agenda. The blue eyes widened langorously at the margins; hard centers spit glassy shards beyond the edge of the TV screen. "Pastor," she said meditatively, rolling the word around on her tongue like a wine that did not impress. "You prefer to be called 'Pastor?' "

Dan should have waited. "It's Greek," he offered eagerly. "It means 'shepherd of the flock.' It's an Old Testament image that Jesus made use of to get across the idea of the caring, loving nature of God, reflected in Christ's relationship with his followers."

" 'The Lord is my Shepherd, I shall not want,' " said Lily Lyle. " 'I am the Good Shepherd. The Good Shepherd lays down his life for the sheep.' "

Dan nodded, too late wary.

"But, Pastor." She came in for the kill. "What is the ultimate purpose of the shepherd, after all?"

"The ultimate purpose" Dan, off-balance, tightened in his chair under the camera stare, like an animal just aware of impending slaughter. I couldn't look away.

"Pastor," said Lily Lyle, almost pityingly. "Pastor, the universal end of sheep, sooner or later, is of course, to be killed. And to be eaten." She paused artfully. "By the shepherd." Beautiful lids extinguished beautiful eyes for a moment, then half-lifted over icy sparkle. "Or his employer."

"Ouch," said Joy, and someone else groaned loudly, me, I think.

Dan looked stricken, and the camera lingered greedily before finally removing itself to focus on Jason Held, whose smooth, doughy face was solemn.

"Pastor, have you a response to that?"

By the time the camera got back to him, Dan had pulled himself together. A little smile sat shallowly about the corners of his mouth, and one eyebrow quirked, but the effect was cancelled by the tic that now pulsed visibly in his silhouetted temple. I was looking for it though; perhaps you wouldn't have noticed it otherwise.

"Well," he said mildly, "Ms Hadley has made her point. I can only say that it is always a mistake to take metaphors to extremes." The camera and Jason waited but, as no more seemed forthcoming, they both started to turn to Lily for the next round. Dan inhaled sharply, and the camera swung back, but he waved it away like a living person. "No, no," he said. " I was going to say something else, but let it go."

"Oh, Daddy," breathed Grace. Psychologically the whole room slumped.

"Maybe we should have had some kind of rehearsal to help Dad get used to being in front of a camera," said Joy.

Only Gil, oblivious, went on crunching potato chips.

Bewildered, the camera came to rest on Lily Lyle, whose eyes were still hooded but already triumphant.

"Pastor," she went on, giving each syllable due emphasis, eye-knives twisting, "Pastor, John Stuart Mill once said that God kills every human being once, and often much more cruelly than human murderers do. What do you say to that?"

Dan looked more at ease, but I still saw his temple twitching. In a wide shot of the three of them, it looked like a fly at his face; you expected him to raise a hand and brush it away. "I'd say it's irrelevant to our subject today. Unless, of course" – he leaned forward in his turn, the little smile reaching deeper now, "unless you're conceding – ?"

"Conceding?"

"That God exists. Because your question deals with the nature of God, but you don't even believe He exists, so how did we get so far so fast? You can hardly argue backwards, that because you don't like your idea of what God is, therefore He can't exist."

"He doesn't."

"Then we'll wait and go into God's shortcomings in the next debate, after you lose this one."

A small cheer went up in the family room, and even Scott looked somewhat gratified to see that his putative connection was not to go down without a fight.

"You leave me little choice then," said Lily Lyle, more carefully. "I really didn't want to get into those hoary old arguments for and against the existence of God, the ontological, the cosmological – I had hoped to get our debate on a more pragmatic level than arguing angels on the head of a pin – "

"Yes, perhaps we can leave the cosmetology argument, and the others, for some other time," said Jason briskly. "Pastor, tell us please, why you believe there is a God." He reached for a light touch. "Say, in twenty-five words or less."

"Because if I didn't," said Dan, "I would kill myself."

Jason crossed his legs, embarrassed. But Lily Lyle seemed genuinely interested. "Why in the world would you do such a cowardly thing?"

Dan hesitated much too long. I could tell from the television purple of his cheeks that his color was high, probably blotched, as it got sometimes, and still punctuated over the outline of his temple by that darn tic. Surely even he could tell that his silences were killing him in this debate. All over Evittsburg, people must be switching to other channels.

"Exactly. Why in the world, as you say? This world that we all live in, with a few little pleasures that we grab with both hands, and the black cloud of pain and suffering and death falling over everything we do and say. The idea that death is the end of life is a mockery of life. It makes achievement and joy utterly pointless, and work and suffering just the punch lines to a rotten joke. If that were the frame around my world, I'd go to bed cursing every night, and yes, I think I would kill myself, once I'd squeezed all the fun out of my existence."

Lily Lyle's face looked a little blotchy now too. She waved both hands in front of her face like fans.

"Wait a minute! Wait a minute!" She fixed Dan with a crystal blue dagger. "You're giving me the old pie-in-the-sky routine." She braced her shoulders, folded her hands, and raising her eyes to heaven, mimicked an impossibly plummy preacher, although no more impossible, come to think of it, than some I've heard on TV. "Hea-vuhn is mah ruh-wahd – "

Dan waited her out, appreciatively. "But you miss the point," he explained patiently. "It's not that we suffer though this world for the sake of a better one as a reward for being good little girls and boys. It's that the assurance of that world transforms *this* one.

"I don't live in the same bad joke of a world you do, Ms Hadley; my entire context is different. The picture's open-ended, there's no frame of frustration around it. It has no boundaries, no dead-end. It's something like the science-fiction world so many people flee to for relief, but God's world is no place of unfettered technology, but of unfettered spirit. God's not just some future prize for being good, but the very present truth that gives point to goodness right now in this life. However one defines goodness." He trailed off contemplatively, diminishing his effect as usual. I'd never known him to be so nervously inept.

Lily Lyle sputtered with fury, thank goodness, which gave him a chance to override her. "Without God, your world narrows down to some little, hopeless exercise of bravado, where you have to go for the gusto before it all closes down on you."

"You're a coward," said Lily Lyle, off-camera.

"Just a realist," said Dan.

Nodding away on the sidelines like a tennis audience, Jason thought he'd made a connection with a more fashionable subject. "You mentioned suicide, Pastor Heyer," he said, brightly, and turned to Lily Lyle. "Ms Hadley, do you think that the unprecedented increase in suicide may have some relationship to the contemporary loss of faith in God?"

Lily Lyle snorted; a good full "Tschn!" echoed through the mike, as she returned her attention to Dan. "A crutch," she said, dripping contempt, "you use religion as a crutch! Real personhood works toward freedom, independence, autonomy!"

"That's *your* crutch," said Dan, but she swept on.

"That whole thing of 'worshipping and obeying' – " she jabbed two fingers on each hand into the air for quotes, "the very mindset that religion fosters and encourages makes people vulnerable to totalitarianism, all the big and little dictators of their lives. It's a total religious mentality that has to be fought. It leads people to follow the Hitlers and Stalins, breaks down their defenses – "

"On the contrary," said Dan, more heatedly. "That religious mentality is built into the human psyche, and if it isn't used toward some close approximation of truth, it will be used toward a lesser one, or a perverted one. The Hitlers and Stalins, yes, or things like drugs or obsessive sex, even something like astrology, or – " tactfully, his shrug only nudged his right hand in Lily Lyle's general direction – "one's own invincibility. Like Chesterton said, 'When people don't believe in God, they don't believe in nothing. They believe in anything – ' "

"More people have been killed in the name of religion throughout the ages – "

"Until the 20th century, when more people have been killed by professional atheists than for all other causes put together in the history of mankind. Congratulations!"

A couple of nervous giggles went up in the family room and a cheer from Doug. "Go get 'em, Dad!" Everyone was finally caught up in the debate. Even Gil had stopped chewing.

Jason uncrossed his legs, looking mildly gratified, and set himself to calming down the fracas. Lily Lyle and Dan sat back, breathing hard,

"Christianity is a failure." Lily Lyle bit down hard on the words, sending them short and sharp into her mike. "The whole world would be better off without it, and without that invented deity that arises only out of neurotic and pathological delusion."

Dan seemed suddenly to have lost his steam. "Now you're getting personal," he said mildly. I felt irritated by his uneven performance. Every time he looked like holding up his end of the argument he dropped it. There was so much more that could be said, and I thought of several things I would have mentioned if I had been up there in the hot seat.

Lily Lyle even waited, but he didn't go on, and she metaphorically shook herself and charged ahead. Time was getting on.

"Tell me, Pastor," she said, and the sound of her voice was almost sensual, a siren call. "You believe in God and yet the whole idea of the God you believe in makes no sense. You say that there is a deity that can, in your words, do all things." Dan opened his mouth. "Tell me, Pas-tor," she couldn't resist oiling that word, "can your God create an irresistible force that can move an immovable object he has also created?"

It was a college sophomore's question, the subject of endless bull sessions down through the ages, but its appeal was still universal. Gil took a swig of Pepsi without moving his eyes from the screen. Doug stiffened. Joy chuckled. Grace sighed, and Scott laughed softly, while Robey and I just sat there and watched.

Slouching in his chair, Dan laughed too. "Oh my God," he said, and raised his head. Almost like an afterthought then he added, "Of course." Again everyone waited, Jason tapping the foot on top of his knee impatiently. Dan sighed. "You're waiting for me to tell you how this can be, right?" He smiled, almost wearily. "Don't ask me. I don't know how. I'm not God."

Lily seemed outraged. "Who needs him?" she snapped. "This may come as news to you, herr-Pastor, but it is perfectly possible to be a good person, a loving concerned person, without any religion whatsoever."

Dan seemed to bestir himself with some effort. This debate was taking more of a toll on him than I ever expected. "I know," he said, almost humbly. "And there are lots of unbelievers around that *are* good and loving and concerned. But you're a triumph over logic, you know, that logic you claim to live by. Because in a Godless world, the highest rule of existence is survival of the fittest. Not all of us are fundamentalists, Jason," he said, as the moderator made a move to interrupt, "but the thrust of evolution without God is that it's an unending struggle between various strains of selfishness. Where's your logic then in "being good?""

"We are all Cartesians," said Lily Lyle proudly. No doubt about it, she knew her stuff. "You're the ones who ignore logic."

"No, no, many of you are Sartreans, yammering about the necessity of good – and also the absurdity of it." Dan sounded impatient, as if time was short, and I glanced at the clock. Still time for some good points, now that he was rolling again. "Christians are logical to the extreme – that's where the angels-on-the-head-of-a-pin foolishness came from. But we're not limited by what appears to be logic by current manmade standards. Whereas you are bound by them."

"And you 'yammer' for goodness, insisting all the time on original sin," said Lily Lyle, scoring a point. I had to admire her, in a grudging sort of way. But the woman had a chip on her soul.

Dan smiled. "Original sin explains why we need God. For Lutherans, anyway, being good is our response to God's love, not a price we pay him in order to get it. That makes great emotional sense. On the other hand, atheists haven't got a leg to stand on logically being good. It's just a doomed, romantic gesture, a last hurrah in the face of a meaningless existence. As Job's wife said, better curse God and die."

"Now you've got it," said Lily Lyle. " I thought you never would." Impish, she looked like good fun. "As far as being good without God goes," she went on thoughtfully, "it's a matter of honor, you know. Standards one arrives at on one's own to contribute to the good order of the world without having to go outside our experience to justify them."

Dan, slouching again, nodded.

"I guess you think I'm going to hell?"

"No," said Dan. "I wouldn't be surprised if I met you in heaven, whatever that may be." Like a master comedian, he timed his last line perfectly. "Of course, Ms Hadley, that would be hell for you, wouldn't it?"

He chuckled and fell off his chair, landing on his face as the camera, belatedly following him, wavered, then bobbled violently and settled on a point somewhere between two of the organ pipes on the wall.

You didn't realize at first, of course, what had happened. You heard gasps in the room, no louder than those on the broadcast, and then you heard somebody's unidentified scream tear though the sound system as the picture went dark.

"What happened?" cried Joy, and then again, grabbing Scott's shoulder, and Doug got up jerkily and started changing channels, as if the explanation could be found somewhere else.

You heard yourself saying over and over, inside and maybe aloud, who knows, and you never asked later, "No, no, no, no, no – "

Doug turned back the channel, and Jason's voice, vibrant with controlled hysteria, sounded behind the gray screen. "Pastor Daniel Heyer has had a seizure of some sort, an ambulance has been called, and he is now being cared for by one of our cameramen with CPR procedures. Everything posssible is being done for him. We will return after these messages."

The context of your world seemed abruptly to shift, to fade at the edges, to withdraw into some timeless limbo; only the immediate held meaning. There on the screen, a woman bicycling though an endless expanse of sand –

CHAPTER 20

Doesn't she think really, someone asks brightly (Irene, is it?) that he wanted to go that way, so he did? Kind of willed himself into it? No, she does not, but she doesn't stop to explain why not, although she finds ridiculous the person's theory that you will your own kind of dying, and It's a Great Comfort to Believe That, You Ought to Try It.

On the other hand, Meredith Busche knows that God's will has been done right there in front of the television audience, so that the whole world would know.

Know what, Elinor asks? That God dumps on those who love him?

"Of course not," says Meredith, pained, "I mean know his will. I mean," she says hesitantly, "I mean, Pastor did say he believed in evolution."

There is no shortage of theories, Elinor discovers. God never gives you more than you can bear. That's the way life is. You gotta have folks to lean on. He is not dead he is just asleep. When your time comes, you go. Let me know if there's anything I can do. Go with the flow. Today is the first day of the rest of your life. We're not supposed to know why these things happen. Don't be afraid to go ahead and cry.

Some of them might even be right. She can't tell.

No person ever lived, or ever will, she muses not very originally (but then death is not original either) who does not finally drain away in the hemorrhage of the world. All those bandaids clapped on the wound through countless eons –

Amd yet they have their uses –

But she doesn't really believe – she tries not to – that it is God's will that Dan should die in such a way. In fact, she remembers, amidst the great numbness that has overtaken her, warring against the concept of God as the Great Chess Player, icily moving human beings around on the board, working out some obscure game plan of His own.

Still, she notes, with dim surprise, how curiously comforting it is to give in to the idea of some Ultimate Ulterior Purpose, instead of having to wrestle with why God would sit by helplessly and, for no good reason, allow a deadly clot to form, or a car to blow its tire. And worse things, far worse, she reminds herself dutifully, but doesn't believe that either –

A limited God, then, who really has no say in human affairs – but limited by whom? Okay, okay, a self-limited God to protect our free will, but why such technicalities, such legalities, the kind of thing Jesus said he went beyond – when people suffer so and couldn't care less about theological nit-picking?

Why, she's only human, much less the God of love – and she wouldn't set things up that way.

The whole church has turned out for the viewing, genuinely solicitous, loving, as this congregation could be, only caught up in the excitement associated with the curious, oh-so-modern circumstances of this death.

Lots of strangers show up, too, more who have heard of the case later than had actually seen it happen live at the time. (Death live on television, there's a thought.) Two networks had shown the tape over and over on their evening newscasts.

Mary Ann Mandible stays by the whole time, spelling Grace and Joy, and Robey too remains at her side under the curious stares of onlookers. And it seems Elinor still takes note of others' reactions to the blacks in her life, so entrenched is her own racist awareness of differences.

Struggling with such nuances at her own husband's viewing? Maybe *instead* of thinking about her own husband's viewing? She sets herself the exercise of actually thinking about him, but the people milling about distract her.

One has to care for them.

Some of the women from Trinity weep as they look at his calm white face. (The funeral director, a good friend, and only superficially the image of funeral directors, suave, unobtrusively cheerful, was too rattled to do his usually skillful job. Her husband has turned out too pale, faintly streaked with nose paint where he had been marked by the fall.) She can't just let them stand there alone and cry.

This is work she knows, if she has never felt good at it. Ideologically constrained from offering those old cliches, she has still in the past hit on some of her own that meant most to her then: he's probably looking down on all this right now and wanting you to take heart. Don't blame God; God hates it as much as you do. Don't forget, someday you'll see him again.

In fact, in the past these never seemed to help others as much as they did herself. Mainly they inspired miserable stares, obedient nods, pathetic grins. Now she understands why. They are the consolations of considered grief, no good for the screaming immediacy –

So Elinor puts her arm around her friends and shakes hands with the strangers, and smiles, and hugs back everyone who hugs her, though embracing is a new-learned skill of her middle age, when it all got fashionable. Still, now is surely the time for it, so she hugs with abandon, and even looks him square in the face, when people join her at the casket, but he just lies there and that does not seem right at all, though people don't mention it.

Ministers from town come in, Lutheran and others too, his friends from the Ministerial Association. Some of the latter seem vaguely defensive, as if she would hold them accountable for his appearance on television and its result.

Dr. Bramer is speedy and surgical, in and out, quick and clean, a handshake expertly tooled to pull her into his arms and out again in one smooth motion, the deep full voice, the direct compelling gaze. (How easy it is to mock these well-intentioned, negligible people. And how easy for one to call them negligible.) "God will wipe away all tears," says Dr. Bramer and is out the door in a flash, but she doesn't even take in the words until Mary Anne echoes them, and they are helpful, she thinks, and forgets them immediately.

The crowd eddies and flows about the casket and about her and the others and Mary Anne who is too soon reliving her own loss. It occurs to Elinor that she is terribly hot, damp springing out on her skin, starting from the left side and spreading over her entire body, so that she thinks she should have slipped out of people's grasp like a Vaselined egg.

A hot flash, and she is astounded and displeased to be interrupted with such a mundane matter at such a time. All that is supposed to be over by now. Still here it is, at its peak, and subsiding already.

Robey gets up from the row of chairs nearby, where he has been fielding the friendly and the curious. He comes over and puts his arm around her shoulders.

"You a hard woman for reachin round, Gramomma," – he offers the old joke – "go sit down and git you a rest."

She checks for Grace and Joy again. She needs to see others mourning him for her, Grace's lower lip tight, Joy's jaw set. Doug is so upset his cheeks shine with tears, and even Scott seems more shaken than she would have expected.

"I wish he'd won," he'd said to her earlier, "I wish he'd won."

"They're over there," says Robey, "with your church secretary, Donnie, and some sweet ol thing, Mildred – "

"Mildred Means," she says. "She probably shouldn't have come out, she has cancer, bad. What will she do now without him, I wonder."

" 'Death is always and under all circumstances a tragedy,' " murmured Robey, " 'for if it is not, then it means that life itself has become one – ' "

It is her husband Robey's talking about –

Gil has brought a friend, a slight black youth lighter still than Gil, and older, too, about 16, she thinks. Clay, he calls him, and she feels it would not be hard to remember that name again immediately on seeing him and then feels the usual twinge of guilt to be thinking anything at all based on the color of skin. They studiously avoid the casket and sit in the corner of the large viewing room, talking together for a long time.

Gil has seemed to get through this better than the others. Before the television screen, he has looked back and forth in bewildered sympathy as others cry, and later he has cried more, steadily and intensively. His cheeks had been wet when the van from the television station arrived at the door to take her and the girls to the hospital.

But he has not cried since. She misses him at the first viewing, and Grace has said he was at a WYC meeting.

Well, that gives him something to take his mind off what has happened. God works in mysterious ways – surely?

She is talking to May, when she hears a small stir from the doorway. Appearing between the fluted white wood pillars that framed it, people falling away before her in surprise, comes that tiny walking firecracker, Lily Lyle Hadley, with Jason Held a step behind. You can't blame them for deciding to join forces to invade this frightening, primitive stronghold; the amazing thing is that they have come at all. She feels warmth creeping over her, but maybe it's another hot flash.

Perhaps it is even anger.

Lily Lyle marches up to her, with Jason still trailing, and shoves out her hand. Elinor has the feeling that if she doesn't shake it immediately, there will be no second chance. "I'm sorry," Lily barks, in a voice little different from her amplified, TV one. "This wasn't my fault, you know." Nearby conversations halt and heads turn, all the way into the adjoining room.

Elinor opens her mouth, but Lily has more to say. "Maybe you think I'd be glad, but it didn't do me any good at all." She pokes Elinor in the chest with an index finger like a pink birthday candle. "They say, 'Lily, for a joke, you told us that God would strike him down, but now he died so how can you say there is no God?' Well, it didn't change my mind a bit – "

"Lily, for God's sake." Jason looks perturbed.

"Never mind," says Elinor. This is certainly the time for the perfect putdown, and she tries to think of one. It doesn't even have to be great; for everyone who has heard her, Lily Lyle has smudged her copybook. They would welcome something that would put her in her place. Not a big assignment for Elinor, the Great Arguer.

But she can't think of anything, and anyway, all she wants to do is get rid of Lily Lyle. She remembers Scott's judgment. "Tell them you won," she says wearily. "After all, you survived."

Lily Lyle seems relieved that Elinor has noticed. Relaxing perceptibly, she gives Elinor another chance at her hand, after all. Holding on, she directs that blue gaze sincerely upward. "It's a shame he died," she says. "I had so much more to say."

CHAPTER 21

Scott and Joy announce that funerals are barbaric ceremonies.

They want a memorial service only. But Elinor remembers thinking long ago that life and its death need to be accepted head on, or what is faith worth? She only hesitates whether to keep the casket open or not. Goodness knows, she used to say, laughing, she didn't want *hers* open, and people looking at her when she couldn't defend herself.

But people need to see, so she compromises. She leaves the casket open, his silenced face a recurring shock, in the funeral home, and then closed for the final hour at the church before the funeral.

It's unfair that his own funeral could not have been like the ones he conducted. He'd have spent hours with the family beforehand, encouraged them to talk about the loved one. (Or perhaps sometimes not so loved). He'd have kept the lost one alive in memory and faith, with a service full of meaning and a sermon suffused with the message of God's enduring presence and love –

His best friend, Don Shires, a Lutheran minister in Pittsburgh, has just been operated on for lymphoma, so Grace asks Dr. Bramer instead. He breezes in a minute before the hour, leads the service in an appropriate sepulchral tone, delivers a sermon that, despite a few personal touches referring to my dear brother and colleague, sounds straight out of the generic barrel.

Doug has asked with tears in his eyes, if he can play the organ for the service. He sits rigid and still on the bench, his elbows clenched to his body, even when he is playing.

So different from relaxed, expansive Doug. And the music is different too, for he isn't using his left foot yet, and without those pedals there is no bottom to anything, nothing to stand on. Her own elbows tighten in sympathy, and carefully she sets about loosening them, willing the muscles to relax.

This last hour with him is endless, yet over too soon. Grace and Joy sit on either side of her, and Scott next to Joy, his first time in church here. She tries to appreciate the effort Scott is making, but when he opens the hymnbook, it seems to her that he handles it with disdain, like some tainted and dubious object. His silence during the hymns seems to her less the natural reluctance of an unbeliever to join in such sentiments than a contempt for the whole state of mind that faith requires.

What if he is right?

Joy's feelings, she suspects, are mixed, but now Elinor needs more, and finds herself turning to Grace. She hopes they don't feel rejected; she forces herself to share Joy's hymnbook when she offers it, while Grace, and Gil and Robey down the line, hold separate ones. Though Robey's boom cannot be heard during the hymns either – she listens for it – and Gil's silence is almost as complete as Scott's.

She hungers for affirmation, but only Grace sings steadily beside her.

Meanwhile, she survives on her own surface, observing carefully, grateful for the lethargy that seems to have descended like a weighted veil since the debate. His death seems sure enough, but filtered through a glass window, brought to her by courtesy of EVTV, through switches and cables – some modern technological improvement over the old traditional ways of dying among loved ones in fevered deathbeds amidst the smell of vomit and failing body processes.

Drifting off into little brown studies (cozy dens with cheerful fires in fireplaces, leather furniture, filled bookcases along the walls), she comes and goes along the edges of the service, almost laughing aloud at one point when she notices that the candles on the altar are the longest possible – Irene must have won a battle in her endless war with Maudie Gibbon of the Altar Guild. Maudie had once been church treasurer for a congregation in Omaha that must have been very thrifty; she protested on principle every time a candle was replaced while it still had a flicker left.

Another time she notices Vera Finch holding on as usual to the last note of some response and it occurs to her that old Myron Hart from their first congregation, who had invariably anticipated the first note of every chorus by at least a half-beat, would have made Vera a fine husband. What would their children have been like, probably perfectly punctual, she thinks, and stops herself just short of giggling, shocks herself back into the present –

Aside from Dr. Bramer's cold efficiencies, she has to admit that the funeral service carries its own consolations, if she only pays attention. In the absence of bitterness, who could possibly hear without a shiver of acknowledgment words like, "Blessed be the God and Father of our Lord Jesus Christ – He comforts us in all our sorrows so that we can comfort others in their sorrows with the consolation we ourselves have received from God"? God known as Jesus knew him, as a loving parent – if Christianity had contributed nothing else to the religions of humankind, that would be enough. The rest would follow. At least, for those who had experienced loving parents. What about the others? She was grateful for hers; what would you think of God if yours had been abusive – ?

" 'O God of grace and glory, we remember before you today our brother, Daniel. We thank you for giving him to us to know and love as a companion in our pilgrimage on earth. In your boundless compassion, console us who mourn. Give us your aid, so that we may see in death the gate to eternal life, that we may continue our course on earth in confidence, until, by your call, we are reunited with those who have gone before us –' "

Bramer could never have come up with anything remotely resembling that: another function of liturgy, this, besides continuity? To make up for the human shortfalls of individual pastors, to distribute evenly the conceptual and verbal beauty of the worship of a loving God?

" 'Alleluia. Jesus Christ is the firstborn of the dead; to him be glory and power forever and ever. Amen. Alleluia.' "

Strange word, Alleluia. Doug had said once, laughing, how he had counted the repetitions of the word one Christmas season that was particularly thick with them, in anthems, hymns, liturgy: in the midnight service there were one hundred and twenty one, including the Randall Thompson *Alleluia* by the choir, and the Mozart, and the wild Rorem one by two feuding sopranos, that must have been Natalie Raymon and Sue Pitt; they were giving him fits then, she remembers, fighting over solos and always trying to outdo each other; wasn't it Sue who later tried out for the Met auditions? Never made it, Elinor seems to remember, but she was good – better than Natalie – how in the world could such a collection of undistinguished syllables as "alleluia" come to stand for overwhelming, supernatural praise and joy? From speaking in tongues maybe? She'd have to look that up. Something Latin –

" 'Neither life nor death, nor things present nor things to come shall be able to separate us from your love which is in Christ Jesus our Lord – God, the generations rise and pass before you. You are the strength of those who labor; you are the rest of the blessed dead; we remember all who have lived in faith, all who have peacefully died.' "

What about those who have unpeacefully died, but that didn't apply with this person here, did it, that one up there in the closed casket with the crossed pall over it, a white cross over all-purpose maroon, she remembered the discussion over what color the church should purchase since there was not enough money to get a different-colored pall for each of the church's seasons. Irene had said impatiently, "Oh, get maroon, it's a good all-purpose color. I have a maroon coat and it goes with everything," and it seemed to, except maybe the church festival Sundays when the paraments were bright red, but it looked fine now with the green of the interminable Sundays after Pentecost –

Music helps, music helps, and this music, particularly glorious, hearts swell in spite of themselves, as the voices rise. "When we on that final journey go/ That Christ is for us preparing/ We'll gather in song, our hearts aglow/ All joy of the heavens sharing/ And walk in the light of God's own place/ With angels His name adoring."

Yes, yes, God's own place, whatever it is, angels as this poet saw it, though who needs angels or harps, after all? All she'd need really would be – him, him under there, under the pall – her family, her friends, a pet or two, like Sinnamon – others to learn to know, she'd always wanted to have a good long chat with George Eliot, for instance – and that was strange, an unbeliever, George –

" 'Into your hands, O merciful Savior, we commend your servant, Daniel. Acknowledge, we beseech you, a sheep of your own flock, a sinner of your own redeeming. Receive him into the arms of your mercy, into the blessed rest of everlasting peace and into the glorious company of the saints in light – ' "

But that meant, didn't it, that Dan wouldn't be here anymore, in heaven to be sure and waiting for her, but that was hardly the point right now, was it, the point was that he would not be up in that pulpit as she listened lovingly to his abstruse sermons; not mowing the lawn, sweating and ruddy-faced as they shared iced coffee afterward; not returning from calls with a paper bag of tomatoes from someone's garden, or grim with somebody else's tragedy, or grinning with a new joke, or sharing a rueful bewilderment with her over the girls or Gil; not warm in bed beside her – these were what mattered, not eternity but the good thing they had made of life, together –

She gets up prepared to say she isn't really ready to give that up yet, it is too soon, and then she sees that the family is standing too, ready to walk out together behind the casket. She feels people looking.

She has done that herself in the past, watched the grieving family uncomfortably, turned her eyes away to spare their privacy in grief, full of pity for their burden, then glanced back, curious too, she has to admit, how they were taking it, this one seemed truly stricken, that one bearing up –

Like a million others, she follows the casket, follows him there under the pall as they take him and put him into the hearse. With much ordering about, Ed Waring, the funeral director, shivvies the cars into line – there seem to be a lot of them – and she follows him out to the Evittsburg cemetery, Eternal Rest.

The day is bright and chill, crisp with color, a true October day of the sort he loved, but then who doesn't, and what does it matter? The hole is deep, and the earth that has been taken out of it decently covered with green artificial turf, but that doesn't make anything better. Nor worse, to be honest. The casket, with him inside, lies silently on straps over the green-walled hole, and she doesn't even remember saying good-bye to him.

" 'For I know that my Redeemer lives,' " she hears Bramer's neatly articulated voice, not too fast, not too slow, and feels Doug's hand tight on her elbow. " 'I am the resurrection and the life … he who lives in me, though he die, yet shall he live –

" 'We commend to Almighty God our brother, Daniel, and we commit his body to the ground, earth to earth, ashes to ashes, dust to dust' " -- she is vaguely surprised the old words are still being used –

Apparently, however, they don't shovel dirt over the casket any more. At least not while anyone's around. It strikes her forcefully that there are no flowers to go with him, and she turns to a white wicker basket full of spider mums Ed has laid against the green earth pile and pulls off some heads, thinking that cherry and orange are certainly inappropriate for a funeral, more like a football corsage, and throws them on the casket. All but one slide down the side into the dark, and she keeps her eyes on that one where it rests, willing it to remain, and it does.

" 'The Lord bless him and keep him. The Lord make His face shine upon him and be gracious to him. The Lord look upon him with favor and give him peace.' "

The flower holds. Doug seizes her arm even tighter; Joy and Scott take Gil's hand as he stands silently next to Robey.

" 'Let us go in peace.' "

The flower holds.

CHAPTER 22

The Ruth/Naomis have organized the luncheon afterwards at church, covered dish, of course, an article of faith in the Lutheran confession: "I believe in covered dish suppers as the Great Healer," perhaps a sort of human channel for the Holy Spirit. The warm smell of noodle casseroles and coffee hits her, and she carefully remembers to think of these funeral baked meats, as she always had before, as encouraging signs of vitality and life renewed.

Flanked by family, she sits and eats quite heartily, she thinks. Gil, grave as King Tut's mask, dispatches large portions of assorted salads and hot dishes with dedicated zeal; he seems more meditative about his choices for second helpings than about the funeral he has just witnessed.

She sees people she hadn't noticed before. Those who hadn't already spoken to her come and do so now, and she is touched at the number who have stayed on for the luncheon. Many times they have other places to go after a funeral, she thinks warily. (Thinking is to be engaged in only with caution). Once they've taken the time off they like to spend it usefully.

"These luncheons are a good idea." Joy sounds approving. "Sound therapy for times like this, knowing people are behind you all the way."

It seems appropriate to confirm the sentiment with a smile.

Scott is even more of a surprise. "Garrison Keillor knew what he was talking about when he said Lutherans believe you can't get into heaven without a covered dish." He is quite taken with the Butlers and their two little boys, DeWitt and Dewayne, across the table and expands visibly, but Doug, next to Robey, seems still pinched and raw-edged.

He says little, Grace even less.

A man Elinor has never seen before puts his arm over her shoulder to shake her hand. She follows it to find his face, an anxious one, leaning solicitously above her. "I'm Henry King," he says. "From Station EVTV. You have no idea how terrible we feel about this, Mrs. Heyer."

Her neck hurts from twisting to see him. "Thank you," she says. "It's kind of you to come."

He looks relieved. "We have been hoping," he says, and pauses. She tries to look encouraging, but has to turn her head around at last, facing the table, her half-eaten chicken leg, Doug's full plate, the silhouette shapes of the Butlers' faces, within her vision.

"We were hoping," King goes on more smoothly, his voice reaching through both ears now it hits her hearing aid, "that you would not be initiating any court action about your husband's – er – experience."

Court action.

"We have, hm, investigated," he says, more quickly now, "and we have found out he was in the hospital recently for a possible heart attack, so that, mmm, in effect, he took on the debate with knowledge beforehand of certain negative conditions in regards to his health."

She has never even thought of court action.

Turning her head around again, she says, "But – "

His eyes harden. "I warn you, Mrs. Heyer. The law is on our side." His hand drops from her shoulder. "Let me assure you again, Mrs. Heyer, of our deepest sympathies in this unfortunate matter." She feels him move away.

"They're trying to scare you," says Scott scornfully. "He couldn't have realized there was a lawyer within hearing. I didn't want to bring this up yet, but I'd say you have a good case. You know, there are all those steps to get up the hill to the station – I'd be glad to take it on for you."

"You must be joking!"

Scott shrugs. "Just a suggestion."

Another presence moves behind her; Robey has gotten up from his seat down the table, where, as usual, he's been performing in high gear, if slightly subdued for the occasion and the white folks. His warm hand falls on her shoulder from where Henry King has just removed his.

"'The chief defect of Henry King/ Was chewing little bits of string.'"

"Who wrote that, Robey?"

"You askin me, Gramomma? You know I only quote em, don't never credit em. Unless they be black."

"Of course," she says. "I knew that."

The first day after Dan's death, Elinor awakes chilled, only a sheet, a layer of cold air lapped about her body, no warmth anywhere. After that she has added an extra blanket to the two she and Dan used, which helps.

There is nothing she can do about the other. Every morning Dan dies all over again; and, every day afterward, death strikes him down again as mercilessly as ever the first time. There is always the good, clean waking, warm now in bed, a sleepy opening to the new day, and then, a blow to the heart, Dan dead.

Dan dead, Dan dead, an aching bruise across the day until it fades in sleep. Every morning Dan dies, and then again the next morning, and then again, and again –

She has always loved silence before, even made a fool of herself from time to time, arguing in this desperate noisy world that, without quiet to think in, one is less of a person, addicted to mere sound, that music itself is devalued when used to cover up the disturbing tinnitus of thinking. And if there ever was a time for thinking, surely this is it. She takes her hearing aid out and wraps it carefully in a tissue, lays it on the dresser.

She takes up embroidery - flame stitch, they call it - but she hates it. And silence doesn't help when she has something *not* to think about, Dan dead only the start of it. So she soon capitulates and uses music to fill up the space. First she tries tapes of the kind of music she loves most, great choirs, beginning with the one at Gettysburg College she had always dreamed of singing in, but never made.

She's bought all their records, the ones made primarily for choir members' nostalgic reminiscences and the later public ones. So she plays them, pretending she has been singing with them. Then she puts on the Mormon Tabernacle choir, and the Robert Shaw recordings, and tapes of the Bach chorales and the Passions, and the Mozart and Verdi Requiems – but they don't drown out the kind of thinking she doesn't want to do, either.

So she switches to secular things, symphonies and operas, which should do the trick, turned up so loud she can hear them without her hearing aid.

They are not loud enough.

One day she accidentally tunes in to MTV and sits there for an hour of full-length distortion of reality, in a hellworld of orange frightwigs, purple walls, and obsessed, apparently predatory, people. Seen thus, who would want to live in this world, or ask someone else to – having the chance to leave it behind seems nothing to rail against after all.

So she goes out and buys a rock record of her own, "Highway to Hell," by AC-DC, and she puts it on daytimes, and sometimes nighttimes, to deaden her nerve ends and put fiber into her life, as she puts it wryly to herself, to help the hours pass quickly through her gut, so as not to grow fat on grief.

Not that it works.

For one thing, she can't stand it very long, even without her hearing aid. The noise is muted but the beat is still punishing. For another, Grace is appalled, and Joy, curiously, takes on almost as much about it. She is coming in a lot these days, and she catches Elinor in the middle of it one day. " 'Highway to Hell'? For God's sake, Mom, what's gotten into you these days?"

Grace is even more upset, but then in her way, she seems to be upset about a lot these days. "I took that record away from Gil last month," she said furiously. "Now his own grandmother – "

Elinor turns it off and listens as Grace frets, loudly so that Elinor can hear her, that Gil hasn't come by to visit his Nana, that Doug is so busy he seems to have no time for anything or anybody anymore, that Robey visits Elinor more faithfully than he did any of the other Carliers, and "he's only an in-law of an in-law for you."

"We talk a lot." In fact, for some reason, he seems to be the only one she can talk to. "And we watch birds."

Just last week she asks him idly, "What's that bird there?" about a brown and boring bird she sees out the window, chasing other brown and boring birds away from a scrap of bread on the ground.

"Seen it all my life, Gramomma," he says, loud so she can hear him. The bird flies away. "No use you askin me that. I ain't never inquired. Maybe it's a Jubjub bird. 'The bird flies out, the bird flies back again.' " But that's no help in this case, and that evening she goes to the store and buys a bird book with beaky faces on a flexible cover, and they start to look up birds together.

Elinor gets a feeder and hangs it from the maple tree in the side yard near the kitchen window. Afternoons, Robey drives up in his old Ford, and pounding punctiliously now on the front door first, comes in, and she puts on her coat, and they sit out on the plastic porch chairs, watching until it gets too cold. Then they remove to the kitchen, to drink coffee and watch some more.

They agonize regularly over all the different sparrows, which they feel they should be able to tell apart at once, out of respect – not just lumping them together as sparrows – but the cardinals are an easily identifiable joy.

Finally, she put her hearing aid back in so she can hear them, although that time of the year they don't have much to say.

That made "Highway to Hell" too loud so she stopped playing it.

By then it was almost Christmas.

CHAPTER 23

We started arguing again, Robey and I. He was too hard on Doug, I thought.

"After all, Robey, he's not you. His generation has had it easier. It's not necessary for him to be a professional black any more. I should think you'd be proud of that, your generation. Wasn't that what the civil rights struggle was all about?"

"You talk as if the struggle's over, Gramomma. You think it's all peaches and cream now for black folks? 'If there is no struggle, there is no progress,' and I know who said that. I named my son after him. Frederick Douglass said that."

"Yeah, back in the 19th century. The physical struggle is over now. You're in, don't you understand that?"

"Oh, Gramomma." His voice batted every syllable with real exasperation. "You remind me of the early explorers."

"The what?"

"The early explorers. The ones that paraded around in the wilderness with their European ideas, thinking all they had to do was impress the natives and they'd take over the place." He paused, hit the quote key of his computer brain. "Like Jean Nicolet, the French guy, who came across what's now Wisconsin, and thought he was in China. 'He leaped ashore, clad in mandarin robes, firing pistols in both hands.' " Robey gave a great roar of laughter. "Did he ever realize what a fool he must have looked like?"

"Okay, so you're saying – I just don't get it, Robey. You're saying – what it's like, being black, right? – and that I don't get it?"

"Now you got it, Gramomma."

"Look, Robey." I lowered my voice. I needed to. "Robey, I'm not saying there's no more struggle. But it's in a different arena. A lot of things had to be dumped along the way, like ballast, to be lean and mean enough to win. Now we've – you've – " I always felt as if I were tightrope-walking, trying to talk to Robey about racial matters, so he wouldn't get insulted, though I never noticed that he felt the same with me – "we've got to hold on to the victory, but pick up what was lost in the process." I looked at him suspiciously. "You're laughing at me."

"Gramomma, would I do that? Jes that it be wunnerful how white folk think they know what black be like. Anyway, Douglass don be strugglin none. He want to be a universal nigger – take the best out of the black, the best out of the white. But it don work that way. Jus lak it don work that way with religion. You take little dabs here, little dabs there, you lose the connections."

I couldn't believe my ears. "That, from a man who loves the Bart?"

He ignored me. "Douglass thinkin he fit into the white world, with his white wife and his yeller kid, everybody makin way for him. 'Here come the boy, don he look like us?' laughin behin dere hans – "

I rebelled. "It's a new world for all of us, only I say there aren't enough blacks like Doug who are willing to enter it. Of course, there aren't enough whites either, but they're not very organized anymore. You'd rather do all the things that are guaranteed to turn people against you and then you complain because you see yourselves as being left out!"

" 'The destiny of the colored American is the destiny of America.' He know his stuff, that Douglass."

And that was that.

For about a month after Dan's death, I didn't go back to church. People called on the telephone to chat, and Mary Ann came by several times, and so did Irene and the Butlers once.

We talked about inconsequential things. Mary Ann and Irene were born Lutherans, and the Butlers were not, but they all shared the good Lutheran tradition for burning at the stake in preference to any suspicion of religious talk outside the church walls. They never urged me to come back, only said they missed me.

Still, I got the message. Once the Pastor's Support Committee called by, to ask how they could help. Robey was there at the time, and when he heard who they were, he said to them, shortly, "Good. Get her back to church."

They laughed as if he had cracked a joke, and looked covertly at me, and discussed at some length the children's Christmas pageant this year, which was to be an animal's eye view of the Nativity. Ted Tilton's three-year-old daughter was to play a little black lamb, and he was hilarious about her adeptness at elbowing her way into an honored position close to the manger.

"But he's white," said Robey, when they had gone, relieved at accomplishing their duty call with so little stress.

"Well, of course he's white," I said. "Some of us were born that way, you know."

"Gramomma, don't bite. I mean, why not get a beautiful little black chile to play that black lamb. Don't they want it to get close to the little white baby Jesus?"

"Oh, Robey, maybe there aren't any little black kids that age. Let me think, the Butler children are out of the nursery now, then there's Eugenia Hempley, and little Sussie, but I haven't seen them for months – Dan – Dan said they were moving to the north end, I think, and Mim Sorrell has no grandchildren – and that's all the blacks we have except for old Harry Martin who hardly ever comes."

His look was contemptuous. "And you call yourselves an integrated church."

I felt like hitting him. "Well, blacks aren't exactly knocking down the doors to get in, you know."

"Maybe you haven't made them feel like they'd get much of a welcome if they did." He chuckled. "Calm down. How that white face do communicate – "

When I did go back to church, it was awkward.

Trinity was going through the methodical mainstream process of evaluating the congregation and deciding on long-range goals. People felt disloyal to turn their attention toward the acquiring of a new pastor when the relict – grand word – of the old one was still showing like a dark cloud not yet sufficiently disappeared over the horizon. So I got in the habit of arriving late, after the announcements, and leaving after the service, with only minimal socializing.

When people asked me to their homes, and they did at first, I would thank them and invent urgent jobs of work for myself, a column that must be written, the house to clean, Christmas to get ready for. This hardly persuaded them. They read my columns and knew how I hated housecleaning and any other kind of physical labor as well. Still, the excuses were socially acceptable, and the offers died down.

I minded that, too.

Mostly I would sleep. Or lie there wide awake as the case might be. One afternoon, I remember drifting between consciousnesses like a slow-motion tennis ball, back and forth, fuzzy and white, bouncing between floor and ceiling. It reminded me of times when, as a child, I had been wholly involved in dreams while still awake, and knowing the difference without losing my sense of reality of either one.

Back then I used to stare at the ceiling and imagine myself walking there with the chandelier jutting up from my feet like a big mushroom, and my bare toes curling around the blossoms and tendrils of the plaster moldings. There had been no sense of anything awry; the serene real world of sofa and lamps and end tables remained in their accustomed places to mark the ceiling world as special, and for coming back to.

This time it was different. When I walked upon the ceiling, sofas and lamps and end tables rained on me, and the bookcases themselves, and finally the rug, smothering all.

I lifted my arms to protect my head, and to my horror I saw only one mole there on my forearm, where there had once been two with an inch of clear skin between them.

As a child I had always used those two moles as an assurance of my own identity. When I got up in the morning, I would check them to make sure they were still there, that it was still me. They were a great comfort because I believed that if I were ever kidnapped, I would always be known by them to be Elinor, even if I had changed out of all recognition in the meantime.

Willing myself against swelling panic, I saw that the other mole was still there, after all, but had faded almost to invisibility. In these later years, I had never noticed.

Was I then still me?

Thank God, the doorbell rang.

It was Grace and Gil, all unaware they had saved me.

"Well, at least, you don't have that awful record on," said Grace, eying me on the sofa and motioning Gil to open the curtain where I'd drawn it. "I thought there for awhile you were going to get a Sony Walkman."

"I may yet." I felt as sullen as Gil looked.

"Come on," she said shortly, heading for the kitchen. "You're coming home with us for awhile."

"No, I'm not. If you're worried about my getting over – what happened, I'm better. Really." I laughed merrily. "I don't play the record anymore. I have my hearing aid back in. I can stand silence again. And the birds help a lot. And Robey. I'm fine really."

She shouted above the rattle of the dishes in the sink. "You and Robey can watch the birds just as well at our house, even if it is in town. To tell you the truth, I'm embarrassed. Irene had to call and help us to see that you need more company than you're getting. I know you want to stay here, but I haven't got the time or the energy to argue with you right now. As soon as I finish the dishes, I'm going to pack your bag and Gil will check the doors for you. Where are the timers Dad had for the lights? Gil, you know how to set them, don't you?"

"He showed me once."

"Speak up, Gil," said Grace irritably. Her plump figure disappeared up the steps, and Gil slouched off in his new teenage shuffle to find the timers.

I looked at my arm again, with its lonely mole, and felt very sorry for it. Someday it would be shut up in a box, lying on a soft white satin lining, comfortably enough. But I wouldn't be along. For the first time ever we would be separated from each other. Then what would happen to those little moles, to the inch of skin between them?

And where would I be myself?

Somewhere?

Nowhere?

It didn't bear thinking about.

"I think they're in that cupboard to your left, on the third shelf," I called out to Gil.

CHAPTER 24

Living at Grace and Doug's was like being turned around bodily and faced in another direction. Not forwards versus backwards, or future versus past, just different. Here we were oriented toward town instead of suburb, Our Saviour instead of Trinity, and back into the school calendar as I hadn't been since Joy graduated.

Gil still was not his old cheerful self, and Doug too seemed less open, more constrained. I marveled to think that I had not been the only one permanently marred by losing Dan. I think I could be forgiven for rather rejoicing over that inside, not knowing what was to come.

The days went by haltingly, with everyone else busier than I. It was surprising to realize that I missed Trinity, although Mary Ann and Irene called occasionally, and the Cohicks, a family Dan had taken into membership at Easter, asked me over to dinner. This was a real surprise because they had never been particularly friendly before.

"We wanted to have you and Pastor over," Paulina said, and got stuck there.

Jerry Cohick had recently bought the local prestigious dress shop, Barretti's, and Paulina had started a support group for large women, called Big and Beautiful Enthusiastically, or BABE, which, it turned out, she wanted me to join. Conversation at the dinner table consisted mostly of Paulina urging me to join her in persuading Jerry to stock more larger sizes at Barretti's. It sounded like a good idea to me, but death to a shop which had built its reputation on catering to the rich and skinny, so I tried to stay out of it.

Paulina was full of fascinating gossip, including a long tale about the Weight Watchers' group she had belonged to in Cleveland. It seemed the president there had aimed to lose forty pounds to regain her husband's affection, after he started running around with his secretary. She succeeded, and the secretary started gaining weight out of frustration. She joined Weight Watchers in her turn, and the president quit.

So the secretary lost weight and got him back, and quit Weight Watchers, the president returned, and by this time the husband was so confused he ran off with a waitress from a pizza parlor, who was fatter than either of the others but proud of it. This was supposed to be some kind of a parable to explain why Paulina founded BABE but it seemed to me that it needed some work done on it for inspirational purposes.

Still, I enjoyed it, and Dan would have loved it.

I let myself in to Grace and Doug's Columbia Street house around 9 PM, and Grace called from the kitchen. "Leave the lights on for Gil, please, Mother."

She and Doug were sitting around the breakfast table drinking coffee with Joy and Scott, and the air was blue with smoke.

"Cut your way through, if you can, Mom," said Joy, with heavy irony "Grace has gone back to the coffin nails, as you can see, or not see, as the case may be."

Grace looked guilty but determined. "Just until I lose some of this weight," she mumbled, looking quickly at Doug and then away. After Paulina's story, I couldn't help but wonder if there was something wrong between them, but Doug had never been one to wander, and his and Grace's marriage had always felt so good to me, once I'd got used to the idea.

"Got one for me, Grace?" I surprised even myself. The girls had scolded me out of smoking years before, but I had never forgotten how satisfying it was, especially social smoking. Just sitting around talking and smoking together, not like drugs with reality distorted, but as an aid to concentration. Cigarettes were like worry beads to finger and mouth while thinking over your next contribution to the conversation.

The smoke too was a consolation, the feel of it, lemon-tart on the throat, the look of it, like silver ribbons floating, as pleasant as blowing bubbles with an eight-year-old. I had once tried to smoke in the dark, and it was astonishingly boring, not to see the smoke --

"Mom, for heaven's sake." Joy was shocked and Scott looked offended.

"Oh, Joy, stop being such a Puritan," I said, lighting up with a comforting familiarity.

She was speechless at this ultimate insult.

"I bet you aren't even half as disapproving when your friends sniff coke." I took a big drag and choked. It had been a long time. I took the next one more cautiously.

Doug looked as morose as the others. "So what's the problem?" I asked, carefully easing the smoke down my throat and back up again. It tasted rather awful, like newspapers left down for the dog.

"His father." Joy pointed a shoulder at Doug, who smiled apologetically. "Giving him a rough time again."

Doug lifted his shoulders and took a breath. "The same old thing, Mom," he said. "Dad, you know. He's always told me You Are What You Are, boy -- "

"I remember. Popeye and God."

"Well, it's seemed lately, the last year or so, that all the things I read into that phrase weren't necessarily what he had in mind. Or, at least, not now." He paused again, the folds of his jawline lifted as he swallowed.

Grace took up the story. "Robey's been putting pressure on Doug to get out of Our Saviour and work in a black church somewhere."

Doug's voice sounded stronger now. "Maybe all the time he was saying, 'You Are What You Are, boy, and that's black. You ought to be working for our people.' I had to go and get all intellectual about *both* my cultural heritages, and about being made whole by a God who is a loving universal presence, who loves both sides of me equally, and that is what I am. And all the time Dad just meant my congregation was too white for *him*, the Lutheran church's too white for *him*, my music's too white for *him*, and all he cares about is my black self."

"Maybe he's changed since he got older," I ventured. I hadn't known Robey before Doug and Grace got married, but it did seem that just recently he'd hammered away more on the accent, the black mannerisms –

"There's this church in Atlanta he's been trying to get Doug to apply for," said Grace. "They're looking for a minister of music – "

"Carrie Bivens Zion does the whole gospel bit, and that's fine and I love it – but I love Bach better, and Palestrina, and Randall Thompson – and, ok, Gilbert and Sullivan –"

Grace put her hand on his arm, and I remembered that they had first gotten to know each other producing a youth "Pinafore" at Trinity.

Scott sounded hearty. "He's got a point, you know, Doug. Roots and all that, an obligation to your own people."

"Look, man!" Doug turned his face to Scott and slapped his own brown cheek. "I got some white folks back in there too, you know. My own mother's heritage. Should I spit on that? And even if I didn't, I have a right to choose what I love, don't I? Not because it's any better – I never said Bach was better than gospel – but because it happens to appeal to me." He fumbled for the glass coffee pot on the ceramic tile in the center of the table. "It speaks to me, Scott. I'll never forget the first time I heard a Bach chorale – " he fell silent, but his hand trembled, pouring. "At Carrie Bivens Zion, I could never direct one again."

"I'm sure there are some black churches that like a good mix of all kinds of music," said Joy helpfully.

"That's not what Dad wants," said Doug. "We've always had this difference, you know. Back during the civil rights activism, he'd have long fatherly talks about getting out and demonstrating. We were always close after Mother died" – his voice choked up – "and I didn't want to disappoint him. In fact, the three times I did go out were because he shamed me into them. And each time, all the time, in all the screaming and the hosing and the raw naked fear, the only place I really wanted to be was back at my organ. He didn't understand, but he tried to, and I appreciated that. But lately, the last year – and I may be inagining this, Mom," he said apologetically, "it seems just since Pop died, Dad's been really pushing me. 'Get your black back,' he keeps saying. "He reached out a hand aimlessly, and Grace took it in one of hers, and then, stubbing out her cigarette quickly on the ash tray, in both. "I don't know what I'm going to do," he said, and closed his eyes, but two round drops escaped beneath the lids anyway, as we all sat there frozen. We always say, men should never be afraid to cry, but when they do –

The front door opened and closed quietly.

"And then there's Gil," said Grace.

Grace and Doug had grounded Gil during school nights because his grades had dropped precipitously, but he was allowed to go out on Friday nights, usually with Clay.

"Oh, over to Clay's house," he answered airily, when I asked him the next day where he'd been.

"And what did you do at Clay's house?"

"Oh, things." When he could see that wasn't going to stop me, he added sulkily, "You know, television, and they have a pool table in the cellar. And we go out some – "

"Where's 'out some'?"

"The movies, sometimes."

"What movie did you go to last night?"

"We didn't go to any last night. We went to Andre's house."

I didn't know Andre, and neither did Grace. Later, Doug said he'd met him; he was from Gunther Park. His father was white, his mother black, and the parents agreed it was probably a healthy thing for boys who had so much in common to get together with each other.

I no longer noticed any golden in Gil and no one called him Nugget any more. He was growing up. Up and away.

Doug was busy with rehearsals for the Christmas programs. The Junior Choirs were doing a Clokey cantata, using a knockout boy soprano Doug had been working with for some time. A youth handbell choir, a senior handbell choir, and the senior choir were doing a Bach tricentennial program, and of course there was the regular children's Sunday School program which was not even so original as Trinity's animal's eye view, but just a simple Nativity enactment, set to black spirituals and white folk songs, complete with shepherds and sheep, wise men, angels, the works. And finally to top things off, the Christmas midnight service.

Grace was working steadily now at her real estate job. "Not selling much, but getting lots of experience," she said, quite gaily. She liked getting out of the house, as I liked staying home now.

I bought another bird feeder and hung it outside the kitchen window, and, even in the city, from the trees in the back yard, birds came. Sparrows mostly, but a cardinal couple, and titmice, and some chicadees – I knew the names now – going for the extra sunflower seed I mixed in for them.

I had gotten back to my columns since the break after Dan's death. It seemed that the least I could have expected after that was a new depth to my writing, but they were still the same chatty trivial affairs they had always been, lightweight and detached. I could not, it seemed, sit down and write about the things closest to my heart. Not that the newspaper would have published them very long if I had --

Robey came by to this house too, and we worked on our life lists – thirteen birds we could recognize now on sight – and I tried to talk to him about Doug, but he clammed up at once.

"Yeah, Gramomma," he said stiffly, at his blackest. "I be at Douglass for goin white on me. Honkeyfyin hissef "– a gamin grin slipped out, but he stopped it before it could harm his image – "You be too, was you me – "

"I suppose you have a quote," I said angrily, "to cover how you're tearing him apart."

" 'First fight,' " he said. " 'Then, fiddle.' " Ever Robey, he couldn't resist the little twinkle, the tiniest glimmer of satisfaction at coming up with a perfect one. He was incorrigible.

"I suppose, as usual, you don't remember who said it?"

"Gwendolyn Brooks. Told you. I remember the black ones."

CHAPTER 25

After I moved to Doug and Grace's, I went back to Trinity only twice. They still had not replaced Dan, and I felt I really should go back, but I hated the strange voices of supply pastors in Dan's pulpit, and the unusual bustle of people who made a point of crowding around. They were loving and concerned, and I appreciated that, but where I had once reveled in their warmth, I just wished now that they would let me go in peace. I knew that things would shake down to normal after I came back another time or two – but after that I went with the family to Our Saviour.

Sometimes I even stayed home.

I didn't smoke again

But I wanted to.

Days were easier now, even bedtime, when Dan and I had been accustomed to discussing together everything that had happened during the day. Sometimes we ended up in total agreement, but other times, well – "The Ad-Hoc Heyer Clarification Committee," Dan had called us once as we battled our way to quite different positions on some subjects. (That time, as I recall, it was about technological progress as a value. I said it wasn't; he said it was.)

I missed our right-brain, left-brain exchange, and, most of all, I missed his easy laughter, his fond liking as well as love for me, more precious than I had known at the time. I had begun to miss the sex too, but much more than the physical lack, I missed the joining of heart and mind that made the joining of bodies so good.

Getting up was still the worst way to start the day.

Sometimes I prayed at night before I went to sleep that the next morning I would wake up already knowing that Dan was dead, before I had to remember it. It didn't work; every morning he still died all over again.

I quoted some of the Bible verses to myself that had helped me get through the time my father lost most of hinself to Alzheimers, but they seemed old and platitudinous. They *were* old and platitudinous. Though what can you expect about death, surely the oldest, most platitudinous event in human experience?

I felt like Robey quoting the Biblical passages from the Bart, which he claimed were the cream of the Bible anyway, although I argued that learning only the best parts missed all the connections. "The Lord is my Shepherd – " but the TV debate had spoiled that for me. My old lifesaver, "If the vision seem slow, wait for it " – but we hadn't really wanted visions, Dan and I, only assurance – blessed assurance. "I am the Resurrection and the Life," "Let not your heart be troubled, neither let it be afraid," "O Death, where is thy sting? – "

Why did none of this mean anything any more?

Somewhere in the middle of one of these sessions with myself, Gil and Joy walked in the door together.

"Gil's off for spring vacation now." Joy sounded as happy as if the vacation were hers. "What are you going to do with all that extra time, Gil?"

He seemed livelier than he had been for some time. "Dad's giving me twenty-five dollars to sort out the choir room at church and put everything in order," he said happily, almost sounding thirteen again. "The place is a mess with the music from all the choirs piled around since fall. One thing you can say about Dad," he said, obviously parroting Doug, "he is not an organizer."

"Seems to me he has to be one to get everything done," I said. "How about something hot after all that cold air?"

In the family tradition, Joy chose coffee, and Gil took tea, which he'd been trying lately in his efforts to grow up. "How do you drink that stuff?" he asked Joy, shuddering extravagantly.

"Just wait until you have to stay awake all night to study for your exams in college – "

"Really, Joy?" I was as delighted as if I had just discovered that we both had had the same professor. "That's where I started too."

Gil was into weightier things. He assumed a thoughtful look over his mug of tea. "Mom said I was to decide on my own gifts for everybody this year; she doesn't have time to get them. And Dad's advancing me the money for doing the choir room. What do you want anyway?" He looked impartially from Joy to me.

Joy thought. "Scott and I had decided we were going to ask people to give contributions to AIDS research for Christmas presents," she said, darting a look at me. "But you know, Gillie, what I'd really like from you?"

He shook his head, a little warily.

"Write me something." She waved her mug and the coffee slopped alarmingly. "Anything. Another play. A short story. How about an essay of some kind? You took creative writing in that advanced class last year, didn't you? How about a poem?"

He looked intently at his tea, put his finger into his mug and pressed something against the side. Triumphantly, he delivered it on his finger tip, then said, disappointed, "I thought it was a bug." He wiped his finger on his jeans. "I haven't written anything since that play for school."

"Just sit down and write what comes. It's called stream of consciousness, and it's a good way to get started."

She smiled at him, and once again I was wracked by a fierce love of her, this Joy of my heart, who tried so hard and did not really mean to be so trying.

Gil drank off the rest of his tea and turned to me. "How about you, Nana?" He set the mug down on the table with a bang and flushed. His child's coordination had recently begun to give way to teenage awkwardness. He lifted the mug and set it down again silently to prove that he could. Then he turned to me again and lifted his shoulders.

"You know what I'd like to give you, Nana?" he said in a rush. "I'd like to give you Grandpa back again." For the first time ever, his voice cracked on the last syllable, a high ratchet that split the air, amazing us all.

Oh, I didn't want to laugh at him, but the laugh came anyway. I knew I couldn't stop it, so I changed it on its way out, and I cried instead, and then, once I had started, it was silly but I couldn't seem to stop. I didn't even try. Dan had died almost two months ago, and Gil was growing up, and everybody knows it helps if you can cry.

Joy had taken up jogging and wanted me to join her. She promised me it would solve all my solvable problems, but after a quarter of a mile I decided it would only add to them.

"I know," I said, when she protested. "My body will get used to it. But my mind never will. Jogging, running, any deliberate bodily disturbance just for the sake of exercise reminds me of Sherry Willis."

Joy crossed her eyes, being funny. "Oh yes, Sherry Willis from church. I remember her brother Bob. "She uncrossed them. "He was cute."

"So is Sherry. Very sweet girl, too. But not a brain in her head. She says things like 'Don't you just love babies?' and then for fifteen minutes she tells you why. She's the kind of person who says, 'This may sound stupid, but I really think Elizabeth Taylor is pretty.' She is probably the most dynamically boring person I have ever known. After fifteen seconds with her, I panic. It's like a reflex action. I would just automatically scream if I didn't manage to get away from her by then."

Joy looked at me doubtfully. "That's what jogging does to you?"

"That's it."

So she jogged alone, or with Scott, and I went for an occasional walk, where I didn't have to think in step.

I got going at last on my Christmas shopping and found some real bargains, a tape recorder on sale for Gil, and a lamp I bought for Grace and Gil to replace one Gil had knocked over recently on an end table. I wasn't sure they'd like it. I'm afraid I really got it for myself. It was one of those useless novelties that fascinate me; you only had to touch it to turn it on, and before I wrapped it, I had a good time playing with it myself.

I made a contribution to the AIDS fund in Joy and Scott's name, and also bought them a record of *The Messiah*, although I suppose that was uncalled for and a tad nasty.

Shopping at Sears for the lamp, I met Meredith Busche and Jan Barry. Meredith looked smaller, bonier, ropier, more concentrated, as if she had simmered down to double-strength. I couldn't think whom she reminded me of now, and then I did. Lily Lyle Hadley. I felt like ducking around the imitation-wood kitchen unit on display before they saw me. Too late.

"Elinor!" cried Meredith. "I've been meaning to call you!"

Jan's broad face with the features spread unevenly over it, beamed as she grabbed my hand. "How *are* you, how *are* you?" Her grip was so hard, my ring bit my fingers.

"It's 11:30," said Meredith. "What are you doing for lunch?"

I tried to think of something.

"Nothing, I'll bet," Jan answered heartily. "There's a McDonald's right next door. Why don't we all eat there together?" One on each side they bore me off, talking all the way.

Over the soggy hamburgers, which, I'll admit, I like better than my own, they asked questions. How was I? How was the family? Had we gotten over the terrible thing that had happened?

"It *is* a terrible thing, God's punishment," intoned Meredith, but I didn't rise to it. "The world is a terrible place." Terrible was her word for the day. "How do you account for all this terrible sin anyway?"

I wanted to say, what sin? but God knows I believe sin exists, and I opened my mouth to make a more thoughtful answer, although I hadn't yet figured out what it would be. "And the starving people in Africa," she went on. "That case down in Maryland, where the mother killed her two children and then she killed herself? All those immigrants over the border?" It sounded like a Scottish bagpipe tune. "And those Russians. Oh, it's the end of the world coming, for sure. We've left Trinity, you know.".

"No, I didn't know."

She looked pleased, probably at having finally achieved equal attention with my hamburger. "On account of – um – Pastor Heyer's death, you know."

I felt absurdly touched that someone had so valued him, though they showed it so foolishly. My eyes moistened.

"You don't hold it against us?" she asked.

"Why should I hold it against you?"

"What we wrote in our letter?"

I didn't ask because I didn't really want to know.

"They didn't tell you." Meredith was disappointed. "Jan and I have joined the Sole Congregation of Jesus Christ in Gunther Park. We made a decision that we couldn't stay at a church where the pastor had obviously sinned so grievously against the Holy Spirit that God had to strike him down before the whole world. We don't mean to hurt you, dear," she said anxiously, and the strange thing is, I believe that.

"But why else would it have happened?" asked Jan, genuinely puzzled.

After all the frantic Christmas activities, the choir concerts, the children's pageants, the Sunday School class parties (they invited me to Trinity for some of these things, so I did double-duty), the Christmas Eve midnight service at Our Saviour was like a refreshing dip in one's own cool bath after a hot day on the beach.

The hour promised rest, the candlelight, healing. The air smelled of pine and candle wax, and the jeweled lights of the stained glass window, lit from outside, showed God entering this world on our terms, and not His, an idea that seemed suddenly not so outrageous after all as I had been thinking lately.

We sat in the back, near the organ, and I smiled without much pain at the thought that Dan would have disapproved, since there were still seats left in the front.

Dr. Bramer intoned the service, something Dan always hesitated to do because he didn't trust his musical ear. So I didn't see Dan superimposed on the figure in alba and stole in the chancel. If Dan could not be with me, I felt sure I knew where he was. I am getting better. I'm not losing everything I once had, I said to myself. My world still has that meaning Dan talked about, even if I'm not sure what that meaning is.

In the antiqued Christmas glory, Grace looked rested, Gil glowed again, Robey watched him proudly. Even Joy and Scott hummed along, not committing themselves to the foolishness, but willing for the moment to table their opposition.

Doug looked more relaxed on the organ bench, and for the first time since the accident used his left foot freely on the pedals. No doubt he was relieved that the Christmas pressures were over now. The beginning of wisdom is learning to savor small advances.

During the Silent Night at the end of the service, the congregation held hands and I made a promise. "I'm stronger now," I said. "I know I have to believe in you, God. So I promise I *will* believe in You. No matter what, I *will* believe in you. No matter how I feel, I *will* believe in You."

It seemed enough at the time.

CHAPTER 26

Christmas Day was not so restful, more like a hangover.

In this Age of Irony, you don't dare take anything seriously over any sustained period of time, lest you be accused of losing your sense of humor. So Joy and Scott took pains to prove that last night's sentimentality had been only a momentary lapse, and slapped gifts into everybody's hands like surgeons' scalpels at an operation.

When Gil handed Joy a notebook page half filled with lines written in a small, neat hand, she glanced at it hastily and patted him on the back. " 'Twenty Questions.' Oh, that sounds very good, Gil," she said. "The beginning of your *ouevre*. I'll keep it forever, and maybe someday someone will offer me a million dollars for it."

Scott was not so intent on underlining the silliness of the season as its grotesquerie, starting the day with a jolly reference to the beast slouching toward Bethlehem to be born.

"The rough beast," corrected Robey. He was in a good mood though quieter than usual. And, almost like a gift in itself, blessedly free of his mocking black dialect. His gifts this year were Mahalia Jackson records all around, and a copy of black history written for teenagers for Gil. He also gave me a long stocking-like nylon net bag, closed with a drawstring and filled with black seed.

"Let me guess," I said. "Thistle for goldfinches?"

He nodded. "Imported," he said, adding with a touch of his usual mischief, "Nigger seed."

I didn't even want to touch that, so I just raised an eyebrow, a handy talent to cultivate.

"Well," he conceded, "niger seed. Or nyger seed. Spelled with one g. But very very black. Goldfinches love it."

"What is this, International Race Awareness Day?" But I was pleased. We had mentioned several times branching out from the usual birdseed, and he had remembered.

The Christmas tree was real, but smaller than we ever had at home. They were getting so expensive now that we had even talked about getting an artificial one, but agreed to a real one for another year. Dan had loved the real trees, swore he would never go artificial, and secretly I vowed the same, however small it might be, no matter what the rest of the family did.

Grace seemed to agree, and so did Doug, although we had hesitated to bother him about it. Now, on Christmas Day, he should have been at least as relaxed as last night, but the jaw lines cut deep into the sides of his face, and he looked worn and limp, like a much-loved teddy bear.

"Shouldn't he be in bed?" I asked Grace. "Remember when your father looked like that, and we didn't do anything about it?"

But I guess she didn't hear. She was basting the turkey, typical of Grace, who sometimes did things that didn't always need to be done. I didn't mention it, but turkey takes care of itself under aluminum foil. Maybe she needed work like I need silence. Or like I needed silence again, after that nightmare month under the cauterization of noise.

Was it a hallmark of our time that we all looked tired? I remembered a book review I had read in the POST once of an English novel: In English novels, people under heavy stress invariably look tired. In American ones they throw up.

"We're being unAmerican," I murmured, but again she didn't hear, went on basting the turkey, hunched over the oven like a little old woman.

Still, everybody felt better after dinner, and the lamp was the hit of the day. No one could resist the allure of tapping it through its three-way light cycle time after time, testing speeds, pressures, materials.

"At this rate," I laughed, childishly pleased at the success of my gift, " I may have to go out and get one for each of you." I made a show of picking up my purse. "Lucky I have a Master Card."

"The Charge of the Light Brigade," said Robey, setting off one of those barrages of aimless puns some families fall prey to from time to time.

"When I consider how my light is spent," said Doug, and Grace offered, "No doubt, she'll make light of it."

"Angel of Light," Joy said sweetly, and Scott said, laughing, "All I can think of is 'Let there be light.' "

Gil won the match though, gesturing at everybody gathered around the lamp. "Many hands make light work," he said, and grinned with delight at the cheer that followed.

No one could solve the puzzle of how the light worked. (None of of us were electricians.)

Gil continued to investigate it long after everyone else had given up. "Look, Mother," he called. "It works with a banana."

Scott rolled his eyes, and Joy giggled. "Warm or cold?"

"Room temperature," said Gil seriously. "Unpeeled though."

Robey was frankly baffled. "Ugamma Jackson – you remember him, Doug – he worked with me for years before I retired – he has one of these. He discovered that his telephone turns it on, and so he'll call and turn it on in the evening when he's not home to make it look as if somebody's there."

"Let's try it." Gil was ecstatic, and would not be satisfied until the lamp was moved to the outlet nearest the phone. But no one chose to call, and so finally, around 10 PM, Doug was forced to go out to a public phone and try to turn the light on. The phone rang and rang but the light stubbornly remained dark.

Finally, Gil lifted the receiver. "Thanks, Dad. Nice try, but no cigar."

Grace looked relieved when Doug reappeared, bringing along a wave of cold air with him and muttering, "I can't believe the things I do for my family. Do you know I had to drive several miles just to find a pay phone?"

"Come on, face it," she said fondly. "You were as curious as he was."

"I won't argue the point," he said loftily. He touched the lamp with his finger and it leaped into light. "I can't imagine how it works."

Scott shrugged. "That's only because we don't know the principles it operates on. Everything makes sense," he explained, "once you know how it fits into the real world." He looked at me slyly. "Even the so-called supernatural."

"I couldn't agree more," I said cheerfully.

By March Doug was looking more relaxed, and working on the spring junior choir festival. Grace's real estate job had picked up, with two commissions to her credit in the last month.

It seemed to me that Robey hassled Doug less, too. Joy was very busy at the paper, and, although we talked on the phone regularly, we actually managed to avoid arguing. In fact, it seemed that I had given up argument for peace and quiet, although I wasn't sure how long that would last. It never had before, no matter how many resolutions I'd made. For some reason it seemed easier to will yourself to believe in God than to stay out of arguments.

After school started again, Gil seemed quieter. Grace thought he was happier too.

"Don't you, Mother?" she asked, anxiously. "Of course, I'm feeling guilty about getting back to fulltime work again, so I want him to be getting along fine. Do you think I'm fooling myself?"

"I'm not sure. He does seem contented, more his old self since Christmas, but there's still something missing. I'm not sure what it is."

"You just miss that little Nugget we used to have," she said fondly. "I do too, but they do grow up, Mother. You of us all know that."

I determined briskly not to get caught up in futile nostalgia. There had been too much of it in my life lately, and I willed it away. Will power was working beautifully these days.

"By the way, Grace," I said. "I'm going back to the house next week."

"Oh, Mother, not so soon!" She sounded truly dismayed.

"Grace, I'm not doing you any good here and I need to be back with myself and work out my new life. You helped heal me, and I'm so grateful, darling, but it's time to go back. Gil stays at school for those drill team meetings most afternoons, and you don't need me here for him. Something else, too, Grace, Doug hasn't been home during the daytime at all lately, between rehearsals for that musical, and lessons, and calls, and things. Do you think he's worried he'll run into Robey?"

"Does Robey come by much during the day?" Grace unfolded the pie crust she had taken from the refrigerator and carefully sprinkled flour on it.

"He drops by every other day or so for a cup of coffee and an hour with the birds."

"Nothing wrong with that." She patted the dough meticulously into the pan and pressed some holes together in the middle. "It's embarrassing," she said cheerfully, "not to be making my own pie dough. This is the best I've found yet, but I always enjoyed doing everything from scratch."

She hesitated. "Sometimes I really do wonder if I'm being fair to Gil. Oh, I know, most women work now, and long before their children are as old as he is. But I always said I wouldn't." She folded the overhanging edge of dough back under itself on the rim of the pan.

"It would be different if I didn't like housework. But I like it as well as real estate, I think." Expertly she crimped the edge of shell between her thumb and index finger, the middle finger bracing beneath.

"Well, you might not be so fond of it if you did it full-time," I said, out of my own experience. "I seem to need both the domestic and the professional. You know how I hate housecleaning, but my two happiest days were always Thursdays when I finished the column and cooked a big dinner for – your dad and me, and Mondays when I shut off the house and got back to my typewriter. I seem to need a change of pace, and I suspect you do too."

She dumped the apples she had cut up into the shell, took a breath, and spoke carefully. "Did Doug tell you what he heard in the church parlor yesterday?"

I shook my head.

"He was taking a nap on the sofa before going out to do some calling. (Yes. He's still doing pastoral calling, Mother, because Bramer never gets around to it.) And he got waked up by hearing voices over on the other side of the room. It was old Orville Wahle and Joe Nyberg, installing a new TV in the cabinet for the adult

Sunday School's new video series. Anyhow, he heard his name, and they were talking about the music in the church, and Orville said, 'Well, I'm a country music person myself, ' and then Joe, good old Joe, he says, 'What's a nigger doing playing Bach anyway? I'd like him better if he'd do his own stuff. It would be more honest than pretending he knows how to do ours.' "

She poured the crumb topping over the apples and shoved the pie in the oven, closing the door with a bang. She turned to face me. "What are we supposed to do anyway, Mother? Fit ourselves into other people's little boxes all our lives, just to keep peace?"

But I, who had always had answers for her, had no answers.

Except will power, of course.

CHAPTER 27

It was a relief to get back to my house again (our house, I mean, Dan's and mine), and it was easier than I expected. Getting through the first Christmas without him had helped.

Mornings were still split in two, though: before and after the remembering. But now the blow, when it fell, seemed muffled, as if, even though I couldn't get awake in full possession of grief, I expected it.

I had always liked being alone. Living with Dan had been like living with a larger part of myself, which sounds either insulting to him, or else very self-absorbed, but wasn't either one, I think.

Now, after Grace and Doug and Gil, and all their affection, I needed to be back alone again. I was even eager to test my strength. I knew now I could depend on my will power, pull myself out of my moods, maybe even get to work and do some writing beyond those trivial columns.

Right away I started.

After I finished my column for that week, I sat down and rewrote three old columns about the family and sent them off to a family magazine. I wrote a sample book review and sent it to the *Philadelphia Inquirer*, and wrote another article about the death of loved ones and sent it off to *The Lutheran*.

"Not that I expect anything but rejection slips," I said to Robey one afternoon as we sat with our coffee, birdwatching. "That's how experienced I am."

"That be experience all right, Gramomma," he said admiringly. I gathered this was to be a black day.

"I'm just so glad to be back to even trying to write. At this point, I don't need to be published."

"Sure, Gramomma."

"Well, it's just therapeutic to get some of what I'm thinking down on paper, attack it where it is and face it down."

" 'No, I do not weep for the world. I am too busy sharpening my oyster knife.' "

"That's a beauty, Robey. Who said it?"

"Zora Neale Hurston."

"I read one of her books, but I don't remember that. Well, anyway, I think writing is all I need really. Who needs readers?"

"Zora wrote that for me to read, and you too. Think you could write it all down? And then burn it up right off?"

I thought about it. "You're right, Robey. I could never do that in a thousand years. I save it all, the littlest scrap."

"So your writin ain done til the readin?"

I sighed. "Well, that's true, but it's annoying. I want so much to be independent, not to have to rely on anyone else for anything – "

"Independent!" He blew a gust of laughter. The cups rattled in their saucers, and a titmouse flew off the feeder in alarm. " 'Independence? That's middle-class blasphemy. We are all dependent on one another; every soul of us on earth.' "

One must make allowances for a tempting quote, but that one sounded odd from Robey. "I won't even ask who said that."

"Don even know."

"Robey, at the risk of repeating myself, you know, you don't make sense at all. You come and visit me, a white woman, at least every other day. You read the Bart all the time, and other books too, and you seem to get a lot of good out of everything in there, and not just the black writers. You get along well with whites, you even seem to like us a lot of the time. What *is* all this black stuff with you lately, anyway, the talk that isn't really you, the pressure on Doug – ?" My voice trailed off at the expression on his face.

He stood up. "What the matter with you, woman? Don you got eyes? Don you know when you see it 'the continuing despair of the goodness of the Lord?' I gettin old lately, Gramomma, and when you get old, you don get brave. You learn 'what is Bull and what is Truth,' and you get to be more what you is than you ever was before, and you take pride in it, cause there ain no time to take pride in what you gonna be." He hit the table with a deadly-controlled fist. "Your Dan done teach me that."

He looked at me with that hint of self-mockery back on his face. "Don make me leave, Gramomma, cause I purely do love your company. Jus let me be what I is. On any given day."

I gritted my teeth and turned to the window. The titmouse had returned.

"All right." I took a breath. "One of these days I'm going to buy that Audible Audubon. With the little records of birdsongs you can play on it? Would you like to go in on it with me?"

His chair creaked as he leaned back into it. "Anything we can 'make summertime out of,' Gramomma, I be proud to join you."

Besides the Audible Audubon, I bought a new hearing aid, one that didn't compete so loudly with what I wanted to hear. And I visited the Social Security office every week or so, trying to clear up some problems that, I was told, had arisen because I had neglected to apply for my money immediately after Dan's death.

I thought briefly about getting a word processor, until the manuscripts all came back again within two weeks. Robey helped me paint the TV room. And I thought of getting a dog, in the summer when the weather was better. It had been a cold spring and I wasn't eager to go out in it several times a day with a dog attached. Perhaps I should get the yard fenced in instead.

Only Gil remained outside the little puzzle I had willed together with everyone firmly in place. Sometimes he came by full of affection and nervous energy; other times, when I came on him at Columbia Street, or twice at the hardware store while I was buying paint, he seemed sullen, unwilling to linger. But then teenagers are notably unstable and probably have to hype themselves up to visit grandparents. I was pretty sure he wasn't on drugs, for I watched him closely when I saw him. I couldn't help being suspicious of the music he listened to, but then everybody insists it doesn't matter because the kids don't listen to the words anyway. (Many of these people deal in words for a living. They are the same people who rage at the negative subliminal influence of tobacco advertising, say, or discussing religion in school.) And who was I to condemn that music anyway, after its service to me in November?

Gil must find his own way, as I had found mine.

But Joy called up the first Saturday in April, talking at first about inconsequential things, and then finally getting down to the heart of the matter.

"Mom. Did I ever show you that poem Gil gave me at Christmas?"

"No, and I forgot all about it."

"Well, I was going through some things, and I came across it today." Pause. "Now that I read it again, it's worrisome."

I really didn't want to hear it. "Okay. Read it to me."

Paper rattled. "He calls it 'Twenty Questions.' Remember that year, he must have been about eight, wasn't he, when he loved to play that game? Wouldn't let a person alone." She cleared her throat.

'Twenty Questions

'For answering the next nineteen
It takes the first,
To say later, why and where
And what and how,
A lifetime's so-on,
Animal, vegetable, mineral?
Who needs to know?
Why, everyone, for planning;
And if you don't they say
Take your place,
Or make your place.
If you must,
Light a fire,
Do what you have to do
To wave your color.'
Answer the first, and like magic
Too good to be true,
Animal, vegetable, mineral,
There's you.'

There was a silence. "What do you suppose he's talking about?"
I hesitated. "Animal, vegetable, mineral – the basic nature of things – "
"The old finding-yourself problem, I guess. The teenage dilemma."

How should I know? As a teenager, I had never considered myself
lost, and I'd never had much sympathy for the platitude of "finding
yourself." Only lately – "I've always thought this 'finding yourself'
business was ridiculous," I said briskly. "Kids going on and on about
finding something that doesn't even exist yet. It's like happiness –
finding yourself is what happens while you're doing other things. You
don't just go out and find yourself, you make yourself through what
you do and think while you're busy living life."

Joy sounded doubtful. "Well, but I think Gil's trying to say, you
have to start with something, and that's what the question is all
about, what are you to begin with?"

We were so close to it then; why didn't we push it through to the
logical end? But the whole racial thing had been part of our lives for
so long. It never occurred to us how new and singular an issue it was
to Gil. And I was too caught up in my own conflicts to imagine how
confusing it must be to carry two battling heritages in one young
boy's bloodline.

Actually Joy did touch on it, for a moment.

"That 'Wave your color' line. Is he active in some black
consciousness group, or something in school?"

"He's in a flag drill team called WYC, Wave Your Colors," I said,
dismissing it. "That's probaly what put the phrase into his head."

"Well, we probably should look into it."

"I'll tell you what. I'll see him at the dress rehearsal tomorrow
for that children's musical of Doug's – "

" 'Our FourFathers,' " she said, audibly repressing a chuckle.

I had to laugh too. "It is funny to see them all lined up there
on the stage, like steps, from Doug as Abraham, right down to
Charlesene Walters as Joseph – they had to use a girl because they
couldn't get any of the smaller teenage boys to take a speaking part.
So they used them all up as the sons of Jacob who don't say a word,
just run around pulling poor Joseph in and out of the hole. They put
a beard and a mustache on her, and she's doing just fine."

"Sounds weird, but okay. I can't wait to see the show."

"It's one way to get some Bible history into the kids' heads, even if the patriarchs do end up dancing the cha-cha, carrying Charlesene on their shoulders."

Joy choked. "Forgive me for being so old-fashioned, Mom – but with the frames of reference so many kids have nowadays – the way they don't know anything about anything except their own lives plus what they see on TV – do they really know that this is, well, exaggerated a little? For fun?"

"We can only hope." I envisioned all the children growing up to think for the rest of their lives that Abraham and Sarah had gone into mildly rock hysterics at hearing they were going to have a child at their age, that Jacob had conned the rights to his father's business from his brother for a pizza, that Joseph had been the vice-president of Egypt –

"It's true it's not Doug's Bach chorales," I said doubtfully. "But he knows the composer, and the music's clever and lively, like Abraham's song, 'I See Stars.' That one's really quite lovely, where he sings about seeing the future God promises when his children will be as numerous as the stars of heaven, and all the nations of the earth will be blessed through him."

"Mmm. I guess you have to be there. When's the performance again?"

"Next Sunday morning in the Fellowship Hall."

"Maybe we'll come."

"Doug would appreciate it. He needs some encouragement."

"I'll ask Scott." The phone went silent. "I'm writing it down."

"I'll catch Gil at the rehearsal. About this Twenty Questions thing."

"Good. The sooner the better, in my opinion."

CHAPTER 28

The rehearsal was, as they say, a hoot, a million little kids running around to no apparent purpose, and the grown-ups in varying stages of self-control. Doug, who was usually terrific at this sort of thing, looked harried; he barked at two of the fourfathers like a drill sergeant.

"What the hell's the matter with you, you can't keep in step? See, we put our right foot out and then back, and then the left, and I pick up Joseph here and pass her down the line, and then – where's Isaac anyway? – Right now, Jacob, you set her on her feet on that last beat. Damn it, we're black! We're supposed to have rhythm! Jacob, just because you're going to be a CPA doesn't mean you can't keep time. Dance!"

I'd never heard Doug swear at the kids before; they hadn't either. Some of them were looking a little uncertain about it all, and I had the feeling that could have been one reason for those two fourfathers' ineptness, which was truly outstanding.

Robey was on the other side of the stage, looking on with a frown. I picked my way across, through pieces of a deserty-looking set, all sand dunes and distant high peaks. "Doug sounds a little het up," I said casually.

" 'Beware the easy griefs that fool and fuel nothing.' "

"Do you know something I don't know?" My tone was a little waspish.

"No, I don't have any idea what's going on with Doug. I'm just talking to talk."

So we stood silent, watching the uproar.

A child, a little girl with no-nonsense brown-bobbed hair, who looked to be about three-and-a-half, hove into view on the other side of the large Sunday School room that flanked the right side of the stage. She struggled to push a huge white woolly sheep on rollers. His name was Jarvis, and he was a fixture at every Nativity reenactment since Doug had come to Our Saviour.

"And I do mean fixture," said Doug once, explaining Jarvis's origin to me. "You can hardly move him, he's so heavy. I asked old Neff Demling to put together a small flock that first Christmas I was here. He's an old-school carpenter, you know, nothing but the best materials. Well, he got so carried away putting out a really good sheep, he overdid it. Didn't have time to make any more either, so I had to get Jim Hotchkiss to throw together a couple more out of plywood. They look like a different breed." He had surveyed his little herd, standing or lying where the children last left them, and slapped Jarvis on the rump. "Jarvis looks like the genuine article, no doubt about it."

The little girl pushed and pushed, but Jarvis wasn't going anywhere. She spied us across the room and toddled over purposefully.

"Help push Jar's?" she asked and took Robey's hand trustingly.

"Okay," said Robey doubtfully. He allowed himself to be marched across the room, and together they pushed. Jarvis barely began to move.

"Jar's won't go," said the little girl in disgust.

A young woman in long skirts and straight brown hair rushed into the room and looked around. Spotting the little girl at the other end, she ran over and plucked her away from Robey and Jarvis without a glance. She turned the child around and held the little face in the vise of her right thumb and forefinger. "What did I tell you?" she asked tightly.

The child could hardly have answered if she'd tried.

"Haven't I told you time and time again DON'T SPEAK TO STRANGERS! If you ever speak to strangers again, I WILL HAVE TO TAKE STEPS!" She shook the child's face in time to her words and looked up at us.

I was petrified, but Robey seemed unperturbed. "I'm Robey Carlier, and this is Elinor Heyer."

"Glad to meet you," said the woman, sounding just the opposite. "I'm Dot Mackey." Turning the child around again, she pushed her toward us. "Now, Flower, I will introduce you to these people. This is Mr. Carlier, and this is Ms. Heyer."

The little girl looked down at the floor.

"Now, what do you do?"

Flower grabbed her mother's skirt and pulled, but Dot Mackey detached her from it as if she had had practice.

"This is something you must do, Flower. And we always do what we have to do, don't we? Apologize to them, Flower."

"Apologize for what?" I said. But Dot Mackey paid no attention.

"Flower. Apologize for talking to them when they were strangers."

"Sor-ry," she mumbled. Dot Mackey grabbed her hand and marched her off.

"That's okay, Flower," I called after them. I turned to Robey. "Whew."

"Do you suppose she would have been so upset if I were white?"

"Oh, Robey. Yes, I suspect she would. This not-talking-to-strangers thing seems to have taken over for a lot of the young parents these days, and I think, on the whole, it's not a racial thing at all."

He shrugged and moved past me to watch the action on stage.

Doug had whipped the group into a semblance of order by now, or as much as he was going to get. "Sing out," he yelled at the chorus, which was laboring through a version of "We Are Climbing Jacob's Ladder" without much enthusiasm.

It was hot in Our Saviour's Fellowship Hall, and everyone was sweating. Doug waved his arms in what seemed almost a despairing gesture, and the music fell off the piano rack as the pianist made a futile grab at it. Doug caught it and slapped it back so hard the rack collapsed. A collective nervous giggle ended the song, as everybody watched to see what he'd do next. He stood there obviously boiling inside, as Robey moved over quietly and leaned down to examine the rack.

"No problem, Douglass," he said easily. "Just a screw pulled out here." He took out his key chain and, picking up the rack, leaned down to screw it back in with a key, as Doug looked on with an unreadable expression.

Robey straightened up. "There." He tapped the rejuvenated stand lightly. "Treat it with love," he said to the pianist, who smiled at him perfunctorily, keeping an anxious eye on Doug all the while. "It's just getting old, like the rest of us."

Doug turned impatiently to the chorus again, and in carefully monitored tones, explained to them what he wanted. He listened quietly as they gave it back to him. "Good," he said then, "good, I think it's going to work." He turned to the group. "Final runthrough," he said, "and then we'll all go home and rest up for tomorrow." He smiled in a strained attempt at apology. "Sorry about all this, by the way." Relieved, they all smiled back at him.

Robey and I left together without a word.

Finally, "That boy do be uptight," he said. I opened my mouth and then closed it, but not before he noticed. "No, Gramomma," he said. "I be layin off of him; ever since you give me all them pieces of your mind."

"I'm glad, Robey." Something else struck me, far too late. "I just remembered. I wanted to talk to Gil. Did you see him?"

"He spose be Isaac, but he never show up."

CHAPTER 29

I thought of phoning Grace when I got home, but I was hungry, so I decided to make myself a decent meal first for a change. I actually went to the bother of cooking for myself: shrimp in garlic butter, I remember, and delicious even if it was only the cheap miniature variety of frozen shrimp.

Then I took it into my head to sit in Dan's chair and watch the news.

No one had sat in it since the night he had died, the family consciously, and strangers accidentally. I had deliberately avoided it myself, I wasn't sure why.

But, musing over my shrimp, I moved my mind along precarious pathways, like a checker piece avoiding the enemy very carefully. I thought that maybe one key to waking up in the morning, knowing Dan was dead, might be to sit in his chair.

So I calmly moved there to watch the evening news, and I found it wasn't that hard, after all. It was harder to watch the news, the daily quota of rapes and murders and accidental bloody deaths and dishonesties channeled out of Washington and New York to all the attentive viewers within a radius of several hundred miles.

Locally, a boy had shot his sister accidentally, and a rapist was working over Lake Estates, but kept getting scared off. There was some breaking news about some minor bombings lately; the police seemed ready to close in on the perpetrators, who had caused far more fear than damage with their attempt at terrorism. The network news zeroed in on more findings on the Challenger disaster, which were uniformly distressing. Afterward the Wheel of Fortune did its anesthetic duty, and I had just finished a Cousteau special when the phone rang.

It was Grace. "Mother," she said, in one of those tones so obviously designed not to alarm that it scares you to death, "Mother, Gil's all right. Remember that. But the police are here with him, and he's in a lot of trouble. We – I need you."

When I got to Columbia Street, the worst seemed to be over for everyone but me. The policemen sat in the living room easily, coffee cups in hand, discussing how to pronounce "Gorbachev" with Doug, who looked no more rested than in the afternoon. Perhaps because the policemen were very black, I thought hopefully, the grayness of his face and the pale butter yellow of Gil's struck me sharply. Smiling, the men got up when I walked in and shook hands, ready to go.

"See you Monday, at eleven," said one to Doug, and he nodded tightly, and showed them to the door.

Grace jumped up quickly and made me sit down. "All right, Gil," she said harshly, dragging him to his feet from where he'd been sitting on the floor.

He took a big breath and choked, his eyes avoiding my face. Then he took another breath and forced the words out, his whole body, which I suddenly saw must have put on another inch I hadn't noticed recently, slumped before me. He straightened abruptly, and met my eyes before looking away again.

"Dad brought me home; the police just came along," he said defiantly to the end table.

Grace waved her hand impatiently, and Doug came back into the room. He braced his hand on the door jamb and looked at Gil with eyes that seemed changed somehow, in a way I could see and fear but not identify. It was disturbing. "What in God's name did you think you were doing, Gil?" It might have been better if he had shouted.

Gil swallowed and then shrugged, turning back to me, his hands hard by his sides.

"We were making a place for ourselves," he said, almost inaudibly.

I opened my mouth, but Doug got his question out before I did, in the same strangled tone. "A place for yourself? Damn it, Gil, your mother and I have been making a place for you all your life. What do you think we've been living and breathing for but to ground you in the best of both possible worlds. And your Grandpa – "

Gil whirled on his father. "Both possible worlds! Neither of your worlds is possible with someone like me. I'm different! I need my own world, and there isn't one ready-made for me like the one you chose, the white one. And Grandpa didn't create his either." His lip curled into a sneer and his head snapped back. "You just bought into worlds that someone else made." He took a step backward as Doug's hand came up. "We're creating our own world and our own people!"

I was bewildered. "What world, Gil? What people are you talking about?"

He turned back to me, keeping a wary eye on his father. "A world for people who aren't black or white, either one," he said, faltering for the first time, as he looked at my face and saw God knows what.

Doug took a step toward him, and Gil moved toward Grace. Her arms went out as she looked into Doug's convulsed face, and her own paled still more, and I prayed, God, I didn't want this for her, and I saw her, in a snapshot I had taken once, in her little blue-checked sunsuit, sitting in her sandbox, absorbed in her own small world, and I prayed that all this had not happened, but it had.

"Doug, calm down," I said. "Grace, I still don't know what happened."

"About 8:30 o'clock, the police called," she said in a monotone, still watching Doug, who had sagged onto the nearest chair and sat there like a large robot with the battery gone dead. "Gil had permission to go over to Clay's and that was when he was supposed to be home. You lied to us, Gil," she said sadly, and he opened his mouth. "I'm talking now. You'll get your chance." She stopped to think. "They wanted Doug to come down to the police station. They just got back before I called you, Mother."

Doug in his chair sighed deeply, almost a sob, and at the sound Gil turned toward him, then caught himself. His face set, and his jaw tightened noticeably with, I saw in surprise, a hint of his father's folds around the line of them.

"Gil, you hadn't been at Clay's house at all. Mother, they were both over in the furnace room at school with some other boys and the man who advises WYC. I had thought they were both teachers at the school, but it seems one of them had been kicked out of a school in Maryland and had come up to Evittsburg and gotten a job as a janitor at the school."

"Who cares, Mom?" Gil's voice was husky.

She snorted incredulously. "Well, obviously, you don't." She turned to me and waved her hands in front of her, as if she never wanted to hear another word about it. "They were picked up on suspicion of terrorist activities."

"Terrorist activities!" I had thought it was drugs or some sort of sexual experimentation, and I tried to think whether this was better or worse.

"You don't understand, Mom." Gil's impatience had the sound of his old teenage fretfulness. "It's not the terror part we're doing it for. That's just what we decided we had to do, to make the really important thing happen."

"What was that important thing again?" I asked.

He looked surprised to have to explain any more.

"Make our place, Nan."

I felt dumb. "Who's we?"

"Nana, you know. Our mixed race. 'The first generation of men and women, who are not *both* black and white,' like you, Dad – 'and neither black nor white.' " He was reciting words he had obviously learned by heart, a liturgical rap that had evangelized him – " 'to carve our own place, make our own taste, not blindly cruise, to pick and choose – ' "

Doug's voice, interrupting, sounded dry as old wood let to cure a thousand years. "Do you actually think you're the first generation that was 'neither black nor white?' And what's this about your own place? You mean like the Colored in South Africa? Below the whites, but above the blacks? Is that what you had in mind?"

"Oh, no," said Gil, earnestly. "Of course not, Dad – "

"That's what you'd get, more or less, especially with your bombs and things."

"Bombs!" I couldn't believe it.

"It was the only way we could get attention," explained Gil hastily. "We were only going to do a few of them, and not hurt anyone. Just at night when the streets were clear. And we were absolutely impartial and did both a black and a white place. Just property damage, Mr. Sides agreed, not people," he went on, in a rush. "Clay and I said to be careful about that."

"And what were you going to do when you got attention?"

"Why tell them just what I told you." He looked from face to face, but I could see that the others' were as blank as mine felt.

"Tell us again," said Grace, tensing her hand on the back of the rocker.

"Well, you know how, when people are arrested, they always cover their heads and stuff? But we weren't going to do that, Clay and me, we were going to look proudly at the camera and say, 'See, we're not black and we're not white, or red, or yellow either, we're just people like everyone else, so for God's sake will you stop dividing us up into races all the time and hating each other all the time and just accept people for what they are and not for what color they look like.' And everyone would have listened. Except there weren't any cameras there," he ended ruefully.

His innocence was like a tremor in the room, after which everything settled down again in the same place, but changed forever. In the silence that followed, Gil seemed to be waiting for validation. His eyes moved anxiously from his father to his mother and back again.

"Uh, how many bombings were there?" I asked finally.

It was Grace who answered. "Last night and tonight; they were on the evening news. One of the kids tipped off the police, Mother – I wish it had been you, Gil – and they raided the furnace room before they could do anything more."

"We put out the fire right away," said Gil.

"The fire?"

"During the scuffle, a fire broke out somehow," said Grace. "It was a miracle the whole school didn't blow up. The police think Rick Sides set it before escaping out the back way, but the boys put it out before it got to the explosives, thank God, and they caught both of the teachers, if you can call them that. Gil did help with putting out the fire, the police said, and they think he'll probably be put on probation. Oh, Gil," and she reached out and brought him to her, and the two of them clung together, faces hidden against each other's shoulders. I watched, wondering what Dan would have made of all this, and then my eyes met Doug's strange ones. They looked flat, slotted into his head, and I don't think he even saw me.

CHAPTER 30

The show must go on, of course, and "Our FourFathers" took place as scheduled at the 11 o'clock service the next day. That is, the time was as scheduled.

Robey and I stood together in the Sunday School room again, helping to pin up costumes and push little kids out into the rigged-up floorlights, when they were too frozen with fear to get out there by themselves. Little Flower Mackey had no such problems. She wouldn't look at us when she came through the room to wait for her cue with the other little girls who were doing the Daughters of Ur Farewell Dance, but she bounded out in front of the audience readily enough when the time came.

Neither Robey nor I said much. Grace had called him late last night about Gil, but he hadn't mentioned it since he'd arrived at the church this morning.

I finally broached the subject, after we'd sent out the last quivering Daughter. We watched them dancing about on stage with pots on their heads and scarves fluttering, rather like Salome, I'd thought yesterday, but hadn't dared to mention to the wardrobe mistress-choreographer for the show, Corinne Heinz, who taught dancing at Rita Durbin's studio, and also taught the 5th grade Sunday School class.

"Do you feel as guilty as I do about Gil?" I asked.

" 'It is reserved only for God and angels to be lookers-on.' "

"I guess that means yes. I'm feeling guilty because I think I should have seen this coming. Gil was giving signals all the way, but I didn't take any notice. I was too wrapped up in my own problems."

Absently he watched Flower, jiggling her little hips in what looked suspiciously like a childish version of some modern fertility rite from TV. He turned suddenly. "Yes, I feel guilty, if that's what you want. But I won't stand aside. Neither does Gil. That's his problem. He's only got to control it, get rid of some of the idealism. And this has given him a good scare. He'll think twice about doing anything so radical the next time." He turned to watch the stage again. "It's Doug I'm worried about."

All the little Daughters skipped past us, and Doug as Abraham (none of the boys seemed to come up to the job, he'd said) dominated the stage. I couldn't see his eyes from this angle, but before the show they had looked the same as last night, silhouetted from within. "I always thought all the attention to eyes in books was a lot of poetic bunk," I said loudly, to rise above the crowd's enjoyment of Abraham and Sarah's syncopated "I Laughed Till I Cried." "Did you see Doug's eyes, Robey?"

He nodded, tight-lipped, and the crowd roared louder. Abraham seemed to respond to the racket, leading Sarah, a little befuddled by it all, through a wild impromptu dance upstage, bucking and turning to the beat.

She came running off at the end with obvious relief, grinning shyly as she passed us, but I was paying more attention to Doug. At this point he was supposed to proceed into a fatherly heart-to-heart with Isaac, which was to run simultaneously into the discovery across stage of Rebekkah at the well. (The musical's authors had obvious problems to solve, both with time and with Abraham's domestic irregularities, and had chosen to establish his dominance and then move on to his successors quickly.)

Isaac (that was Gil) had started out from the left wing, but I saw him stop suddenly as Doug strode toward him. I didn't remember that at rehearsals.

"What's going on?" I whispered to Robey.

He tensed. Doug barked something and I saw Gil come forward in response, bewilderment in his eyes.

"Goddam," muttered Robey, and clutched my arm. Doug pulled Gil out front with a twist that thrust Gil against him and disclosed, in his right hand, a knife of some sort, a butcher knife from the look of it.

"What would you be without God?" he shouted, and the crowd roared at the familiar words.

"I Am What I Am," cried Doug, and a man shouted from the back, "Praise the Lord!"

"God loves us," Doug almost crooned, lifting Gil up effortlessly, it seemed, in his left hand. Gil seemed to have given up struggling, supine against his father's arm, looking sick and bewildered.

"Alleluia, praise the Lord!" other voices sounded.

"I Am demands a sacrifice," yelled Doug, and some in the crowd still responded, "God wills it, Your will be done," but others now saw that this was no playacting, and, stunned, remained silent. Doug threw Gil to the floor and raised the knife and I heard Grace scream then and the commotion of her struggling to get past others from the back, where she always organized things for Doug.

Robey held me back. "We can't fight that knife! 'Abraham, Abraham!' " he shouted toward the stage, in his most sonorous voice. " 'Do not lay your hand on the lad or do anything to him!' " The knife faltered.

With one thought, our eyes not even meeting, Robey and I dashed over to the corner and got behind Jarvis and pushed. He was heavy, all right, and, as we labored, Robey shouted again, " My son, God will provide Himself a lamb for a burnt offering!" Thank God, it worked, and I saw Doug hesitate again, please God, let us get out there in time.

Both of us were panting now; that darn Jarvis *was* a fixture and seemed to have been installed permanently, but we got him moving at last and pushed him steadily along toward Doug, who, thank You, watched our progress with the knife still in the air, awaiting Jarvis's arrival like Wagner's Siegfried looking out for the Swan. We must have seemed like some Monty Python version of Genesis, as Robey roared, " 'Now we know that you fear God, seeing you have not withheld your son, your only son, from me!' "

"The Lord has provided," said Doug-Abraham quietly, and plunged his knife into poor Jarvis. The audience stared and no one thought to pull the curtains.

All hell broke loose then, and, of course, it *was* hell. Someone called the police, and three of them led Doug away, unprotesting, the dark sun still backlighting his eyes.

Grace went with him, shocked bloodless but unweeping, and Gil stood in the back of the milling stage with his hands so tightly held over his eyes that the marks showed, ten tiny tan imprints, when he took them down.

He was dry-eyed too, but his body shook with sobs, and I sent the kids away who flocked around him out of sympathy and curiosity, and led him to the music room behind the stage. Robey opened the door for us and then turned to help direct the excitement into some sort of ordered conclusion, always the male priority, but then I never was one to question entirely a reasonable division of labor.

Gil looked at me then, for the first time.

"Did I do that?" he asked. His lips shook on a shiver of breath.

My first impulse was to deny his part in it, to comfort, console. But I nodded instead, and then shrugged. "I guess so, Gil, a little," I said. "But then so did I. And so did Grandpa, and your mother, and lots of other people we don't even know. And so did your father." I hugged him to me.

And so did God! Now that it was over, I was so angry I suddenly tasted blood in my mouth. "Life is like that," I said, and I heard it resound in the room, an accusation. So I spoke over Gil's head, to Whoever might be listening, in case He cared at all. "Damn it, why?"

CHAPTER 31

Doug, dear and gentle as a Bach fugue, was worn out from years of responding to all the different signals in his life. I knew that as well as the next armchair psychologist, but, in my opinion, it didn't get God off the hook. The more I thought about it, the angrier I got.

I didn't really believe that God had actually reached down and pushed Doug into that megalomaniac assumption of deity, dealing out life and death as if he were the I Am Himself. Assuming He existed, which I think I always had deep down under everything, even after Dan died, because otherwise what right did I have getting mad at Him?

But, if He cared as much as I'd always been taught, as Dan had fervently preached every day of his life one way or another, He'd have done something. Wouldn't He? And He'd have done it for us recently. Not two thousand years ago.

It's that maddening Absence that angers so. Where is He, for goodness sake, when we need Him? I only echoed the old questions, added nothing new to the old arguments. Except the experience of God's absence in my own life. Hearing of His absence in the lives of others, even 6 million Jews, or on the Cambodian killing grounds, never carries the weight of one's own personal want. That's not good, and it's not right, but that's how it is.

So, angry as I was, it didn't take long to dispense with the willpower bit. One thing I've always been able to say for myself, and that is, when I make a decision, I act on it. No hanky-panky about it. Maybe God exists – maybe He doesn't – but if He was going to act like this, I didn't have to pay attention to Him. I stopped praying. I stopped going to church. I stopped arguing religion, even in my head.

It made things harder for Grace, who hadn't stopped believing, by any means. I respected her for it. (The detached agnostic attitude was surprisingly easy to come by, I discovered. One doesn't really have to *do* anything or make any reality come out of one's beliefs, if one just shrugs shoulders.)

At first, I don't think she even realized what was going on with me, and why should she? She was busy visiting Doug at the state hospital, and had virtually given up her job for the time being. After Doug's initial period of medication, she was permitted to see him whenever she wanted, and she went over several times a week.

I went with her the first few times, but Doug's eyes were still dark, one- dimensional circles charred by the fire within, and between that and the dismal surroundings, cheerful as they tried to make them with bright yellows and oranges and browns, with other hollow-eyed men and women staring around corners and skittering nervously ahead, I was relieved when she said she would rather go by herself for a while. Joy tried it once or twice too, but "I start to shiver" she confessed, shamefaced, and after that we went with Grace only when she asked us.

With all my inner commotion going on, I wasn't being of much use, however, so I moved back in to Columbia Street where I could help Grace with running the house and keeping an eye on Gil. He did not recover quickly, but he was willing to talk about it. "I didn't mean it to happen that way," he kept saying, and he was very surprised when it came out that the whole WYC thing was simply a ploy for drug-dealing that had gotten out of hand.

Both Rick Sides and the other man, Jerold Jackson, had considerable records in other parts of the country for drug felonies, and apparently were setting up the boys as go-betweens for their burgeoning drug trade in Evittsburg. It was pretty funny, if you could see it that way, that neither Sides nor Jackson had had any idea that Gil and Clay were hoping to be arrested to get their message on TV. God knows what turn the plot would have taken if they had suspected.

Gil, of course, couldn't believe the new revelations. "Honest," he insisted, so earnestly I had to believe him, "honest, Nan, they never tried any drug stuff on us. It would have turned me off so fast."

Aparently bombing didn't, but I let it go. Why shouldn't bombs appeal to any red-blooded American boy? Guns were defended like God Himself in every state of the union and in the popular culture, and what are bombs but less accurate, more efficient guns? Gil was a child of his time, and he was on probation, like a lot of other children of his time.

I thought of laughing about it.

Something else was funny too. How upset everybody got when I stopped going to church. Except Grace, who never seemed to notice.

My coming over to their side seemed to unnerve Joy and Scott. As for Robey, " 'We real cool. We left school!' " he grunted when he found out I had missed church for the third Sunday in a row.

"Stop grumbling. You almost never go, even though you say you 'might' believe in God. Well, I don't anymore. So why should I go to church?"

He didn't say anything more, just stared at the cardinal singing away out on the tree limb. "That bird makin mighty strange sounds," he drawled finally. "Ain't none of them on the machine, what he's spose be singin. I miss them old songs." He got out the cardinal card and inserted it into the handheld player, and we forgot our quarrel in our mutual bewilderment at all the songs they don't include on the records.

Life regained a precarious balance, like one of those children's toys with the sand in the bottom, that you punch and it comes as close to falling as possible and then, gradually, swing by swing, rights itself. Gil and Grace and I bobbed and swayed and lost a lot in the game (Lucy Lockett lost her pocket), innocence, sweetness, and faith, but we started straightening up again in spite of ourselves.

It helped that the congregation was so decent about the whole affair. Dr. Bramer, surprisingly, had come out the Sunday afternoon of the disaster. Grace was with Doug, but he shook hands with me, sympathized, consoled, and prayed some. He had little to say to Gil, who stood by miserably. Dr. Bramer meant well and I appreciated his visit, although he had no clue at all as to God's possible course through the ruins. But then none of us had, and so we left that issue well enough alone.

The evening of the disaster, the Church Council held an emergency meeting with the Worship and Music committee and decided to put Doug on "disabled status" and find a substitute organist meanwhile. Not the easiest thing in the world in a city where organists were in such short supply that they played musical benches among the churches when one left a job. And Easter was coming up.

Furthermore, they continued Doug on full salary for a month's vacation plus a month's sick leave. After that he would be on half pay until further action was taken, which relieved Grace of having to make hasty decisions under financial pressure.

She had just gotten home the night of the disaster, when they called.

"Thank you," she said over the phone, with more composure than I had expected after the day's events. "Yes, he's doing as well as can be expected, they tell me." She listened, lifting the hair off the back of her neck, as if it weighed too heavily. "You might try Mrs. Venable, the wife of the minister at Grace Methodist. She used to be a Lutheran, and I heard she did well enough with the liturgy several years ago, when Doug was on vacation."

She listened again, her face gradually falling into a mask of weariness, like the sad twin of the theatrical masks, the planes of her nose and cheek and chin in the same high stylized relief. At that angle, it looked as if she had lost weight even since morning.

"Oh. Well, if you tried her already – I don't know. Let me think about it. Maybe you could ask Dot – no, I don't think so – Twyla, I just don't know." Her knees seemed to sag and I shoved a chair under her just in time. "Yes, please. Thanks. Maybe I'll have some ideas by then." She hung up the phone and smiled a very small smile at Gil and me. Being just naturally nice is harder on the "nicer" than the "nicee."

Gil went over and stood by her silently, and she reached out for his hand. "Your father asked about you," she said. Tears glinted behind her lower lids before she blinked. "He really didn't remember much what happened at the cantata, seemed to think you had chicken pox."

Gil's hand went up to the small scar under his nose, and she smiled more broadly. "How old were you then, seven? I remember, he was so worried about you, took two days of vacation to stay with you, you were so sick."

She took him to her then. "Oh, Gillie, Gillie." Again, they sobbed in each other's arms, but I just got madder.

Easter came and went at church. But I didn't.

I couldn't believe the relief. That effort at will power had really taken it out of me. How could I have been so dumb? To will to believe in a loving God! It was so much easier just not to care about Him any more, one way or another.

Joy, strangely, wouldn't let it alone. She was no happier than Robey, actually seemed to fret about it.

"It's just not like you, Mother," she said, after inquiring about my church attendance like an old-fashioned maiden aunt. "You're not the same at all."

But I was through with all that foolishness, that crazy blind trust, that God-scam. Again the great wave of relief burst over me, not to *have* to believe any more, just because I always had. I felt so free, of having to do, to feel, to believe, free to "curse God and die." It felt so good and the dying would happen anyway. I had already learned that.

I was suddenly filled with an intense throbbing energy. That afternoon I washed all the windows downstairs in the Columbia Street house. I could hardly contain myself for wanting to *do*!

Dan still died for me every morning though, and only at those times did I think about what he would have said about my new conclusions. Finally I decided it was better just not to make such hard work of it mentally and concede the irrelvance of everything and go on from there. Dan, and faith, had been, but they were no longer, and I was getting over them, getting on with my life, a rational, down-to-earth, sensible life, without any folderol.

It was good solid stuff to hold on to, nothing beyond what one can taste or touch or smell, one's own experiences. That little quiet moment in my earlier life, that "religious" experience during my father's suffering, which had meant so much for awhile, had faded long ago. Anyway, when one is upset, as I had been about Daddy and his Alzheimer's, one's mind does strange things. Everyone knows that.

"God is only indigestion," Scott had once said, laughing, "think about it." In my fury at that patronizing phrase, I had failed to consider the truth he uttered. Now my energy could be turned to more constructive tasks, the Martha-jobs that supported life. I had been silly Mary long enough.

The next day I started to clean house, all but Gil's room, before which even my newborn vigor quailed. I washed all the windows upstairs, and scrubbed and waxed the kitchen floor. I cleaned and polished all the furniture, and then I indulged myself in a childish memory – bought some of that pink wallpaper cleaner that was the play dough of my childhood, and enjoyed myself thoroughly moving furniture, climbing ladders, wiping and kneading day after day. I only worried about what to do next when the walls were all clean.

I couldn't have been happier when the sewage backed up.

CHAPTER 32

Grace had gone down in the basement to look for a foam cooler to carry lunch over to the state hospital for herself and Doug. "It'll be our first time out of the building," she said, her voice receding into the depths of the cellar. "I want so much for it to go well – oh, Mother!" She wailed, and my heart plunged suddenly, unexpectedly, pitching me into total darkness for a split second.

"Oh, Mother." She scrambled back up the steps, like someone fleeing hell. "Aach! It's awful!" Her face twisted in disgust. "There's water inches deep down there and stuff floating in it – and it smells awful."

She was right. There was and it did. I made her keep her date with Doug, but after that nobody had time to think about anything else for two days as we pumped and sluiced and swept and cleansed and sanitized, and then sluiced and swept and cleansed and sanitized again. Meanwhile, sorting out, washing, putting out to dry, discarding or storing furniture, books, memorabilia – you couldn't rest a minute. It was wonderful.

When the sewage backs up, you find out who your friends are. Ron Henderson, a plumber in Trinity congregation, said promptly over the phone, "You need that like you need a hole in your head right now," dropped everything, and came over with a young assistant and a pump, and snakes, if that's what they're called, to get in and ream out the pipes. "Tree roots," he diagnosed laconically, standing inches deep in muck as the pump churned away.

Grace and Gil didn't seem nearly as excited as I was. Robey had dropped in to birdwatch and volunteered to help the first day, and in time we managed to get the work done, the others laboriously, me with this unaccustomed sense of furious fulfilment.

On Thursday afternoon, Robey and I finally finished the job, carting the last bag of hopelessly soaked trash to the street for pickup. "My high-school yearbook," mourned Grace, "that wind-up music box you got me for Christmas when I was twelve – if I'd only remembered they were there, I'd have gotten them out long ago and they'd have been saved." Sure, and if we knew at the start all the things we know now, how different our lives would be. Maybe.

Joy mourned things too, all the toys she had carefully put away many years ago that had belonged to our old brown dog, Sin. (The name was Joy's first joke on the minister's family she had been born into.) She bewailed the old ice-cream freezer too, hopelessly rusted and tainted, but carrying the most delicious memories of her childhood, she said, weeping tears more copiously than one might imagine for such an object.

Gil was in school, and Grace, truly thinner now, more silent, had gone over to the hospital to see Doug for the first time since their picnic, which had turned out to be a fairly successful venture into the outside world. Robey and I, showered and dressed in clean clothes, sat again, like old married folks, across the table from each other as we did so often now, coffee in hand, birds in sight.

"That shit soup pretty near done me in," Robey groaned, as he leaned across the table for the sugar.

I moved it closer. "We're not as young as we used to be." Now there was an original thought for you. I looked out at the feeder, swaying violently under an onslaught of starlings. "I've been trying to decide whether to go back or not for my 35th college reunion, Robey," I said, trying in the back of my mind to figure out what a large gray bird, not a starling, with a sleek brown head and neck could possibly be. "College was so big in my life, and it seems so little now."

He shrugged. " 'D'ye think 'tis the mill that makes the wather run?' " he said, lackadaisically.

"I don't get the connection," I said impatiently. "Oh, it's a cowbird! Shoo, get away!" I carried on behind the window, scaring away the cowbird at once and all the other birds along with it, while Robey watched absently.

I felt ridiculous, making such a fuss all by myself. "If she gets an egg into the phoebe's nest this year, so help me, I'll shoot her."

"Sure you will, Gramomma." He smiled into his cup and then stopped smiling. "You feelin mighty fretful about strangers in your neighborhood." A squirrel ran up the tree trunk and brazenly hung himself across the distance over to the feeder and gobbled down the bird feed upside down. "But we think a lot alike, you and me, Gramomma." His upturned hand slashed white, explaining: "Jarvis and all? We made a good team."

The two of us hadn't really discussed Doug's breakdown together in so many words – had left it to our eyes to do the healing work with tears, our bodies as props for weeping together, and later, tools of hard labor. Our mouths and our minds, inextricably combined, were still out on this case. Finally I nodded. "Jarvis went easier for the two of us, didn't he? We must have something in common after all, Robey, believe it or not, since he's the first thing that popped into our heads."

"I've been thinking," he said, "I'm glad it wasn't any worse."

I thought about it, but it seemed inconceivable. "Doug could have succeeded, you mean?"

Impatiently, his hand swatted down the irrelevancy. " 'The great act of faith is when a man decides that he is not God.' "

I still didn't understand. "But that's exactly what he did decide, to be God, to take life – "

"Oh, Gramomma," sighed Robey. "Not the way he shapin up. He coulda done Jonestown all over again, man." Within the infinite sadness of the tone rang a note of pride. Robey noticed it, I think, shook his head anyway, smiling wryly at himself.

I had to gasp, the sound or more likely the movement, scaring the birds away again with a great flutter against the light.

I remembered Doug's gift with people, his way with crowds, his evangelical charisma – "You mean, he chose the lesser of two evils?"

"He tryin to end the sufferin instead," said Robey confidently. "He say later when I see him, 'Dad, I gonna kill myself too, but you don let me' – he puttin an end to the trouble, not spreadin it out."

"That's one way of looking at it, I suppose. But playing God for one or a hundred hardly seems to make any difference – "

" 'Poor dear God,' " said Robey gently. "Ah, El, 'even bein Gawd ain't a bed of roses.' " Mischievously he looked up. "Anyway, you might be right about our having things in common. You never even noticed what I quoted when we were hauling old Jarvis onstage."

"Being God yourself," I said acidly.

He grinned with glee. "I read the Bible too, you know. You and I both have God in common, after all."

"Speak for yourself," I said heartily. "I gave Him up for Lent." I looked away, concentrated on the birds. "I don't want Him back either. I'm doing just fine without Him." Robey's stare unnerved me. It seemed conmingled with concern, and, yes, love, a love that seemed to want more from me than I was prepared to give.

"It's Gil we have to think of now," I said hastily. "He still needs help. I've been thinking" – the words slowed down – "it might have been easier for him if the old pattern had prevailed, if Dan and I had stayed out of the picture entirely. He might not have had that feeling of 'twoness' you've mentioned. He might have grown up much more secure if he could think of himself as black, instead of us harping on and on about equal time for his white heritage. It's not right, or fair, or healthy to ignore such a large part of yourself, but maybe he wouldn't still be struggling to put two halves together into a secure whole." I faltered. "But we couldn't have stood it, not having Gil."

"Hell, I don't know," said Robey. "I used to think I did, but I don't. I used to rail at the system and the whites who made babies and then had no part of them, but I'll have to admit I resented you and Dan being so big in Gil's life. But 'there are years that ask questions and years that answer' and this was one of the asking years."

"Hurston again," I said. "I just read that the other day."

He smiled again. "One of my favorites. Speaking of asking, Gramomma – " I stiffened, and he noticed at once and smiled again and shook his head.

"Don't worry. I'm no threat to you. Or whatever you're thinking." He put the cup down, took hold of both sides of the table and stared into my eyes, unsmiling now. "If I were 20 years younger, you couldn't stop me asking, Gramomma." He laughed softly. "In those days I could stand on my head and hum fine songs to the stones as they dreamed of heaven, and I thought I give up my nobodyness. And I did, Gramomma, get that straight. But you pay the price to be somebody. My hummin all choked up now." He leaned back and shook his head. "So romantic, all this, after the shit. But I need you to know I could have loved you, Gramomma." His use of that name now was deeply mocking of himself, I felt, more than of me. "Long time ago, I threw out my own thoughts and wantings, for the harm they do me. It works, Gramomma, it works. I got my proud shoes on. And I'll never give them back because they take me where I want to go." His steady gaze shifted to the noisy, embattled feeder outside where a cardinal was threatening a hovering house finch.

"I'm too old now, Gramomma. Black and white can mix when you're young, I learned that. But I'm too old for the guff."

He got up from the table and picked up the plastic bag of smelly clothes he had worked in this morning. "We're 'cracked plates,' Gramomma" – Hurston again? – "and I need to get away for a while to mend." He leaned forward. "And give you time to mend too."

I got up in time to hold the door open after him and watch him down the steps. He walked woodenly, putting his feet down deliberately, on each step shifting his weight to the other leg before putting the first one down again, as if he knew it would not bend. My own joints, suddenly, were feeling none too good.

"Robey," I called, but he didn't turn around. "Robey, I understand about that. I know exactly what you mean." I had to talk fast as he reached the second flagstone. "But, Robey, I need to know." He still didn't answer, moved on, straight-legged. "Robey, are you coming back? Please, Robey?"

Mrs. Zindell slammed her screen door hard next door, as Robey walked stiffly down the street, not looking back.

CHAPTER 33

The sewage crisis seemed to have dampened my need for physical activity, and writing was still a problem. Anger is not a suitable fuel for the kind of columns I write, and, starting with Doug's breakdown, I'd been having a lot of trouble with them. I thought of handing in my resignation to *The Evitts County Viewer* in the summer.

May is one of the best bird months, but I didn't seem to enjoy watching them so much alone, so I took to walking to school with Gil until he protested. I was still worried about him, but not for the same reasons. Now he was home most of the time, stayed in his room a lot, and often came out red-eyed and strained. He never said much any more and spent hours a day practicing the piano, though without much visible enjoyment. You're never satisfied, I scolded myself. It seemed as if I had been worried about him for years now, with no gains, only losses in that time.

With the warmer weather, I took up tennis for the first time in my life and hated it. Still, I made some new friends, and in time my body made some adjustments of its own to the new regime, though under protest.

I still looked at want ads.

I thought of running for the school board.

Grace was back at work now, going over to the hospital between appointments. Once when I went with her, Doug smiled at me and said, "Hi, Mom," and we lived on it for a week, although the next time he paid no attention to Joy at all. But the doctors said he was definitely getting better and began to talk of releasing him. I'd noticed his eyes were Doug again, mild and beautiful.

One reason I really noticed Robey's absence was because I missed arguing with him. He was the only one, besides Dan, that I had ever argued with in perfect amity. I first noticed the old form returning when Joy and Scott came in for coffee, the family drug, after our latest trip to see Doug, which hadn't been a complete success.

"The old boy still has a way to go," said Scott, stretching out his legs and tilting the chair back on two legs, a male trait I had found endearing in Dan, but vaguely vandalistic in Scott. "But I think he's going to make it." I poured the water into the coffee maker and turned the switch to "dark."

Scott angled a look at me. "Got any beer around, Elinor?" he asked suddenly. "I hate to say it in this family, but sometimes coffee just doesn't hack it."

"Haven't bought any since Dan died," I said.

"Never mind. Just thought I'd go for the gusto, you know." He slumped down in his chair and looked at me sideways again. "Like they say, it doesn't get any better than this."

I poured the coffee and handed it around.

"Why settle for less," said Scott, "when you can have it all."

I got up again. "I bought some sesame sticks the other day." I put the box out on the table.

We sat silently for a while, and then Scott reached over and turned on the radio. "Since you're into rock now," he said, "you don't mind, do you?"

Cacophony poured out.

I couldn't help it. I stiffened. "Great music to visit asylums by," I said. "But we're home now."

"Oh, Mother," said Joy.

It sounded so automatic my mind seemed to leap instinctively into action. "I'll admit it did something for me back when your father died. But I think I was half mad in a quiet way at the time, and it expressed how I felt. At one end or another of that kind of music, there's a nervous wreck, and sometimes at both ends. And if you aren't one before you listen to it, you're one afterward."

I swear Scott looked smug as he leaned over and turned the radio off. Had he just wanted to get me started again? But then he often looks smug. "So you believe in censorship."

He knew better than that. "I just wish that once instead of saying 'porn may be disgusting, but I'm against censorship,' you'd say, just once, mind you, 'I'm against censorship, but porn is disgusting.' "

"Well, I kinda go for both rock and porn," he said.

I knew he was just giving me a hard time, but Joy laughed, and it really got my goat. "A lot of rock is the 20ᵗʰ century's Emperor's New Clothes," I jabbed away, feeling strangely at home in my new form. "A hundred years from now, if anybody's still around, they'll look at the words and the noise and the videos and the condition of our society, and they'll marvel that we could so ignore the connections. Rock groups – and oh yes, that new rap – holding concerts to help the miserable of the earth, but singing songs that glorify self-indulgence, drugs, violence, loveless sex – all the things that produce still more miserable of the earth. Every advertiser knows better, but you still think there's no connection?"

Joy interrupted hastly. "Mother, we really have to go. Scott, didn't we tell Sharon and Mike we'd meet them at six?"

And they left, looking particularly self-satisfied, I thought.

I cleared the table and ran water over the cups. I set them on top of each other, watching them flood over the sides.

Until I turned off the faucet, but that was some time later.

Because, as if it had been jump-started, my mind began thinking again. I thought that anger, basic dysfunctional anger at the core, distorts and deforms. It obstructs God the way certain substances block nutrition, and the creature that lives on it is wizened, less than her potential.

For someone like me, maybe, fervent good-natured argument leached out some of the poison. Allowed God and people through. Without the safety valve, someone like me could be a time bomb, sputtering frantically around more harmful outlets until they could no longer contain the energy.

Someone like me. (Had Doug been angry?) What was I when I wasn't distorted and deformed?

A truism. The greatest cliché of all. A creature of God. Yearning like a sunflower toward my Creator. Made in His image. Not in looking like Him, but in knowing Him. Only God and Humankind know God.

Holding on for dear life, I was getting back to normal. Back to my safety-valved, argumentive self. And getting back to normal is coming back to God.

Continually.

Forever bitching. Forever doubting. Forever demanding.

The religious experiences.

Or the lack of them.

The questions.

Even the answers, until they are replaced again, by further answers. They're the navigational corrections that we make, when we allow ourselves, on this life voyage. But beyond them all is that one simple fact that fills in the unknown spaces like a great North Star – that I must love God.

It's built in. As St. Augustine said, " Our hearts are restless till they rest in Thee."

The world is not made up of people who need God and people who don't need Him. It's made up of people who know they need God, and people who don't know it.

Whether I wanted to or not, I had to have Him.

I was stuck with God.

Just as He was stuck with me. I wondered if He had ever regretted that splendid idea of Creation. (However He did it. And does it.)

I sat and thought, yes, and I prayed, for a long time, until Gil came home from school, and then some more, as I listened to him at the piano, practicing almost desperately, it seemed. As if something entirely separate from music might be accomplished by it, if he worked hard enough.

CHAPTER 34

The next day I cleaned Gil's room. I felt rather guilty at having missed it before, and had to force myself to get it done, because I had just put out a hummingbird feeder and wanted to keep an eye on it.

It had been disconcerting to find out that, for me, mental and spiritual health might very well involve physical inertia – not being at all a child of my time in this respect. It was depressing to contemplate, especially without Robey around to share the insight.

So I forced myself to do the work, which is how I came across the scribbled poem on notebook paper, lying out on his desk. Perhaps I shouldn't have read it, but I did.

Hot from heaven
Aggrieved goddess,
Scorched saint:
"Why do you tempt God?"
She says, "and doubt His will?
He has His reasons,
For your dad and all."

Well, if that's God,
They lie
That He is good and loves,
So why not kill yourself,
As readily
God kills.

No birds that afternoon, and again no Robey. At 2:30 PM, after Grace left for the hospital, I walked over to the Blaise Hill school to wait for Gil. He came out the porticoed entrance looking like any of the other teen-agers, shoving and shouting like the children they won't admit to being, pounding each other on the shoulders and arms as if life held nothing more than the promise of boyish laughter forever.

But I had read Gil's poem. If the details were obscure, the thrust was unmistakable.

I wondered how many of the others, Clay, for instance, as bouyant beside Gil as any of the others, struggled in deep waters inside. Not all, certainly, I thought, remembering the confirmation classes I had taught for years. On the whole, although they and the popular culture thought differently, that age was still wading in the children's pool of life. Wasn't it?

Gil looked displeased to see me, and I could hardly blame him. What boy needs Nana waiting for him when the guys are around? And the girls – I noticed Tammy hovering in the distance, her eyes on the knot of apparently indifferent boys, before she caught sight of me and discreetly faded away.

His face cleared as he came closer. "I thought you were someone else."

It might be a good idea to get Grace to make an eye appointment for him. "Who did you think I was?"

He looked around, hunching his back, making a joke of it, his guardedness. "Mrs. Busche," he said.

"Meredith? She comes here?"

"She's been meeting me lately, after school. A lot."

I was astonished. "What in the world for?"

He shrugged. "She says to save my soul."

"She says what?"

"To save my soul."

I seethed as we fell into step together. "And how does she propose to do that?"

He hated to tell me. "She wants me to come to her church."

"And will you?" I marveled at the nerve of her.

He looked uncomfortable. "I said I would Sunday."

I had a mental image of two old biddies, Meredith and me, ripping Gil apart between us. But it was an image born out of the modern reflexive contempt for the opinions of older women. Whatever our rivalry was, it wasn't comic strip stuff. Gil had grown-up problems and he needed to deal, whether accepting or rejecting, with grown-up concepts.

I slowed down. "Gil," I said. "Meredith doesn't have to save your soul, and neither do you. It's already taken care of, thank you."

He looked at the ground. "But I did that to Dad – "

"Oh, Gil," I sighed, "I told you before – give up the guilt, dear. God knows we all do wrong things."

He trudged along beside me, not saying a word, and I tried again. "It's God who makes the difference in our lives she called being saved, not you or me or Meredith."

"We have to do something."

"We do. We *let* Him. And then, by God, we try to live those lives the way He means us to! Don't you see, Gil? It's really the other way around from Meredith's idea. She thinks we have to be good and then God will love us. But being good has nothing to do with it. That comes afterwards. Knowing God loves us – *then* we want to try to be good."

I shuddered to think what Joy and Scott would have to say if they heard this conversation. Mother, you're so naïve. Goody-goody. Superstitious. Fanatic. Lutheran.

But all I could say was what I had learned about life to this point. I tried to think how to put what I had arrived at the day before, as my cups overflowed in the sink. "What I tell you, Gil, is what I've learned about myself. Human beings are religious, if they just let themselves be. Because being religious comes of being human. And that's because being human means growing into consciousness. Like the hunter-gatherers in the Garden of Eden."

Gil would never remember all this. It came before he was ready. But it seemed terribly important that I should tell him anyway, a natural function of my age and relationship to him.

So I barged on, working it out as I went along. "Somehow, there's a blind spot, a closed window in that consciousness, so we can't see the face of God. But when that blindness is wiped out, then the window is opened – for Christians it's Christ who did this – then we're closer to what God meant us to be in the first place: in the image of God, conscious of His Consciousness."

I have to admit that Gil looked at me a little suspiciously. If I was going too fast, I couldn't stop it because I was still working on it myself.

"It's a natural mindset, not an abdication of the brain. Because once you know *that* God is, you have to use your brain to open up to the truth of *what* God is. You may not have the whole truth. (I think even Christians don't have everything right – it's not possible to fully plumb God.) Or you may misunderstand some of it, but you've got to use your brain as well as you can. And as long as you can."

A dog in the yard we were passing barked heartily. I liked him. I would go to the pound tomorrow and get me one, a puppy with big feet and warm eyes you could soak in like a Jacuzzi. I would build a big fence around our yard so he could run free and still be protected.

Gil said. "Mrs. Busche says I'm never supposed to doubt God or ask any questions – just trust that He has reasons of His own for making people suffer and die."

I would look into getting my teacher's certification too. I didn't feel as free as I had before – almost nostalgically I remembered the exuberant relief I had felt for a while, when I thought I had dumped God once and for all. But only the animals, who don't know God, are free like that, and their freedom is called innocence. When we grew out of being animals tens of thousands of years ago, we grew out of being innocent.

I am setting my own boundaries, which is a work of freedom. My faith is no longer a reflex, or a hand-me-down, just because it runs in the family. It's not a matter of tradition any more, or custom, or default. And I'm simply not up to the frightful burden of nihilism. No one is. But I admit it.

Good God! I choose to believe in God! With Jesus as His face on earth!

Belatedly, I replayed what Gil had been saying. "No, no, no, Gil! Never stop doubting. For believers some of the best growth comes out of doubt. Besides, you have to keep on doubting so you can doubt doubt, when its turn comes. There's no law that says you only have to doubt God, you know."

"Mrs. Busche says God made us suffer to draw her attention to me," said Gil. "So I could join the Elect Minority."

"The Elect Minority?"

"That's the name of the new church she's starting."

I had to choose between smiling and grinding my teeth. I decided to smile, at some boys on a stoop who did not appear to be engaged in any illicit activity and deserved to be rewarded. They hardly knew what to make of it.

"I don't believe God makes people suffer, but I don't have any answer about why He *lets* people suffer. Except a very old one, Gil, that makes more sense to me all the time. He deliberately limits Himself to give people the freedom to live their own lives and make their own choices. What a relief that must be for Him," I mused, surrendering to whimsy, "to have someone to argue with. The angels can't do it."

Gil burst out. "It's bad, being in the middle. When you're not black and you're not white, you want to be *something*."

I put my arm around his shoulders as we walked – he was getting so tall – and he didn't protest. "Gillie, I know. But you can still be yourself in the middle without destroying others, and yourself too. You might even be able to help bring both sides together." I thought of Doug. "The real temptation is trying to be everything – " but I saw that I had lost him.

"I wish there were some perfect answers to all this," I said, feeling tired. "But I do know one thing – I still believe in playing Spite the Devil."

"Playing what?"

"Spite the Devil." I hadn't thought of it for awhile. "Your grandpa used to play it. He said nothing made the Devil madder than somebody stopping the spiral of evil in its tracks. And then for good measure, making something good come out of it instead. 'God loves the game too' he used to say, and quote Romans 8:28: 'In all things God works for good with those who love him.' And he would emphasize 'all things,' meaning both bad and good."

I tried the Socratic method. "And what came out of Grandpa's death?"

Gil looked down at the sidewalk disappearing under our feet. "Dad – uh – "

"Dad what, Gil."

"Dad, uh, trying to kill me?" He stepped on a flapping sneaker lace, stumbled, caught himself, trudged on.

"It certainly played a part in it."

"Was that the Devil?"

"I don't know. I don't even know if there is a Devil. But there is evil, and what your dad did was to let evil recycle itself. We all do that, all the time, and if there is a Devil, he must love it. Because it goes against all the ways God made us to be human."

Gil sighed. "You mean, if I were to, say, well, to kill myself – " I knew then that he had left out the poem for someone – anyone – to see – "that I'd be making more evil come out of evil?" He looked sideways at me.

I nodded, afraid to react any more forcefully. "Uh-huh."

"Spite the Devil," he said. His grin was almost grown-up. "I always like games. What's for dinner?"

"Meat loaf."

If there were no food, we would not hunger. If there were no loving God, we would not so thirst for One, to plead with, to thank, to curse, to bless. To be made real by.

Cogitor ergo sum.

I am thought.

Therefore I exist.

We got to the house just as a car drove up, Robey's Ford. He got out and looked puckishly at us over the roof. " 'Keep a green tree in your heart.' " he called, and came around and did high fives with Gil and turned to me. " 'And perhaps the singing bird will come.' " He stuck out his arms like wings and pumped them up and down. "Tweet, tweet, Gramomma."

"I know," said our grandson. "An old Chinese proverb."

The next morning, I woke up already knowing that Dan was dead. I thanked God for him and got dressed to attend my thirty-fifth college reunion.